THE SECRETS OF
THE STORM VORTEX

THE LIGHTNING CATCHER

THE SECRETS OF THE STORM VORTEX

ANNE CAMERON

The Lightning Catcher: The Secrets of the Storm Vortex
Copyright © 2015 by Anne Cameron

Black-and-white illustrations by Victoria Jamieson

The text of this book is set in 12-point Times New Roman.
Book design by Paul Zakris

Library of Congress Cataloging-in-Publication Data

Cameron, Anne.
The secrets of the storm vortex / by Anne Cameron.
pages cm.—(Lightning catcher ; [3])
"Greenwillow Books."
Summary: "Now-twelve-year-old Angus McFangus and his friends encounter a storm vortex and a stranger from the crypts"—Provided by publisher.
ISBN 978-0-06-211283-5 (hardback)
[1. Weather—Fiction. 2. Schools—Fiction. 3. Adventure and adventurers—Fiction.] I. Title.
PZ7.C1428Sec 2015 [Fic]—dc23 2014035854

15 16 17 18 19 CG/RRDH 10 9 8 7 6 5 4 3 2 1
First Edition

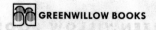

GREENWILLOW BOOKS

To Paul, Pat, Don, Anne, Cameron, Duncan,
Amanda, Harley, and Eden

PROLOGUE
THE DARK CASTLE

If you have ever been chased to the top of Mount Maccrindell by an abominable snowstorm, you will know that it is the best place on the whole Isle of Imbur from which to see Castle Dankhart. It is also an extremely dangerous spot to linger. And unless you are a fully qualified lightning catcher, you should make a hasty retreat the instant you've chipped the icicles off your eyebrows, taking a solemn vow never to return.

If you *are* a lightning catcher, however, fleeing from an abominable snowstorm, then you would be well advised to take a different route. Follow a concealed path until you reach a deep crevice in the mountainside that leads to a

secret cave. Inside the cave you will find two of your fellow lightning catchers, Azolla Plymstock and Morton Knapp, discussing the weather patterns over Castle Dankhart.

Catcher Plymstock had just completed a long two-week stint on observation duty, making notes on every temperature change, cloud formation, and shower of rain that had fallen over the dark castle in that time. Catcher Knapp had arrived twenty minutes earlier to take over.

"I'm happy to report that the last fourteen days have been remarkably calm and quiet," Catcher Plymstock said, pulling a coat on over her stout frame and buttoning it all the way to the top.

She was now heading back to the Perilous Exploratorium for Violent Weather and Vicious Storms for a hot bubble bath and an evening with her favorite book about cake baking.

"There has been no sign of the icicle storms returning?" Catcher Knapp asked, studying the neat chart that Catcher Plymstock had already handed over.

Catcher Plymstock shook her head. "There were several abominable snowstorms on Tuesday morning, followed by a brief scattering of pale pink snow at 1:15 p.m., but it didn't last long. We have run out of chocolate cookies again, I'm afraid, so you'll have to make do with plain for the time being."

She pointed to a neat desk at the back of the cave stacked with weather sample canisters, spare candles, and a cookie tin. A small fire was burning in a log stove next to an armchair. The camp bed had been freshly made.

"There's also a herd of wild mountain fog yetis camping close by, so I've left you some earplugs in case they start howling in the night."

"Thanks for the warning," Catcher Knapp said, making a swift note of it. "There's nothing worse than a late-night yeti yodeling session. I'll try to—"

BOOOOOM!

A powerful shock wave suddenly rippled through the walls of the cave.

"What in the name of Perilous—" Catcher Knapp toppled over sideways with a startled expression, twisting his ankle as he fell. Catcher Plymstock stood her ground, feeling the floor of the cave shake violently beneath her feet. She waited for the worst of the vibrations to stop, then dashed to the cave entrance, where a sturdy pair of binoculars was kept at all times. The binoculars, however, were completely unnecessary. She stared at the calamitous sight before her, with her heart thumping hard against her rib cage.

Castle Dankhart, which had been sitting benignly in the sunshine all morning, had now disappeared beneath a huge, tumultuous cloud, an explosion of weather so thick and threatening it had obscured all turrets, gargoyles, walls, and the very rock upon which the dark castle sat. The cloud began to spin in a treacherous whirlpool of lightning bolts, unstable blizzards, and what looked like violet rain. Azolla Plymstock gulped. It was the most violent weather vortex she'd ever seen.

"Azolla, what is it? What's happening?" Catcher Knapp asked, hobbling across the cave to join her.

"There's no time to explain!" Catcher Plymstock sealed the crevice in the mountainside hurriedly with an inflatable doorstopper before the weather could force its way inside. "We must send a message to Delphinia Dark-Angel immediately! If we launch one of the clockwork messenger pigeons from the south entrance, it might just make it back to Perilous without being pulverized."

She hurried to the back of the cave and flipped open a wicker basket where a row of feathered mechanical messengers stood waiting. She grabbed the largest pigeon, lifted its wing, and extracted a small canister nestling underneath that contained a slip of paper.

"Prepare the pigeon for flight!" She thrust the fat bird at Catcher Knapp. "I must compose a message."

"But, Azolla, what on earth is going on?"

Catcher Plymstock thought hard for several seconds before scribbling her message with a shaking hand: "Urgent! Castle Dankhart explosion. Total weather catastrophe!"

1

THE STARLING MUSEUM OF STORM SCIENCE

Many miles away, on the busy streets of London, the weather was behaving in a perfectly normal manner. A heavy shower of rain had just begun to fall on fleeing tourists, shoppers, and nonmechanical pigeons. Angus McFangus, however, had already escaped the downpour. He was standing instead in a gift shop at the Starling Museum of Storm Science, staring at a row of very odd teacups. Each of the cups came with a tightly sealed lid and was decorated with lightning bolts, storm clouds, or snowflakes.

Angus picked up the first cup warily and read a label dangling from the handle: "From the famous storm-in-a -teacup range, this is Dewdrop. Drink tea while you watch delicate drops of dew form on the rim of your cup and listen to the sound of gentle rain without the need for rubber boots."

The cup next to it, Summer Squall, promised a "sudden sparkling downpour with a genuine rainbow, buzzing bees, and a lingering scent of meadow flowers." And then there was Snowflake: "Set your teeth chattering with this frosty cup of freezing winter."

Angus grinned. He'd only ever seen a genuine storm in a teacup once before, at the Perilous Exploratorium for Violent Weather and Vicious Stormson on the secret Isle of Imbur, where he was training to become a lightning catcher. On that occasion the encounter had led to a hair-raising incident with some silver lightning moths and had almost landed him in serious trouble. But maybe this time . . .

Angus glanced over his shoulder. The gift shop was empty apart from one bored-looking shop assistant slouching behind the register. He reached out and picked up the last cup on the shelf. "Lightning bolt boneshaker. Drink tea in fear for your life with realistic lightning flash and thunder rumble sugar stirrer." The cup rattled

ominously. Angus dug his fingers under the lid, opening it warily and—

FLASH!

A thin streak of orange lightning shot past his left ear, singeing his hair.

FLASH!

Another lightning bolt whizzed across his left shoulder, and struck a tall display of paper snowflake lanterns behind him, instantly starting a small fire. Angus thrust the cup back onto the shelf. He yanked off his sweatshirt in a panic and quickly used it to smother the smoldering sparks before the whole display went up in smoke. He grabbed a thick book on hurricanes, and wafted away any lingering smell of smoke. A tinny rumble of thunder echoed around the gift shop.

The shop assistant was now watching him with a scowl. "All breakages, floods, and fires must be paid for!" he warned.

Angus hurried away from the lanterns, pretending to study a harmless-looking wall chart until the assistant turned away from him at last.

He pulled on his slightly singed sweatshirt, zipped it up

the front, and breathed a sigh of relief. As a trainee lightning catcher at Perilous he encountered dangerous weather on a daily basis, although he still didn't have a clue how to deal with most of it! Perilous, in fact, was one of the most exhilarating, dangerous, and unpredictable places on the planet. Angus now found it impossible to imagine his life without storm vacuums, deadly lightning bolts, and cold-weather survival lessons where he'd learned how to build an igloo, boil up an emergency survival stew, and indulge in a spot of accidental iceberg hopping.

When he and his two best friends, Dougal Dewsnap and Indigo Midnight, eventually became fully qualified lightning catchers, they would help protect humankind from the worst ravages of the weather across the globe, just as the secret organization of lightning catchers had done for hundreds of years now.

He walked around a large table full of cuddly clouds, wondering when he'd see Dougal and Indigo again. At the end of the previous term Principal Dark-Angel, the head of the lightning catchers, had sent all lightning cubs home for two weeks so the Exploratorium could be thoroughly decontaminated after some violent ice-diamond

storms. Two weeks, however, had somehow stretched into the entire month of June, which had then extended all the way through the summer holidays without a single word as to when it would be safe to return. Angus had missed Perilous and his friends terribly.

He glanced around the gift shop, trying to decide if he should buy them each a present. He could see a stack of fascinating books about storm science that Dougal would kill to get his hands on. Indigo would be thrilled if he bought her a Pop-Up Iceberg Obstacle Course; she was far braver than any other lightning cub he'd ever met and never flinched in the face of danger.

"Angus?"

Angus spun on his heels. His uncle Jeremius stood in the doorway behind him.

"If you've finished messing about with teacups, we've got an appointment with Trevelyan Tempest, and I don't think he'd be too impressed if you flooded the gift shop." Jeremius nodded toward the teacup, which had finally stopped rumbling. It had now created a large wet puddle on the shelf where it sat.

"Oh, right, yeah." Angus hurried away from it. "Who's

Trevelyan Tempest anyway? And why are we meeting him?"

"Trevelyan is someone I've known for many years," Jeremius said.

"So he's a friend of yours?"

Jeremius grinned. "I wouldn't exactly call him that."

Jeremius McFangus was a lightning catcher from the Canadian Exploratorium for Extremely Chilly Weather. Angus had met him for the first time just a few short months ago. Before that, he'd had absolutely no idea that his dad even had an older brother. Jeremius was tall and broad with rugged features and a deep, jagged scar across his chin. He enjoyed spending his days trudging across glaciers in ferocious blizzards, camping out in subzero temperatures, and trekking to the North Pole to collect deep-snow samples. He also had the same gray eyes, small bear-shaped ears, and brown hair as Angus, making it obvious that they both came from the same family. Angus liked his new uncle immensely . . . except when he was being cryptic and refusing to explain things like why they were meeting someone called Trevelyan Tempest. Still Angus was certain he'd heard the name somewhere before.

He followed Jeremius into the museum foyer, where several groups of visitors were milling about, studying floor plans and brochures. The tiled floor and thick stone pillars had an impressive air of age and grandeur. The glass domed roof above was magnificent. Angus twisted his head around, staring straight up through it, trying not to bump into anyone as they made their way through a heavy set of double doors and down a corridor.

"Where are we going?" Angus asked, not really expecting an answer.

"According to the directions I've been given, we're heading over to the far side of the cloud gallery. The last time I visited the museum this section was full of ice sculptures if I remember rightly."

"You've been here before?"

"Many times." Jeremius smiled. "They've got one of the best collections of fossilized hailstones in the world."

"But I don't understand," Angus said, jogging down the corridor after his uncle. "What have hailstones got to do with anything?"

Jeremius didn't answer.

Angus sighed. It had been the same all summer. Ever

since Jeremius had taken him back to the Windmill at Budleigh Otterstone, Devon, he'd been refusing to answer questions about anything remotely interesting.

Angus had spent much of the previous eleven years living at the Windmill with his other uncle, Maximilian Fidget, while his parents, Alabone and Evangeline McFangus, worked away at Perilous. Angus had been told about the exciting secret life they'd led only a year ago. He still found it impossible to imagine his normal, ordinary parents winning Lightning Catcher of the Year awards or thundering through the celebrated fog tunnels of Finland. He was desperate to ask them every little detail about their adventures.

Unfortunately Scabious Dankhart, the most notorious villain on the Isle of Imbur, had kidnapped them and trapped them in a dungeon beneath his castle, so Angus hadn't seen or heard anything from them in over a year. The only evidence he had that his parents were still alive was a secret message sent to his uncle Jeremius and an amazing three-dimensional picture, called a projecto-gram, that had been taken in their dungeon. Angus had spent many hours staring at the projectogram over the

holidays, studying their pale, hollow-cheeked appearances, desperately hoping that someday soon they would be rescued.

He'd spent the rest of the holidays helping his uncle Max, who possessed an extraordinary talent for creating dangerous weather machines. His latest invention, an instant icicle slicer, had deliberately cut the legs off every pair of pants Angus owned, forcing him to wear his pajama bottoms for several days instead.

His twelfth birthday, on the fifth of August, had come and gone without much fuss. Uncle Max had baked him a special beet and corned beef birthday cake, which Angus had continued to burp up for several days afterward. Jeremius had bought him a brilliant ball game with springy elastic tentacles and tiny bats, which they'd played together on the lawn in the hot summer sunshine. For the first time ever there had been no card, present, or phone call from his mum and dad.

The rest of the holidays had been uneventful, give or take the odd explosion bursting out of Uncle Max's workshop, until this morning. Jeremius had woken him early with news of a surprise visit to London, immediately after which they would finally be returning to Perilous on a late-evening ferry. Angus had packed hurriedly, stuffing as many socks, sweaters, and pants into a bag as he could carry. Then they'd caught the first train from Exeter and emerged from a packed station some hours later into a wide tree-lined square called Thunderbolt Plaza. From there it had been a brisk ten-minute walk to the huge Starling Museum of Storm Science with its impressive pale stone facade and domed glass roof.

It was only when Jeremius had left him in the gift shop, muttering something mysterious about "confirming arrangements," that Angus had become suspicious about the real purpose behind their London trip.

He followed his uncle nervously as he pushed through another set of heavy doors at the end of the corridor . . . and froze.

They'd walked straight into a thick, swirling foglike substance. It was exactly like stumbling through the middle of a no-way-out-fog on the Imbur marshes.

"What's happening?" Angus asked, accidentally swallowing a mouthful of cold, damp air.

"According to the museum guide, this is supposed to be

what it feels like to walk through the clouds," Jeremius explained, appearing close beside him.

Angus wasn't sure he liked it. The soggy surroundings made him feel mildly claustrophobic. He stared down at his feet, hoping there was something solid beneath them. Thankfully, he was standing on a wide walkway with tiny lights on either side to guide him further into the gallery.

The haze thinned after a few paces to reveal a large room beyond. Giant wobbling cloud exhibits surrounded them on all sides with names like cumulus, stratus, and cirrus. Each cloud was remarkably soft and fluffy-looking, almost as if it'd been caught fresh that morning and dragged inside. Angus reached out and stuck his finger through something called a castellatus cloud as they passed it; it was castle shaped, with turrets, and felt strangely sticky, like cotton candy. He wiped his hands on his jeans, hoping nobody would notice the finger-shaped hole he'd just poked through one of the fluffy turrets.

At the far end of the gallery, Jeremius led the way through yet another set of heavy doors and into a deserted corridor.

"Angus." Jeremius turned to face him at last. "Late last

night I received a message from Principal Dark-Angel."

"Oh," Angus said, feeling slightly nervous. Messages from Dark-Angel didn't always bring good news.

"She has asked me to escort you to the Starling Museum today so that you can learn more about being a storm prophet."

"Oh," Angus said again, suddenly understanding.

In his early days at Perilous, he had made the startling discovery that the fire dragon he'd been seeing in his dreams meant he possessed a rare gift for predicting when dangerous weather was about to strike.

Unfortunately, this strange ability had attracted the attention of Scabious Dankhart and his chief monsoon mongrel, Adrik Swarfe, who had tricked Angus into reviving a powerful lightning heart, created in the Great Fire of London. In doing so, Angus had experienced new levels of storm prophet strangeness, which nobody had explained to him yet.

Principal Dark-Angel, however, had promised him some answers and that this would involve a small "detour" before he continued his training as a lightning cub. It was obvious now that this detour had brought him to the

Storm Science Museum.

"There is no need to worry," Jeremius said, spotting the anxious look on his face. "I have Delphinia's solemn promise that you are simply here to *learn* about the storm prophets and nothing more. That is why we are meeting with Trevelyan Tempest. There will be no tests, projectograms, or angry weather to deal with; you will be perfectly safe."

Angus nodded gratefully. Jeremius had already saved him once before from some rigorous storm prophet tests, conducted by Doctor Obsidian, which had involved his being attacked by violent weather projectograms. Principal Dark-Angel had been extremely unhappy about this intervention. Angus, on the other hand, was convinced it had saved him from serious injury or worse.

"Ready?" Jeremius asked.

"Y-yeah, I think so."

Angus took a deep breath. Did one of the exhibition rooms at the museum have a display about storm prophets perhaps? Was that why Jeremius had brought him here? Would there be life-size replicas of fire dragons to poke and prod and fake storms to test his skills against? But

Jeremius strode to the darkest end of the corridor instead and stopped before a very plain-looking door concealed in the shadows.

He pressed a yellow button on what looked like an intercom beside it.

"Yes, can I help you?" asked a crackly voice on the other end.

"This is Jeremius McFangus from the Canadian Exploratorium. I've got an eleven o'clock appointment with Trevelyan Tempest."

Angus could hear the sound of papers being shuffled. And then:

"Please answer the following security questions," the voice asked. "Who wrote the *Pocket Book of All-Season Weather Words*?"

"Cecil Doldrum," Jeremius said, pronouncing the name clearly.

"Name three different types of lightning," the voice asked.

"Skyrocket lightning, tidal lightning, and lightning tarantulatis," Jeremius answered without hesitation.

There was another short pause.

"Password?" the voice asked in a polite but firm tone.

"Snowballs."

For several seconds nothing happened. Then: *click!*

The door swung open, and without another word Jeremius disappeared through it. Angus hesitated for a second, then followed.

⚡ 2 ⚡
A LIGHTNING TOUR

The door closed itself behind them. They had entered a long, narrow corridor lit by a series of dim, flickering lightbulbs.

"What is this place?" Angus whispered as they took a left turn and continued down the dingy passage.

"This is the London office."

"Seriously?" Angus almost tripped over his own feet in surprise.

Dougal had mentioned the existence of a London office during the previous term. Angus had imagined a vast Exploratorium hidden under Hyde Park. But he definitely hadn't expected a gift shop, a Lightning café, and tourists.

"But how long has the London office been inside the weather museum?" he asked, hurrying to catch up with his uncle.

"That's a very good question." Jeremius glanced over his shoulder and smiled at Angus as the corridor took a sharp right turn and continued downward at a steep angle. "The lightning catchers have owned this grand old building for over two hundred years now, and in more recent times it has become a very popular museum. Last year I believe it was fifteenth in the top twenty visitor attractions in London."

Angus stared at the back of his uncle's head as they continued down the featureless corridor, wondering why he'd never heard of it or visited it before.

"Such a splendid old building has given us a perfect opportunity to teach visitors about the science of storms, of course. But it also stops people from asking awkward questions about what else might be happening behind its doors."

"So what else is happening?" Angus stared around, half expecting to see evidence of dangerous weather experiments or escaped thunderstorms, but the bare corridor gave nothing away.

"The main purpose of the London office is to coordinate lightning catcher movements across the globe," Jeremius explained. "There are now hundreds of lightning catchers living in dozens of different countries, and if three teams from different Exploratoriums turn up to tackle the same storm, it's a huge waste of our time and resources. And the London office also monitors the worldwide weather situation and advises Principal Dark-Angel on the best way to tackle any rogue weather fronts or problems. Although she has the final say on any decision made here, of course, since she's head of the lightning catchers worldwide."

"But what if someone accidentally finds the entrance?" asked Angus, looking back over his shoulder toward the door they'd just come through. "I mean, it's not exactly hidden, is it?"

"As I understand it, anyone entering through the door without the correct password is automatically diverted into an empty cupboard with an extremely smelly drain. I believe most people leave very quickly."

Angus was still digesting this information when the corridor finally ended in a set of stone steps that led down into a large cellar. The crumbling vaulted ceiling, stone pillars, and damp, musty, atmosphere were in stark contrast with the splendor of the museum that sat somewhere above it.

"Welcome to the London office," Jeremius said, smiling at the shocked look on Angus's face.

Untidy desks, filing cabinets, and shelves were arranged in a haphazard fashion along one side of the room, where busy lightning catchers were hidden behind tall stacks of papers and box files. On the other side, the stone floor sank by several feet, creating a large rectangular pit where an enormous, highly realistic map of the world had been laid out. Miniature mountain ranges rose up to show the Himalayas and the Alps, with a long chain of mountains whose name Angus had forgotten stretching through South America. There were vast blue oceans with tiny waves crashing against rocky shores, and shifting sand dunes in barren deserts. Angus was convinced he could also make out the Great Wall of China, the Golden Gate Bridge in San Francisco, and the Sydney Opera House in Australia.

It was obvious to Angus, as he followed Jeremius across the room for a better look, that the map showed the exact location of Imbur Island, Perilous, and every other Exploratorium around the world. There was a large structure in India; in America there appeared to be a huge Exploratorium hidden in the middle of a desert. In Africa one had been built beneath a dried-up lake.

"Excuse me, but are you two from the Brazilian team?" A woman with mousy-colored hair, dressed in a neat blue skirt and white blouse, suddenly appeared behind them, looking hopeful. "We were expecting you over an hour ago."

"I'm Jeremius McFangus from the Canadian Exploratorium." Jeremius shook the woman's hand. "This is my nephew, Angus. We're here to see Trevelyan Tempest."

"Ah, yes, Trevelyan's waiting for you." The lightning catcher turned to one of the younger-looking workers scuttling past them with an armful of files. "Charlie, please tell Catcher Tempest that his guests have arrived, and then *do* find out what's happened to the Brazilian team. They've got some extremely import-ant decisions to make about the situation in the rain forest. I suggest you search the new interactive glacier exhibit in the museum first; we had three lightning catchers from Hawaii last week who had to be rescued from a very awkward ice fracture." The woman turned back toward Angus with a friendly smile as the other boy scurried away. "You've caught us on a bad day, I'm afraid. It's absolute pandemonium at the moment. Well, you can see for yourselves."

She pointed to the map, and for the first time Angus noticed that among the mountain ranges, rain forests, and rolling hills there were countless pairs of tiny rubber boots, which were clearly being used to pinpoint the exact whereabouts of all lightning catchers at any one time.

"We've got teams on the banks of the Amazon sorting out a freak snowstorm," the woman explained, pointing to the rubber boots in Peru, which were grouped around a large, glittering snowflake symbol. "We've got half a dozen of our most experienced lightning catchers chasing the tail of a stubborn electrical storm in China. And as for Tasmania . . ." She nodded toward a confusing collection of symbols situated close to the city of Hobart, which included more rubber boots than Angus could shake a stick at. "As you can see, we've got the most enormous problem with a giant—"

"Sorry to interrupt, Celia."

Before she could tell them exactly what was occurring in Hobart, another lightning catcher raced over, frantically waving a piece of paper at her.

"We've just had an emergency weather flash from Greenland and an urgent request for immediate help!"

The woman frowned. "But I thought we'd sorted that whole catastrophe out last night."

"The blizzard cluster has changed direction and is now heading straight for the capital city of Nuuk. And if all the blizzards fall where we fear—"

"Yes, yes, I see." The woman took a deep breath and rolled up her sleeves. "Then we must contact the Canadian Exploratorium immediately. They've got a team of experts visiting from Greenland, so they'll understand the local conditions. Ask Captain Frobisher on the dirigible weather station to transport as many snow plows, inflatable snowshoes, and instant emergency weather shelters as she can carry to the area. And for goodness' sake, somebody talk to the most senior lightning catcher at the Nuuk Exploratorium and

tell them not to attempt any foolish heroics!"

Jeremius pulled Angus safely out of the way as a frenzy of activity broke out all around them. Telephones began to ring like a flock of shrill-sounding birds. Several lightning catchers hurried across the map, moving yet more rubber boots into position around a sparkling blizzard symbol.

"Ah, Trevelyan, at last," the woman said, staring over Angus's shoulder. "We've got another Greenland emergency I'm afraid."

Angus turned around to see a tall lightning catcher striding toward them. He wore a smart tailored suit with a green silk handkerchief tucked into the top pocket of his buttoned vest; his hair was blow-dried to perfection in short, wavy curls.

"You are contacting the weather station and the Canadian Exploratorium?" Catcher Tempest asked.

The woman nodded. "I'll have to speak to Delphinia Dark-Angel, of course. We'll need her approval before we can deploy the emergency blizzard team."

"Might I also suggest that you get an urgent message to Isadora Sleet at the Exploratorium in Alaska?"

Angus instantly recognized the name. Isadora Sleet

had written *The Subzero Survival Guide*, which all the first year lightning cubs had used the previous term in the Rotundra.

"She can offer some expert advice on the course the blizzard might take. Mention my name, and she'll be more than happy to help. I will return as soon as I've finished with my guests." The lightning catcher continued. "McFanguses, if you will follow me, please . . ."

Catcher Tempest led them briskly to the far side of the room. Dodging several frantic lightning catchers, he bundled them through a small door and slammed it shut before Angus could take one last glance over his shoulder. The sudden silence of the empty corridor made his ears ring.

"Jeremius." Catcher Tempest shook Jeremius by the hand. "How nice it is to see you again."

The corners of his mouth twitched with the effort of a forced smile, and Angus got the distinct impression that he was anything but pleased by their presence.

Jeremius nodded once. "It's been a long time, Trevelyan. This is my nephew, Angus."

"H-how do you do, Mr. Tempest?"

"Hmm . . ." The lightning catcher studied him for

several seconds. "Principal Dark-Angel has instructed me to give you a quick tour of lightning catcher London. She seems to be under the impression that you need a proper understanding of our earliest history." He gave Angus a very skeptical look. Angus stared back, blinking.

"As you have already witnessed, you could not have picked a worse time for your visit."

"We didn't exactly choose it on purpose, Trevelyan," Jeremius pointed out. "We're here at Delphinia's request."

"Nevertheless, my expert knowledge will be required if Greenland is to avoid a major incident." He took an ornate-looking weather watch on a gold chain from his pocket and studied it. "I suggest we make an immediate start."

"Not exactly friendly, is he?" Angus whispered as the lightning catcher shot ahead of them and disappeared around a bend in the corridor.

"That might have something to do with the fact that I accidentally trampled on his favorite antique weather watch some years ago. He's never quite forgiven me." Jeremius smiled as they followed at a safe distance. "But he knows more about the history of the lightning catchers and the storm prophets than almost anyone else. And London is where it all began."

Angus swallowed hard. What was he about to discover about the storm prophets? What if he didn't like it, or it made him dangerous, too dangerous to be around Dougal and Indigo? He'd tried his best for a solid year to act as if he were just a regular lightning cub. But after what had happened with the lightning heart, he could no longer pretend, even to himself. The time had come to find out more.

They emerged through another door a few minutes later, and stepped directly into the noisy museum foyer, which was now even more crowded with chattering visitors. Angus glanced through the door of the gift shop as they hurried past it and almost choked. Several members of museum staff were trying to contain the same storm in a teacup that he'd opened earlier. It had now gone completely berserk, firing lightning bolts in all directions.

"Quickly, move those cuddly clouds before the whole display goes up in flames!" the tallest staff member shouted as the others jumped on top of the cup, which was starting to erupt with even greater force.

Angus raced after Jeremius keeping his eyes fixed

straight ahead of him, his head bowed low. He darted through a revolving door that led directly to the street outside and—

"Ooof!"

He'd plowed straight into the back of Catcher Tempest. The lightning catcher glared at him with obvious contempt before stomping off into the rain.

But instead of leading them through the soggy streets of London, as Angus had expected, he headed swiftly around the side of the museum, through another door, up a steep spiral staircase, and suddenly, they were standing on a balcony that ran around the outside of the museum's vast glass dome.

London, immense and bustling with life, stretched out before them. Angus gazed at the incredible scene as Catcher Tempest guided them along the narrow balcony. He could clearly see the Houses of Parliament in the distance, the river Thames, which snaked its way through the center of the city, and the top of St. Paul's Cathedral.

Catcher Tempest stopped abruptly and turned to face them, blocking the view.

"The extremely valuable pair of retrospectacles that

I'm about to give you is normally reserved for important foreign visitors and senior lightning catchers," Catcher Tempestsaid, taking an odd pair of ancient goggles from his pocket. The goggles were thick and chunky with misty-looking dome-shaped lenses on the front and a wide rubber headband. There were several knobs and dials on the side. "A lightning cub has never been allowed to wear them before, and I am letting you to do so today against my better judgment. You will kindly treat them with extreme care and if they are returned to me with any damage—"

"Angus isn't planning to trample them, Trevelyan," Jeremius said, sounding annoyed.

The lightning catcher sniffed. "That remains to be seen. If you will please take the retrospectacles and put them on . . ."

Angus wiped his hands on his pants, took the heavy goggles, and snapped them into place over his eyes. The headband dug into his scalp, pinching his skin. Two flaps extended downward, covering his ears.

London lay before them, magnified to several times its normal size, grand and impressive even in the rain.

He could now see the famous towers of Battersea Power Station and the flag flapping in the wind above Buckingham Palace. He swung his head around and twisted the lens at the front with his fingers; the retro-spectacles zoomed in, allowing him to count the cracks in the pavement outside the Houses of Parliament and every pimple on the faces of the young policemen guarding the entrance.

"Now, observe if you will."

Catcher Tempest bent down, adjusted the lens, and flicked a knob on the side. The image blurred for a second until it came back into focus again and—

"Wow!" Angus gasped. The Houses of Parliament had disappeared along with every other building he recognized. All skyscrapers and office blocks had vanished. There were no neon lights, cars, airplanes, or telephone wires. But a large city lay beneath them still; it had a strange hazy look about it now as if an old painting had been brought to life. A familiar dark river ran through the middle.

"What's happening?" Angus asked, unable to tear his eyes away from the incredible scene.

"What you can now see is the great city of London as it would have appeared over three hundred and fifty years ago. These images have been superimposed over the present-day skyline, giving you an accurate historical layout."

Angus felt his stomach lurch as he suddenly understood. He was looking down on a living, breathing London just as it had been in 1666. He could smell woodsmoke as it drifted on the breeze; the cloying stink of city grime hung heavy in the air. Every modern city sound had faded away completely, thanks to his earflaps. All he could hear now was a pack of dogs barking in the distance.

Angus gulped. Instead of construction cranes and helicopters, he could see a collection of vast lightning towers. They were much bigger than he'd imagined. Skeletal and pyramid shaped, they dominated the old city skyline like a collection of giant leafless trees.

"If you look to the left and follow the green arrow you see on the lens in front of you," Catcher Tempest instructed, "it will guide you to a narrow cobbled street called Lightning Mews, where we will begin our tour of London."

A flashing green arrow appeared as he said it. Angus

allowed the arrow to direct his gaze across the city and then down into a narrow lane with higgledy-piggledy dwellings on either side. The arrow stopped outside an ancient-looking house with crooked timbers, sagging plaster, and tiny windows.

"This is the house where Philip Starling was born," Catcher Tempest explained. "It is also the spot where, many years later, he was introduced to Edgar Perilous by a mutual acquaintance, and they quickly become firm friends. According to journals and letters written at the time, it was here at number forty-two that the earliest lightning catchers met to discuss their groundbreaking ideas and experiments and where the first lightning towers were designed."

Angus stared at the house, flabbergasted. A candle burned low in the grimy window. He was certain he could see shadowy figures moving behind the rippled glass. Was he looking directly at Philip Starling, a strange distant shadow of the past?

"Is the building still standing, Trevelyan?" Angus heard Jeremius ask behind him.

"It survived the Great Fire, but ironically, it was

destroyed some years later after a lightning strike. Now, if you would follow the green arrow once again, you will note that many streets and grand houses in London were also named after the lightning catchers and their brave experiments. Indeed, many of these locations still exist to this day."

The green arrow took Angus on a convoluted tour down a short street called Storm Tower Alley and then into a tree-lined avenue with a large dwelling called Edgar Perilous House. There was Thunderbolt Snicket and a poky-looking inn called The Lucky Lightning Strike, where the green arrow settled and finally disappeared.

"Now, if you will allow me to make a small adjustment." Catcher Tempest twiddled a knob on the side of the goggles so that Angus could once again see the whole of seventeenth-century London before him, with the lightning towers stretching up to the sky.

"All reference to the towers was forbidden after the Great Fire by the rulers of London and systematically removed from those books that had mentioned them. All paintings and pictures depicting the towers were destroyed or were burned in the fire itself. A heavy fine

was imposed on anyone disobeying. All trace of the towers was extinguished, in fact, until Edwin Larkspur's important discovery."

Angus remembered it well. Edwin Larkspur, an archaeologist, had uncovered some twisted scraps of metal beneath an old paint factory, the only remains of a lightning tower ever found. Unfortunately, the remains had then been stolen by Adrik Swarfe in order to revive the lightning heart. Angus suddenly recalled where he'd heard Catcher Tempest's name before. Tempest had been sent to the museum where Edwin Larkspur worked to quiz him for details about the theft.

Angus zoomed in for a better look at the lightning tower closest to him. Complicated metal struts and stairways ran through the open structure. A large lightning rod reached straight up into the clouds to attract any stray electrical storms. The whole thing looked incredibly real.

"As you can see, the lightning towers were a masterpiece of engineering and vision. They were built soon after Starling and Perilous joined a group of scientists who had begun to conduct some revolutionary experiments to capture the explosive force of lightning, to use it for the good of all humankind. As they quickly discovered, however, these forces were violent and unpredictable and could not be controlled. The whole experiment ended with the Great Fire of 1666."

Angus swallowed hard. The skies suddenly darkened to an early-evening gloom.

"What you are about to observe is a reconstruction of the fateful night that London was destroyed," Catcher Tempest said. "Watch carefully as the storm approaches from the west. The images that follow are based upon accurate reports and observations from the time but have been sped up for your convenience."

There was a sudden rumbling of thunder and a streak of golden lightning to the west. Angus swung his head around to the left and fiddled with the goggles until a full panoramic view of London emerged before him again. An immense storm was gathering in the distance and moving rapidly toward the outer edges of seventeenth-century London. He was about to witness the terrible events that had led to the Great Fire and the destruction of the lightning towers.

He watched, transfixed, as bright lightning lashed out, illuminating ancient houses, church spires, and lightning

towers in the distance. He could almost feel the dangerous quiver of ancient electricity in the air. He could sense the mighty storm approaching, even though he knew that it wasn't real, that it had happened hundreds of years before he'd been born.

CRASH!

One of the tallest towers had been struck! The flames took hold quickly, spreading to the structures around it, and then: Angus held his breath as the Great Fire swept rapidly across London with an intense glow like a blazing orange sunset. He watched in horror as everything before him was consumed by the frightening inferno that leaped and tore its way through the helpless city.

Angus gasped as several fire dragons suddenly soared above the rooftops. He twiddled the lens on the retrospectacles, quickly zooming in to see the creatures close up. There was a flash of red, a brilliant swoop of burning yellow, a glimpse of shimmering scales.

"I can see fire dragons!" he said, shocked, unable to take his eyes off the dazzling display. "But I don't understand. Nobody else can see mine. I thought they were just a vision, a warning of danger."

"The dragons are not real." Catcher Tempest reminded him tartly. "You are simply seeing a series of images, created by the retrospectacles, giving you an idea of the events that occurred on that fateful night."

Angus knew that this was what Catcher Tempest had brought him here to see: the beginnings of his own history, the very earliest days of the storm prophets, when their fire dragons had soared high above the ruined city. Each one was larger and more impressive than his own, each one unique with its own distinct colors and form. For one brief moment the dragons lingered, wings blazing in the dark sky above the flames, before they swooped down and disappeared into the fires below. He felt a strange, uneasy stirring in his chest, a twitchy feeling in his fingers and toes, as if some hidden part of him that he'd never even felt before had suddenly stirred at the sight.

And then, in the blink of an eye, it was over. The burned city, devastated, smoldering in a choking haze, lay before him.

"Angus?" Jeremius was gently trying to loosen his grip on the retrospectacles. "It's over now."He lifted the goggles carefully off Angus's head.

Angus rubbed his eyes and blinked, staring out across

the city. He was extremely relieved to see that modern-day London was still standing exactly where it had been just a few minutes before. There were no burned ruins or charred lightning towers, no leaping fire dragons. He'd been looking at a phantom of the past, nothing more.

"I hope you realize how extraordinarily lucky you are to have seen this," Catcher Tempest said, staring down his nose at Angus.

Angus wasn't convinced that "lucky" was the right word. The startling images of a fire-ravaged city had been burned into his memory as if he'd witnessed it with his own eyes, as if he'd stood at the top of the tallest lightning tower in the middle of the very storm that had transformed London into a blackened carcass. His heart was still pounding inside his rib cage.

"You have witnessed the earliest beginnings of the lightning catchers and the storm prophets, just as Principal Dark-Angel requested. Now, I really must go and help sort out Greenland," Catcher Tempest said, glancing impatiently at his weather watch. "Good day to you both."

He disappeared around the curve of the domed roof without a backward glance.

3

CREVICE AND SONS

Angus spent the rest of the day in a strange sort of daze. Scenes from the retrospectacles flashed before his eyes as he and his uncle left the museum and stopped off at the cartographer's, where Jeremius picked up some old maps of Canada, and an antiques shop, where Jeremius rummaged around for rare fossilized hailstones. It was only at the end of a very long day that they finally headed for a private pier to catch a ferry to the Isle of Imbur. After a swift dinner in the ferry's packed dining room, Jeremius led him straight down to a small, comfortable cabin where Angus fell asleep almost instantly. His dreams were filled with magnificent fire dragons that swooped and soared

above the roar of ancient flames. He tossed and turned as London burned before him again and again, as something unfamiliar, something that longed to break free and join the creatures in their fiery dance, stirred inside him.

When the ferry arrived at Imbur early the next morning, he stumbled out of bed and followed Jeremius into the dark, where they climbed aboard an open-topped steam-powered coach. It took them directly to 37 Feaver Street.

"What are we doing at Dougal's house?" Angus asked sleepily as his uncle shuffled him inside. "I thought we were heading back to Perilous?" But Jeremius refused to explain anything at such an early hour of the morning, and before Angus was fully conscious again, he was climbing into another soft bed at the top of the house, where he fell asleep still wearing his socks and shoes.

When he finally woke up for a second time, feeling groggy, it took him several moments to remember where he was. The cramped ferry cabin had gone; curtains were drawn across a tall window; his socks and shoes had been removed and laid neatly on a chair, and—

"Oh!" Angus jumped, banging his elbow on the bedside

table. Someone was staring at him through a half-open door. Deep green eyes blinked from behind a pair of small, round glasses. Angus recognized the familiar face immediately.

"Good! You're awake at last!" Dougal came bounding into his room and perched on the edge of the bed, grinning. It was obvious that his jet black hair had been trimmed recently with the aid of some blunt scissors. He'd also grown several inches over the summer and looked slightly less round through the middle than the last time Angus had seen him. "It's about time, too. I thought you were going to sleep through the whole day."

"Why, what time is it?" Angus asked, feeling extremely disoriented.

"Eight forty-five. Jeremius tried to wake you up an hour ago, but you were still snoring your head off."

Angus rubbed the sleep out of his eyes and grinned. It was brilliant to see Dougal again. It had been impossible to contact his friend over the summer using telephones or computers, because of the volatile nature of the work carried out at Perilous and the strong interference it created.

"Dad says you're staying here for five whole days; then

we're going back to Perilous together," Dougal explained. "He only told me last night. But never mind about that now. What's been going on?" He leaned in, lowering his voice. "Jeremius keeps mumbling stuff to Dad in the kitchen about weather museums. But every time I get anywhere near them, they change the subject and start talking about boring Perilous stuff instead. And why do they keep mentioning Trevelyan Tempest?" he added, frowning. "I thought he was that lightning catcher who worked at the London office."

"He is," Angus said. He settled himself back against his pillows and told Dougal everything about the surprise trip to the Starling Museum of Storm Science.

"So you actually saw London burning? Wow!" Dougal shook his head, looking deeply impressed. "I thought when Dark-Angel said it was time for you to learn more about the storm prophets she meant you'd be reading books and diaries and stuff."

"Yeah, me too," Angus said.

"I wonder what else Dark-Angel's planning to show you. I mean, it must be something pretty amazing, or dangerous, if she's starting you off with retrospectacles."

Angus shifted uncomfortably in his bed. Was Dougal right? Was learning about the storm prophets going to be far more hazardous than he'd realized? He definitely hadn't been prepared for the powerful images he'd seen through the retrospectacles or for the strange effect they'd had on him. He could still feel the spot, hidden deep inside his chest, that had been disturbed by the sight of so many fire dragons and the burning of phantom fires, something that was reluctant to curl up and return to the slumber from which it had been shaken. It felt oddly like indigestion.

"Are you all right?" Dougal asked, frowning at him. "Only you keep rubbing the same spot on your chest."

Angus stopped immediately and let his hand fall to his side.

"Anyway, Dad's taking us into Little Frog's Bottom this morning," Dougal said. "And Mrs. Stobbs came in early and cooked you and Jeremius a huge breakfast."

Mrs. Stobbs, the Dewsnap family housekeeper, had been helping out at Feaver Street ever since Dougal's mum had died. The rest of the time, she worked for Principal Dark-Angel at Perilous, where Angus and Dougal had often seen her bustling about with furniture polish and trays of tea.

"You're lucky; she's already gone into town to do some shopping," Dougal said, hopping off the bed, "or she'd be up here right now, fussing about and trying to force you into an extra undershirt."

Ten minutes later, after a quick wash and a change of clothes, Angus followed Dougal down the stairs. The rest of the house at Feaver Street had a ramshackle, uncared-for feel about it, with peeling wallpaper, faded rugs, and flickering gas lamps. The kitchen, however, was always warm and cozy, and the smell of freshly baked muffins made Angus's mouth water as they entered the room. Just as Dougal had warned, Jeremius and Dougal's dad sat huddled together in the far corner of the kitchen, talking quietly.

"Ah, Angus!" Mr. Dewsnap stood up and shook him cheerfully by the hand. "'Tis a great pleasure as always, my fine young fellow. Welcome back to Feaver Street."

"Er, thanks very much, Mr. Dewsnap."

Mr. Dewsnap was short and rather stout, with the same round glasses and jet black hair as Dougal. He was dressed in his favorite patterned housecoat, which reminded Angus of a bedspread.

"Jeremius has just been filling me in on all the details of your fascinating lightning tour of London"—Mr. Dewsnap continued in a melodious voice— "although I'm not convinced that introducing a young lightning cub to a pair of retrospectacles was entirely appropriate. They're well known for causing nightmares. I remember seeing a famously fierce fognado through some once." He shivered suddenly. "It gave me a severe case of the collywobbles for weeks."

"You've never mentioned that before," Dougal said, staring at his dad in surprise.

"There are a great many things I have not yet told you about my life."

"Like the time you almost got yourself killed in an ice maze, for instance, when you came to stay at the Canadian Exploratorium," Jeremius said as he stood up and stretched.

"You're kidding!" Dougal said, surprised. "What were *you* doing in an ice maze?"

Mr. Dewsnap chuckled. "Not all research for my books

involves sitting about in libraries and reading ancient, dusty tomes. It sometimes calls for a more . . . direct approach. I found a fascinating document that talked of hidden wonders buried in an old, abandoned ice maze from which no one had ever returned. I hired a local guide who was willing to risk rumors of sudden spontaneous snow swamps, and we set off at three-thirty on a Tuesday afternoon in January. You and Angus are not the only ones capable of having thrilling adventures."

"But what happened?" Angus asked, enthralled.

"We heard nothing from Aloysius for a whole week," Jeremius said. It took Angus several seconds to realize that Aloysius must be Mr. Dewsnap's first name. "We thought he'd been eaten by a polar bear, or worse."

"The truth was far more mundane, I'm afraid. The ice maze is famous for the vicious snowstorms that rage through its passages in the winter months, and we were pinned down by a particularly nasty specimen for some days, before we could continue our search."

"But how did you survive?" Dougal asked, staring at his dad, flabbergasted.

"Luckily, I'd had the good sense to pack plenty of

reindeer furs and a small camp stove. We survived by making meltwater lichen soup, which was surprisingly tasty with a pinch of salt."

Angus exchanged shocked looks with Dougal. He found it impossible to imagine Mr. Dewsnap, with his comfy slippers and portly frame, trekking through remote ice mazes.

The corners of Mr. Dewsnap's mouth began to twitch, then. . .

"You're making the whole thing up!" Dougal declared suddenly, pointing a finger at his dad.

Jeremius roared with laughter. Mr. Dewsnap smiled over the top of his glasses at Dougal and winked. "I may have embellished a few of the finer details, just to add to the excitement of the tale, you understand."

"Or you might have stolen the whole story from an old copy of the *Weekly Weathervane* you've been reading," Jeremius said, grabbing a dog-eared magazine from Mr. Dewsnap's chair in the corner of the room. The cover showed a large picture of the famous ice maze.

Angus grinned. The *Weekly Weathervane* was a private weekly news journal for the inhabitants of Perilous.

It reported on everything that happened inside the Exploratorium, from explosions in the experimental division and the achievements of its lightning catchers to nasty outbreaks of snow boot boils.

"Typical, nobody ever tells me the truth around here," Dougal grumbled, folding his arms across his chest as Jeremius continued to smile. "I thought you'd been on a real trek!"

Mr. Dewsnap chuckled. "Sadly, any such expedition would play havoc with my chilblains."

Dougal's bad mood didn't last long. Mr. Dewsnap guided them over to the kitchen table, where Mrs. Stobbs had laid out a substantial breakfast. There were steaming pans of porridge, a large plate of muffins, toast, and pastries the sight of which made Angus's stomach growl with hunger.

An hour later, after four extra rounds of toast and some genuine tales of adventure from Jeremius, who had once been forced to share an igloo on Svalbard with a family of arctic foxes, Mr. Dewsnap hurried them all out of the house for a trip into Little Frog's Bottom. They caught another steam-powered coach, which chugged slowly through a deep swirl of cobbled lanes and deposited them in a lively square at the very heart of the spiral-shaped town.

Angus had been looking forward to exploring Little Frog's Bottom ever since he'd first visited Feaver Street last year in the middle of a treacherous winter. He gazed around the square with interest. There was a row of very crooked-looking shops, all leaning to the left, as if they'd been caught in a stiff breeze for hundreds of years. Cafés, bookstalls, and gift shops spilled out onto the cobbles with tantalizing offers of freshly baked cookies and the latest comic featuring Louie the Lightning Hero. At one end of the square, towering over the roofs of the nearby buildings, stood an imposing statue of two men, bearded and spectacled, wearing long leather jerkins emblazoned with lightning bolts. It took Angus several seconds to realize he was staring at Philip Starling and Edgar Perilous. In the distance, sitting high above the town on a tall tooth of rock, was the Perilous Exploratorium for Violent Weather and Vicious Storms. The stone walls and ornate steel and glass weather bubbles looked magnificent in the soft morning sunshine. Angus felt his heart leap. It was the first time he'd seen it in months. He turned to Dougal and grinned.

"Right, you two, I've got to get my boots mended and this beard shaved off," Jeremius said, scratching the stubbly growth on his chin.

"And I really must return these books to the library." Mr. Dewsnap patted the pockets in his overcoat, which looked weighted down. "I trust you two can amuse yourselves for a couple of hours."

"What?" Dougal stared at his dad, shocked. "You mean you're actually letting us wander about, on our own, for the whole morning?"

"That is correct." Mr. Dewsnap smiled. "I must insist, however, that you steer clear of Ballantine's Bazaar of fortune-telling, Christow's all-weather supplies shop, and the Frog's Bottom Bakery." He pointed to a shop that was advertising prune and cuttlefish pie. Angus grinned. It was exactly the kind of experimental cooking Uncle Max got excited about. "I must also have your solemn promise that you will not enter the Horrible Endings Bookshop, Hazardous Haircuts, or Crevice and Sons."

Dougal's face fell. "But that's half the shops in the square!"

"Those are my terms and conditions. You must take

them or leave them. You are welcome to accompany me to the library, if you would prefer."

"Fine." Dougal sighed, his shoulders slumping. "We promise to stay out of every interesting shop in the whole town. We'll try not to start a sweater riot in Mrs. Dilloway's woolens shop."

"We'll meet you both for lunch at the Yodeling Yeti," Jeremius said. He pointed to a cheerful-looking café at the opposite end of the square and then disappeared into a barbershop where a large pair of scissors dangled over the door. Mr. Dewsnap headed for the austere-looking library, which was wedged between a hat shop called Noggins and a fishmonger's.

"So, where do you want to go first?" Angus asked, feeling amazed by their sudden glorious freedom.

"Obvious, isn't it? It's got to be Cradget's!" Dougal pointed to a tall building close by that was just opening its front doors. "They sell the coolest stuff in town. Come on!"

Dougal led the way across the cobbles. Angus followed, feeling eager to spend some of the extra pocket money he'd earned over the summer helping Uncle Max round up a rogue batch of instant icicle slicers that had run amok in the garden, annihilating a bed of begonias.

Cradget's did not disappoint. Inside, there were towering displays of unusual board games, most of which Angus had never heard of before. His favorite, Pursuit, sounded positively dangerous and seemed to involve some sort of demented compass. They crept quietly past conundrum corner, where an assortment of comfy, high-backed chairs had all been turned away from one another so customers could sit and solve their favorite puzzles and crosswords in peace. Angus bought a large bag of colorful magnetic marbles. Dougal quickly scooped up something called a scare-me-not, which was long and rectangular and appeared to contain a maze with a small glass ball at the center.

"The idea's simple, really," Dougal explained with enthusiasm as he rummaged in his pockets for some change. "The puzzle's covered in secret holes that open without warning, and you've got to maneuver the ball through the maze and down one of the holes before it closes again. It's top of Cradget's best-selling timer puzzle range."

"What's a timer puzzle?" Angus asked.

"Each puzzle is fitted with an internal timer, set to one

day, four months, or anything in between, and unless you solve the puzzle before your time is up, it self-destructs."

"Seriously?" Angus asked, surprised.

"Yeah, that's why they're so popular. You've got no idea how long you've got to solve the puzzle because each one is set to a completely different time. It's brilliant and absolutely barmy!"

They were almost at the register when Dougal hurried back to grab another one. "Just in case the first one self-destructs by the end of the day."

Angus followed, deciding to try the scare-me-not for himself. When they finally made their way toward the exit a few minutes later, Dougal noticed something even more thrilling.

"Hey, look at that!" He darted over to read the large sign that had just been placed next to a stack of crossword puzzle books.

Are you smart enough to claim the title of
Imbur's brainiest brain?
Entries are now invited for
Cradget's Annual Tri-Hard Puzzle Competition

First prize: A year's subscription to Conundrum
Magazine and the coveted Tri-Hard Trophy
Second prize: Cradget's Gift Vouchers
Third prize: Novelty spy pen with hidden camera

"This competition is really famous," Dougal said, staring at the poster in wonder. "It's a real brainbuster. They send you three different word puzzles to solve. Each new puzzle is harder than the last, and you've got to complete all three to even stand a chance of winning a prize."

"Word puzzles?"

"Yeah, they're not like normal crosswords or anything, though. These puzzles have got layers, and tricks, and booby traps that can trip you up and send you right back to the beginning. They're incredibly complicated."

"You should definitely enter," Angus said, seeing the look of excitement on Dougal's face.

"Yeah, I think I will." Dougal was already heading for the queue of people waiting for entry forms. "Just don't tell anyone else at Perilous, okay? Everyone already thinks I'm a nerd."

They emerged into the sunshine ten minutes later.

"This is turning out to be a truly excellent morning!" Dougal stuffed the competition entry form into his pocket. "What shall we do next? We could visit the statue of Starling and Perilous, if you want."

Angus stood and admired the statue properly for the first time. It towered over everything else in the square, the heads of the early lightning catchers reaching above the roofline of the tallest shops as if studying the weather on the horizon.

"Why's there a statue of Starling and Perilous in the middle of Little Frog's Bottom, anyway?" he asked.

"Well, they're both pretty important in Imbur Island history, I suppose," Dougal said with a shrug. "I think the statue's been here for at least a hundred years. You can climb all the way up to the top and look out through windows over the whole town. Oh, wait, I forgot. It's usually closed on Tuesdays for cleaning."

They meandered instead past the shops closest to Cradget's, all of which were on Mr. Dewsnap's forbidden list. At Ballantine's Bazaar of Fortune-telling there was a window display of half-price crystal balls. Dougal gazed longingly through the open door of the Horrible Endings

Bookshop, which smelled like compost. In each of the windows, the same poster stared back at Angus. It was brightly colored with just two tantalizing words in large red letters, "Coming Soon!"

"I wonder what that's all about," he said, stopping to inspect one of the posters properly.

Dougal shrugged. "It's probably just a sale of meat-eating plants at Brabazon Botanicals or something."

"Brabazon Botanicals?"

Dougal turned and pointed to a large imposing building on the far boundary of the square that dwarfed the shops on either side of it. A peaked glass roof had been opened at the top, allowing an interesting assortment of tall trees and palms to burst out into the sunshine, their leaves and fronds rustling gently in the breeze.

"That's Brabazon Botanicals," Dougal said, "and it's only one of the most hazardous shops in town, but Dad didn't say anything about steering clear of it!"

It was like entering an exotic indoor garden. They slipped past a shiny wooden sales counter, crowded with shop assistants, just inside the door and then:

"Whoa!" Angus gasped.

A raging waterfall cascaded down a fake cliff wall. There were banana trees, long trails of purple ivy, and a steaming pond full of giant, carnivorous water lilies, which snapped at their ankles as they hurried past. It was clear that the plant life on Imbur was far more hazardous, and ravenous, than anything Angus had encountered in Devon. They followed the signs to something called the arboretum and stood among the tall trees and tropical palms that they'd spotted from the other side of the square. The breeze coming through the open glass roof above was cool and refreshing.

"This place is amazing," Angus said, catching a brief glimpse of blue sky through the tangled branches overhead.

"Dad's brought me in here loads of times over the summer for manure and plant cuttings," Dougal said. "I really wanted to take a trip over to the mainland instead, to see Stonehenge. But he's been too busy writing a new book on the history of Little Frog's Bottom."

"You could come and stay with me in the next holidays, if you want," Angus said, with a shrug, "as long as you don't mind being chased around the Windmill by pods or blizzard catchers."

"Seriously?" Dougal looked thrilled by the idea.

"Yeah, you can sleep in my room. There's loads of space." Angus grinned, wondering why he hadn't considered such an excellent idea before.

"Brilliant! Thanks. I mean, if you're sure it's okay with your uncle Max and everything. And speaking of uncles . . ." Dougal checked over his shoulder to make sure no one was listening. "Have you found out anything else about Jeremius?"

At the end of the previous term, after many doubts about his mysterious new uncle, Angus had discovered that Jeremius spent much of his time trailing monsoon mongrels around the globe, trying to stop them from spreading dangerous storms and hazardous weather. A jagged scar on his chin came from one such adventure at Castle Dankhart.

"He still won't tell me anything about Castle Dankhart," Angus said with a long sigh. "But he can't have been following any monsoon mongrels around in the last few months; he's just spent the whole summer at the Windmill."

"Hey, watch out!"

Dougal dragged Angus out of the way as a herd of

spiky-looking plants went scuttling past, dragging their long roots behind them, followed by an irate-looking shop assistant.

They spent the rest of the morning exploring book-shops, toffee shops, and bric-a-brac stalls, where they bumped into Mrs. Stobbs, who had just emerged from the fishmonger's.

"It's nice to see you again, my lovely." She smiled at Angus, patting the soft brown curls on top of her head.

"Thanks for the brilliant breakfast, Mrs. Stobbs," Angus said, suddenly remembering his manners.

"You're welcome, my dear. I'm making a delicious fish pie for dinner," she told them, bundling a very smelly par-cel with tailfins into her bag. "But I've got to get home to my Albert first. He's having trouble with his lumbago again, poor dear, and he needs his powdered bone cure from Crevice and Sons."

"Who's Albert?" Angus asked as they left Mrs. Stobbs to the rest of her shopping. "And what's Crevice and Sons?"

"Albert's her husband," Dougal explained. "And Crevice and Sons is a fine-bone merchant."

They stopped in front of a dingy-looking shop in another corner of the square farthest away from Brabazon Botanicals. Moss and lichen grew on the cobbles outside the door. There were no decorations, cheerful awnings, or window displays. "The same people own another shop down Feaver Street; you saw it last time you stayed."

Angus remembered the creepy-looking shop well. He tried to imagine a similar bone merchant on the high street in Budleigh Otterstone, nestled between the bakery and the post office, and failed.

"They've been around for hundreds of years; Dad won't tell me what they sell exactly. But they used to be specialists in mummification."

"Mummification? What, you mean, like in ancient Egypt?"

"Yeah." Dougal shrugged. "I don't think they do it anymore. Although some of the people Dad knows from the Imbur Island Museum look as if they were mummified aeons ago."

Angus stared at the dark-fronted shop. Uncle Max had lent him a book about the ancient Egyptians once. It had contained a whole chapter about mummification that

Angus could still recall in all its gruesome detail, including the section about removing all internal organs from the body and stuffing them into jars. The worst part, however, was the long hook used for removing the brains . . . by wiggling it straight up a nostril. Angus felt sick just thinking about it.

"There was a rumor flying around a few years ago that they had some actual mummies on display inside the shop." Dougal pressed his nose against the grimy glass. "Maybe if we just take a quick look around . . ."

"Er, isn't this on your dad's list of forbidden shops?" Angus said.

"Well, yeah, but it's not like we're planning to get ourselves pickled and wrapped up in bandages, is it? Anyway, I'm not even sure it's open."

Dougal hesitated for a second, then pushed timidly on the door. A small bell tinkled above their heads, making them both jump as they entered. Inside, the shop was dark and gloomy. A narrow walkway disappeared into a twisting labyrinth of shelves and display cabinets. Thick veils of dust and sagging cobwebs covered almost every surface and windowpane. Angus shivered. There was no sign of anything mummified.

"*Urgh!* Look at those!" Dougal darted over to a low shelf where a collection of ugly animal-skull table lamps had been arranged.

Just beyond the lamps was a large display of ornamental spoons, earrings, and necklaces made from cow ribs and rabbits' feet, as well as a whole gallery of anatomical skeletons dangling limply from long rails and arranged in order of height.

"I wonder who Crevice sells those to," Angus said, gulping, as they hurried through the forest of milky white bones. He flinched as his hand accidentally brushed against the knuckles of a large skeleton. Its empty eye sockets watched him as he stumbled past.

There were cabinets full of teacups and saucers made from fine ox-bone china and a vast collection of glass jars containing powdered bone, which they stopped to inspect in more detail.

"According to this label, powdered bone is supposed to be good for rheumatism, muscle aches, lumbago, and all sorts of other stuff," Angus said, studying the contents as they passed each jar.

"Yuck!" Dougal wrinkled his nose in disgust. "Talk about dodgy. How do we get out of this place? I think I've had enough bones for one day."

Angus was feeling just as keen to leave. Dougal led them swiftly back the way they'd just come. After several minutes, however, it was obvious that they'd somehow taken a wrong turning and were now heading even deeper into the choking tangle of shelves and jars. They crept through an eerie alley of animal skeletons, including whole packs of scrawny-looking rats and weasels. There was also something suspiciously dinosaurlike with a long neck and barrel-shaped rib cage that was so enormous Angus and Dougal could have stood upright inside it.

"This place is like a rabbit warren," Angus said, staring around. He glanced at his weather watch. But apart from the fact that they were now headed in a northeasterly direction, it could tell him nothing useful about how to find the exit. He was just about to suggest climbing up onto one of the cabinets so he could get his bearings when Dougal suddenly yanked him down behind the skeleton of a shark complete with vicious teeth.

"What?"

"I think I've just seen Creepy Crevice, the shop owner!" Dougal whispered.

Angus peered through the bones. "His first name's Creepy?"

"Of course it isn't. That's just what everyone on the island calls him."

A man was standing twenty feet away from them behind a dusty shop counter. Creepy Crevice was white haired and withered, his paper-thin skin as pale as the powdered bone that sat in jars on the shelves behind him. His long fingers, sunken cheeks, and scrawny frame gave him the appearance of a living skeleton, dressed in a faded, old-fashioned suit like the ones Angus had once seen at a Victorian Christmas fair.

"Why are we hiding?" Angus asked, keeping his voice low.

"Because Creepy Crevice isn't exactly friendly," Dougal whispered. "Dad had an argument with him once about some bone china. I heard them shouting at each other on the front doorstep. Crevice threatened to pickle Dad's ears."

Angus could believe it. Crevice was scowling in a very

unfriendly manner at a customer on the other side of the counter who was dressed in a dark, flared coat that was so long it brushed the ground. It was also bulky enough to hide more lightning cubs than an inflatable emergency weather shelter. There were three distinctive triangular buttons sewn to the cuff of each sleeve that looked suspiciously as if they were made of bone.

The coat wearer turned away from the counter abruptly a few seconds later, face hidden inside a low hood. Angus sank quickly behind the shark skeleton. For some reason it felt safer not to be seen. He and Dougal waited until Crevice had disappeared into an office behind the counter, then followed the figure in the coat at a safe distance back toward the front of the shop. The door came into sight a few moments later.

"Thank goodness for that!" Dougal said, speeding up in his rush to leave.

"Yeah, I was starting to think we'd have to sleep in this shop!"

As they swept past a pile of half-price dinosaur bones, however, Dougal caught his foot on the edge of the display and tripped.

CREVICE AND SONS

"Ooof!"

He crashed heavily to the ground. Bones scattered in every direction, clattering noisily across the floor.

"Who's there? Thieves! Troublemakers!" Creepy Crevice appeared at lightning speed, having clearly taken a shortcut through the maze of shelves. "All breakages must be paid for!" he said, looming over them both.

"Sorry, Mr. Crevice. It was an accident!" Dougal scrambled to his feet. He brushed himself off and stood next to Angus, quivering.

"Accident or not, somebody has to pay for this damage." The angry shopkeeper picked up two halves of a broken bone, looking furious. "Each of these bones is worth ten silver starlings, so either you two pay up, or you will pay the consequences." He pointed to a sign on the inside of the shop door which said "All Troublemakers will be Mummified."

"M-m-mummified?" Dougal whimpered.

Angus backed away from the bone merchant and rummaged quickly through his pockets. He had precisely two silver starlings left. It wasn't nearly enough to save them from having their brains pickled. He shot a swift look at

Dougal, who had spent the last of his own pocket money in Cradget's.

"I-I'm sorry, Mr. Crevice," Angus said. "We haven't got enough money."

He dragged everything out of his pockets to prove it, including the fluff that had collected in the corners.

"I'll take those." Crevice snatched up his last two silver starlings greedily. "And what about you?" The bone merchant turned to Dougal, his eyes narrowing. "You're Aloysius Dewsnap's boy, aren't you? I've had trouble with your family before."

"We can pay you back, Mr. Crevice," Angus said as Dougal emptied his pockets all over the floor, scattering hard candy and rubber bands far and wide. "If you just let me go and find my uncle—"

"Think I was born yesterday, boy? If I let you out of this shop, I'll never see you again. If you can't pay, you already know the consequences." He nodded at the warning to all troublemakers on the back of the door. "So . . ." He reached into his pocket and slowly pulled out a long hook. "Which one of you wants to go first?"

Angus gulped.

"Maybe you'll think twice in the future about sneaking into my shop and breaking things after you've had a bit of mummification."

Dougal swayed on his feet, looking faint. Angus glanced over his shoulder, wondering if they could make a run for it. At that precise moment, however, the shop door burst open with a loud bang.

"Put that hook away, Crevice." Jeremius marched straight over to the bone merchant. "And please explain why you are threatening my nephew and his friend?"

"I caught these two fair and square, smashing precious dinosaur bones and trying to leave without paying me what's due."

"We didn't smash anything!" Angus interrupted quickly. "We tripped!"

Jeremius took a small money pouch from his pocket and threw five silver starlings at Crevice's feet. "That's more than enough to cover your losses. You've been trying to pass those cheap fakes off as the genuine article for years, and unless you want the whole town to know about it before sundown, you'll take the money and be grateful."

"Grateful to a McFangus? You won't live long enough to see the day!" Crevice scowled at Jeremius with deep loathing. He scooped up the silver coins from the floor, however, and disappeared back into the depths of his gloomy shop, mumbling.

"I think the time has come to leave," Jeremius said, gripping Angus and Dougal firmly by the shoulders. He steered them out through the door, which was now hanging on by a single hinge, back into the sunlight and straight across the cobbled square, only stopping when the Yodeling Yeti café came into view up ahead.

"You two ought to know better than to go sneaking off into shops you've been told to avoid," Jeremius said, staring down at them both in a very serious manner. "Crevice is nothing but a money-grabbing thief. He'll try to sell you your own backbone, given half a chance. He's also got a reputation for being one of the most bad-tempered, sour-natured shopkeepers on this island. It was just lucky I came looking for you when I did."

"Sorry," Dougal said, looking down at his shoes, shame-faced. "It was all my idea."

"We both wanted to see if he had any mummies in his

shop," Angus added, feeling it wasn't fair to let Dougal take all the blame.

Jeremius folded his arms across his chest. "Do I have your solemn promise that you will never enter the bone merchant's again?"

"Yeah, I promise," Angus said, meaning every word of it.

Dougal nodded. "I'm never going near that place again. Crevice was threatening to mummify us!"

"I doubt whether he would have gone quite that far," Jeremius said, the corners of his mouth twitching. "Just stay away from his shop in the future. It might also be a wise idea not to mention this to Mr. Dewsnap, unless you want to spend the rest of the holidays scrubbing kitchen floors and washing up."

They both followed Jeremius into the Yodeling Yeti café feeling as if they'd had a very lucky escape, in more ways than one.

4

THE FEATHERED MESSAGE

Angus was extremely pleased when Jeremius kept his word and told no one else about their adventures in the fine-bone merchant's.

"It's a shame we didn't see any mummies, though," Dougal said as they sat on the floor of his bedroom the following afternoon, attempting to solve the scare-me-not puzzles they'd both bought at Cradget's.

"Maybe Crevice keeps them in another part of the shop, or he only shows them to special customers," Angus suggested.

He moved the ball around his own puzzle, attempting to get it through one of the holes before the hole closed again. So far he hadn't even come close.

"Yeah, or maybe there never were any mummies in the first place. Maybe Creepy Crevice started a rumor just to lure people into his shop so they could buy some useless fake dinosaur bones instead. Do you reckon he meant it about turning us both into mummies?" Dougal added with a shiver. "I mean, if Jeremius hadn't come bursting through the door when he did. . ."

Angus tried hard not to think about how far the bone merchant would have gone to frighten them. Instead, he spent the next few days watching Dougal teach his pet lightning moth, Norman, some new tricks. Cid, his first lightning moth, had been trampled to the ground by Adrik Swarfe, and Angus had persuaded Theodore Twill, an older lightning cub, to give Dougal a replacement.

"I can make him loop-the-loop now, and he does these amazing death dives!" Dougal demonstrated by allowing the moth to zoom around his bedroom ceiling, gathering velocity, before it plummeted toward the floor at lightning speed.

"Impressive!" Angus said as Norman pulled out of the

dive at the last second, wings quivering under the strain. "I wonder if Twill's got any moths left."

Dougal also received the first part of Cradget's Tri-Hard Puzzle Competition through the mail.

"It looks like the first stage involves unlocking the clues on a word pyramid," he explained eagerly, showing Angus a complicated triangular puzzle. "I've got to start solving the clues from the bottom up, unlocking the secret puzzle as I go. This looks really difficult," he added, grinning. "What's a fourteen-letter word for 'something having merely a semblance of truth'?"

"Er. . ." Angus said, uncertain what "semblance" actually meant.

But it was the evenings that Angus enjoyed at Feaver Street the most. Mr. Dewsnap told them long tales of lightning catcher adventures that he'd read about in old copies of the *Weathervane* as they tucked into delicious cakes and pies baked by Mrs. Stobbs. After dinner, Angus and Dougal challenged Jeremius to rowdy games of Snaggle, which Dougal had bought from Cradget's a few years ago.

When the time finally came to return to Perilous, however, Angus was looking forward to seeing Indigo and

continuing his training as a lightning cub. The morning
of their departure was chaotic, with Dougal discovering
at the last minute that his weatherproof coat had been
attacked by Norman.

"How am I supposed to stay dry in this?" he wailed,
holding up a holey hood and nibbled sleeves.

Angus lugged his overstuffed bag down the stairs, being
careful not to set off his scare-me-not puzzle. He'd almost
reached the bottom when the seams suddenly ruptured.
His bag of magnetic marbles burst open and bounced
down the remaining steps, chasing one another far and
wide across the floor.

By the time they left Feaver Street, loaded down with
home-baked cookies and freshly knitted socks from
Mrs. Stobbs, and caught a steam-powered coach back to
Perilous, it was fast approaching lunchtime. Angus kept
his mouth shut and his stomach clenched tight as they
piled into the gravity railway carriage. It was his least
favorite part of life at the Exploratorium, but there was no
other way of traveling up the tall tooth of rock upon which
Perilous sat. He concentrated hard on Dougal's coat buttons as the railway shot upward, whizzing past flocks of

birds and through small puffy clouds. When they finally reached the top, he heaved his bag straight out of the carriage and into the fresh air of the courtyard.

"Hey, Angus!"

Edmund Croxley, one of the older lightning cubs, was weaving his way toward him with a friendly wave. Angus grinned. Edmund had given him a guided tour of Perilous shortly after he'd first arrived on the island.

"Had a good holiday?" Edmund inquired as Dougal joined them.

"Yeah, thanks."

"I hope you younger lightning cubs have been keeping up with your studies over the summer. It's important not to let your brain go soft."

"I think it might be a bit late for that," Angus said, grinning sideways at Dougal.

"Didn't I see you and your uncle at the Starling Museum of Storm Science last week?" Edmund continued.

"Er," Angus said, taken by surprise. He'd never even considered that the museum might be full of other lightning cubs. What if he'd bumped into Pixie and Percival Vellum, his least favorite lightning cubs in the whole of

Perilous? What if someone had seen him being marched out of the foyer by Catcher Tempest? Would anyone have believed he was simply there to stare at the cloud gallery?

"Did you see the new interactive glacier exhibit?" Edmund asked. "Swarming with lightning catchers from Brazil, couldn't get anywhere near it until they'd all cleared off. And then half the museum had to be closed because of a small fire in the gift shop, something about a teacup going bonkers."

Angus gulped. Dougal nudged him with his elbow, grinning.

"Anyway, I can't stand around here chatting," Edmund said. "I must see if my room has been redecorated over the summer. It was completely ripped to shreds at the end of last term by an escaped lightning moth. I'll see you later." And he darted inside.

"Funny how Croxley's room was the only one that got wrecked," Dougal said, still smiling.

"Yeah, I bet Theodore Twill had something to do with that."

A moment later Angus and Dougal followed Jeremius into the entrance hall, where they were met by an incredible sight. Bright, gaudy posters had been plastered over almost every inch of wall, staircase, and marbled pillar, giving the instant impression that the entire hall had been gift wrapped.

"Hey, we've seen the same posters all over Little Frog's Bottom, too," Dougal said, stopping to study one with interest. 'Coming Soon!' That's exactly what all the others said."

"Maybe it's got nothing to do with a plant sale at Brabazon Botanicals after all." Angus stared around the papered entrance hall, trying to imagine what else might be "Coming Soon."

"It could be a weather exhibition," Dougal said. "They had a huge one in Little Frog's Bottom about ten years ago, and Dad went. He said there were lightning catchers from all over the world showing off new inventions and stuff."

"Just imagine if the experimental division invented lightning-proof underpants." Angus grinned.

"If the experimental division has invented lightning-proof underpants, we're all in for a shocking time." Jeremius stood beside them, smiling. "Fascinating though this conversation is, I'm afraid I've got instructions to take you straight up to see Principal Dark-Angel," he added, turning toward Angus. "I believe she wants to ask you about our trip to the Storm Science Museum."

"Can't you just tell her what happened?" Angus asked hopefully. "I mean, you were with me the whole time."

But Jeremius could not be persuaded, and they parted from Dougal, who headed up the stairs to the supplies department to grab a new weatherproof coat without moth holes. Jeremius led Angus down a familiar passageway, with dark paintings of storm clouds hanging on the walls. Before Angus could gather his thoughts, Jeremius stopped outside a door, knocked once, and entered. Dark-Angel's office was sparsely decorated, with a single desk sitting in the center. Dozens of weather maps and charts covered the stone walls.

"Angus!" Felix Gudgeon, one of Angus's favorite lightning catchers, slapped him on the back in greeting as Jeremius closed the door behind them. Completely bald, with a single silver snowflake earring, Gudgeon was distinctive even by lightning catcher standards. His marbled gray beard couldn't hide the broad grin on his face. "Hope you've been keeping out of trouble for once."

Angus thought of the storm in a teacup and the incident at Crevice and Sons but decided now was not the moment to fill Gudgeon in on the details. Standing next to Gudgeon was Aramanthus Rogwood, one of his other favorite lightning catchers. Rogwood smiled at him with twinkling tawny eyes; his long braided beard was tucked into his leather jerkin to keep it out of his way. Standing directly in front of Rogwood, tapping her fingers impatiently against her arm, was Principal Delphinia Dark-Angel. Angus was glad to see that there was no sign of Valentine Vellum.

"Angus, I trust you had a good holiday at the Windmill." Dark-Angel smiled thinly at him, the usual unfriendly expression fixed on her face. Her short white hair and pallid skin looked even paler than normal under the light fissures. He tried not to stare at the bristly mole on her cheek.

"I understand from Trevelyan Tempest that your trip to the weather museum was most informative. And that you have now gained a thorough understanding of the earliest history of the lightning catchers and the storm prophets."

Angus nodded, hoping she wasn't about to ask him any difficult questions. Over the last few days at Feaver Street, a surprising number of storm prophet facts had somehow leaked out of his brain.

"Now that we have started to lay some solid foundations, the time has come for you to learn more about your heritage." Dark-Angel continued, turning to her desk and sitting down behind it. "The storm prophets have played a very important role in our history here at Perilous and in our understanding of the weather. Their unique abilities have allowed us to understand the very elemental forces of nature. A series of special lessons will now teach you all that we know of their impressive skills, which in turn may help develop your own abilities in the future."

Angus swallowed hard.

"The lessons will be conducted by Aramanthus Rogwood."

Rogwood smiled at him through his beard, and Angus felt a surge of relief. Rogwood had already told him more about the storm prophets than anyone else at Perilous, and he'd done so in a calm and kindly manner.

"These special lessons will take place in the Inner Sanctum

of Perplexing Mysteries and Secrets," Dark-Angel said.

"You're kidding!" Angus blurted out before he could stop himself.

Jeremius coughed suddenly, attempting to hide a huge guffaw of laughter. But Principal Dark-Angel was not amused. "I very rarely joke about such serious matters, McFangus. These lessons are extremely important, and if I discover that you have not been treating them with the seriousness they deserve . . ."

Angus gulped. The Inner Sanctum was the most mysterious department in the whole of Perilous. He had never seen anyone entering or leaving the department or met anyone who worked inside it. Nobody knew what lay behind the locked door. And he suddenly wondered why information about the storm prophets had to be kept inside such a heavily guarded and mysterious part of Perilous.

"Needless to say, by allowing you access to the Inner Sanctum and a great deal of sensitive information, I am placing you in a position of enormous trust." Dark-Angel continued. "I must therefore have your solemn promise that you will tell no one about these private lessons or describe anything you might see in the Inner Sanctum."

"I-I promise, miss," Angus said.

"And try not to draw too much attention to yourself in the meantime," she added, giving him a stern look. "The last thing we need is for everyone to start asking awkward questions."

Angus nodded and, ready to leave the office, half turned away from her. But it seemed Dark-Angel hadn't finished with him yet.

"Before you return to your friends, there is something else I wish to speak to you about." She paused for a long moment, shuffling uncomfortably in her chair. "I'm afraid we have received some very upsetting news in the last few days. A series of reports has been sent from Catcher Plymstock and Catcher Knapp via mechanical messenger," she said, taking something that looked like a squashed pigeon from a drawer in her desk. A small canister was attached underneath its wing with a ragged-looking note poking out one end. "I'm sorry to say there has been a terrible accident at Castle Dankhart. It appears that a weather experiment has gone catastrophically wrong, causing untold damage to the castle and possibly killing a number of monsoon mongrels."

Angus felt his insides freeze. The office seemed to shrink around him. "An a-accident? But my mum and dad, are they—"

"Do not fear, Angus." Rogwood placed a reassuring hand on his shoulder. "As far as we can tell, your mum and dad are alive and well. The accident appears to have occurred in upper reaches of the castle. A violent explosion expelled a large debris cloud, which has formed itself into a swirling weather vortex. This vortex is now hanging over the castle, making it almost impossible for us, even in the dirigible weather station, to get close enough to understand the truth of the matter. However . . ."

"We've got another theory," Gudgeon said, picking up where Rogwood had left off. "We think it's possible that Dankhart might have created an explosion on purpose."

Angus frowned. "I don't understand."

"We think that this so-called accident is nothing but a clever ruse," Gudgeon explained. "We've managed to collect some samples from the outer edge of the vortex, and they contain fragments of glass, stone, metal, and all manner of materials you'd expect to find if there had been a real explosion in one of the experimental rooms. But we believe Dankhart is trying to lay a false trail, to disguise the fact that he's up to something much bigger that he doesn't want anyone else to know about."

"But what is he trying to hide?" Angus asked, still struggling to take in the shocking news.

Gudgeon glanced sideways at Rogwood and Jeremius.

"We simply don't know yet," Jeremius said, not quite meeting Angus's eye.

"But it could be anything, with that maniac," Gudgeon added quickly to fill a sudden awkwardness. "Some new kind of diabolical weather he's been working on or a powerful machine."

Jeremius nodded. "We're trying to find out, but it isn't easy. It's impossible to get news in or out of the castle at the moment. All of our usual sources have gone quiet."

"So why are you telling me?" Angus asked, puzzled. Normally, he was the last person to know anything important about his parents, Dankhart, or the monsoon mongrels.

"Rumors have already begun to circulate," Dark-Angel explained. "We did not want you to hear whisperings about an explosion and fear the worst for your parents."

Angus stared at the principal, stunned. Dark-Angel had never been so honest with him before. And yet he also got the distinct impression that none of them was telling him the whole story.

"Very well, McFangus, you may go," Dark-Angel said, checking her watch and bringing the meeting to an abrupt end. "I will inform you if there is any more news."

"If you could wait for me outside," Jeremius said quietly as Angus turned to leave, "I would like a quick word before you rejoin Dougal."

Angus left Dark-Angel's office, closing the door behind him, his head suddenly spinning. What if Gudgeon, Rogwood, and Dark-Angel were wrong? What if there had been a real weather catastrophe and his parents were in terrible danger? Trapped in a dungeon, injured, abandoned by fleeing monsoon mongrels, or worse? Would it be possible to rescue them from such a violent weather vortex? Would anybody even try?

"Did you know about the explosion?" he asked Jeremius urgently as soon as his uncle joined him again a few moments later.

Jeremius nodded. "I got word the night we caught the

ferry back to Imbur, but I didn't want to alarm you with wild rumors and speculation. I arranged this meeting with Principal Dark-Angel so she could tell you everything."

Angus nodded, suddenly understanding the hushed conversations with Mr. Dewsnap back at Feaver Street. He felt grateful that his uncle was no longer keeping him in the dark.

"Principal Dark-Angel, Gudgeon, and Rogwood will do everything they can to find out what's going on and what it means for your mum and dad. In the meantime, we must assume that they are as safe and well as can be expected. Try not to worry. Your parents are both true survivors," he said, gripping Angus by the shoulders. "Did I ever tell you about the time your dad got trapped in a storm full of dark snow and got lost on a mountain in Peru? It took him three days to find his way out again."

Angus smiled sadly, wondering if any of the stories Jeremius had told him about his parents were true. Or were they simply more tales retold from the *Weathervane*, an attempt to lift his spirits?

"This is where I must leave you," Jeremius said as they entered the poster-ridden entrance hall once again.

"Oh, right, yeah. I-I'll see you later, then," Angus said, still feeling shaken.

"I'm afraid it will be a bit longer than that. I'm leaving Perilous."

"What? No way!" Angus burst out. "Why?"

"There is important business that I must attend to," Jeremius said, checking his weather watch and tightening the buckles on his leather satchel.

"Has it got something to do with the weather vortex?" Angus asked, determined to find out something before his uncle left.

"I'm afraid I can't tell you any details, but there is nothing more important at the moment than working out what's going on at Castle Dankhart. I will return as soon as I can, I promise."

"When?" Angus asked.

"In a month or two, possibly, if all goes well. In the meantime, if you have any worries or problems, you can go straight to Rogwood or Gudgeon. I have asked both of them to keep a special eye on you in my absence. So be warned," he added with a grin. "If you, Dougal, and Indigo go chasing off after monsoon mongrels again, I will hear about it!"

Angus smiled glumly. He'd got used to having Jeremius around over the summer. Perilous wouldn't be the same without him striding about the stone tunnels and passageways in his snow boots and furs. It had also been very comforting indeed to have another member of the McFangus family to talk to. Almost like having his dad back again.

"Right, I'd better be on my way. Dirigible weather stations and rogue storms wait for no one!" Jeremius pulled him into a brief tight hug. Then he swept through the front doors without a backward glance.

Angus stood for several moments watching the space where his uncle had disappeared. Then he walked slowly into the kitchens, feeling dazed. The kitchens at Perilous were vast, with long serving tables set against the far wall, groaning under the weight of freshly baked cookies and sandwiches. A gaggle of cooks was busy baking potatoes and slicing bread next to the roaring open fires.

The tables were already buzzing with the excited chatter of returning trainees. Angus dodged quickly past Jonathon Hake and Nigel Ridgely, two lightning cubs from his own year, without stopping to hear what they'd done in the holidays.

He found Dougal sitting at their usual table under one of the large fake palm trees that stretched all the way up to the vaulted ceiling, the scare-me-not puzzle lying on the table in front of him. Dougal, however, was not alone.

"Angus!" Indigo jumped to her feet as he approached, looking deeply concerned.

Indigo was private, fiercely loyal, and painfully shy at times, and Angus was extremely pleased to see her again. Her horse-chestnut–colored hair was pulled back off her face, revealing a strong resemblance to her older brother, Geronimo Midnight. Germ, as he preferred to be called, was training to be a doctor in the sanatorium. Unfortunately, Indigo also looked like her uncle, Scabious Dankhart.

"I've just told Indigo about Creepy Crevice and his stinking shop," Dougal said, explaining the shocked look on her face.

"I can't believe you went into the bone merchant's when your dad and Jeremius told you not to!" she gasped.

"Yeah, well, I wish we'd listened to them now," Dougal said with an involuntary shiver. "Is Jeremius still with Dark-Angel?" he added, peering over Angus's shoulder.

Angus shook his head and sat down next to Indigo. "He's gone. He won't be coming back to Perilous for months." He repeated what Jeremius had just told him in the entrance hall.

"Oh," Dougal said, disappointed, picking up the scare-me-not puzzle and fiddling with it absently. "I thought he might be staying at Perilous again, you know, in the Rotundra."

"Is that why Principal Dark-Angel wanted to see you?" Indigo asked, wide-eyed with curiosity.

Angus had already decided to ignore the promise he'd just made to Dark-Angel. News of this magnitude had to be shared with his two best friends. He swiftly told them everything he could remember about the explosion, the debris cloud, and the weather vortex that was now hanging over Castle Dankhart.

"You're kidding!" Dougal spluttered as soon as Angus had finished. "Me and Dad felt it. There was this strange sort of thunderclap about a week ago. It made all the teacups in the kitchen rattle."

Indigo nodded. "Germ and I heard it, too. We thought there'd been an accident in the experimental division."

Explosions were a frequent occurrence in that dangerous department and had been known to shake the whole Exploratorium to its very core.

"Rogwood and Gudgeon think it's all a clever ruse to fool us. They think Dankhart's trying to disguise something even bigger," Angus explained.

"I can't believe the maniac's at it again," Dougal said, still sounding shocked. "Why would anyone fake a massive explosion? Even your dear old uncle Scabby can't be that mad."

Indigo squirmed in her seat, looking highly uncomfortable at the mention of her uncle's name.

"But what about your mum and dad?" she asked.

Angus swallowed hard. "Rogwood and Gudgeon think they'll be okay. They think the explosion happened in the upper reaches of the castle. But how can they know for sure? We've got to find out more about that vortex!" he said, feeling a wave of anxiety sweep over him once again. "Something strange is going on. They were all being really careful about what they told me . . . as if they were hiding something."

Dougal and Indigo exchanged surprised glances.

"In that case, I bet those feathered messages from Catcher Plymstock and Catcher Knapp are full of important stuff," Dougal said, a thoughtful look crossing his face. "If we could just find out where Dark-Angel keeps them."

"And what about the samples taken by the weather station?" Indigo added.

Angus nodded at his friends, grateful. He'd need all the help he could get if he was going to get to the truth.

"That wasn't the only reason Dark-Angel wanted to see me." He leaned across the table, lowering his voice. "She's sending me for storm prophet lessons . . . in the Inner Sanctum."

Dougal dropped his puzzle with a clatter. Indigo clutched her face with her hands. Nobody spoke for several seconds; then:

"That's the best news I've heard in months!" Dougal said. "You'll be the only lightning cub in the whole of Perilous who knows what's really going on behind that door, and then you can tell us!"

Despite everything, Angus couldn't help smiling. Dougal had been fascinated by the mystery of the Inner

Sanctum ever since they'd first arrived at Perilous. Before they could discuss the subject any further, however, Dougal's scare-me-not gave a small ping.

"That's odd," Dougal said. He picked it up and turned it over in his hands. "It doesn't usually make any noise except when you're trying to—"

Ping!

Dougal's face blanched as the scare-me-not suddenly began to shake and vibrate.

"What's happening?" Indigo asked, scooting her chair away from it.

"I think it's about to self-destruct! They only start to shake when your time is—"

P-ting! P-ting! P-ting!

"Look out!" Dougal dropped the scare-me-not and dived under the table for cover. Angus leaped out of his chair, dragging Indigo away from the puzzle, which was now shaking so violently that it rocked the whole table back and forth.

BANG!

The puzzle finally ruptured, bursting apart in a spectacular shower of frazzled fragments, which then drifted to the floor, smoldering. Several lightning cubs sitting close by yelped with surprise and stood up for a better look.

"Whoa!" Dougal scrambled out from under the table as soon as it was safe. "When they say these puzzles self-destruct, they really mean it."

"There's nothing left except a scorch mark," Angus said, poking at the blackened table with his finger.

He quickly decided to lock his own scare-me-not puzzle in an empty drawer, where it couldn't destroy his other possessions.

5

NIGHT OWLS
WITH BEASTLY WIZ

Angus was woken the following morning by the sound of a clanging bell.

"Whashappning?" He sat bolt upright in bed, wondering if Perilous was on fire. A few seconds later, however, the noise stopped abruptly.

Angus yawned and stumbled out of bed, remembering that this was the first day of a brand-new term. He found some clean socks and pulled on his gray uniform, still feeling extremely sleepy. Then he grabbed his yellow weatherproof coat, just in case he was about to be thrust into a rain-filled weather tunnel, and stuck his head out into the curved hallway.

The door to the girls' half of the lightning cubs' living quarters was already open. Georgina Fox, Violet Quinn, and Millicent Nichols were giggling over the pages of a magazine. Juliana Jessop, a bossy older lightning cub, was talking loudly with a group of friends. Theodore Twill was encouraging his pet lightning moth to circle over the heads of some worried-looking third years. There also seemed to be a small number of other lightning cubs whom Angus didn't recognize, huddled together in a tight knot. Their weatherproof coats were far too long for their short legs.

"First years," Nicholas Grubb said loudly, nodding toward the frightened group, his sandy hair falling over his eyes. "Catcher Mint's about to take them through the weather tunnel to see if any of them come out the other end alive. Personally, I don't fancy their chances if they come up against a fognado."

Several of the first years squealed, looking utterly petrified. But Angus was staring at Nicholas Grubb with a dull thought now throbbing at the back of his brain.

"Hang on a minute. If they're first years, that must mean me, Dougal, and Indigo—"

"—are all second years now. Congratulations!" Nicholas thumped him hard on the shoulder. "It's all downhill from here, until you reach your fifth year, of course, and then you get special study lessons where you can lark about with your mates in the seniors' sitting room. I can't wait! See you later." And he wandered off to talk to Kelvin Strumble and Joshua Follifoot, two of his best friends.

Angus had spent the previous evening with Dougal and Indigo in the Pigsty, a tiny private sitting room squashed between his room and Dougal's, discussing the weather vortex. The fact that they had now made it through a whole year at Perilous and were about to embark upon their second had never entered the conversation.

He made his way through the growing crowd in the hallway to share this startling piece of information with Dougal, who was balancing on one knee, tying his bootlaces.

"Why didn't you tell me we're in the second year now?" he asked as soon as Dougal stood up again.

"I thought you knew. Didn't Catcher Sparks send you a letter?"

"No." Angus frowned. "What did it say?"

Dougal shrugged. "Nothing important. It just kept droning on about setting a good example for the first years, and we had to sign a good-behavior pledge and send it back."

Indigo joined them a few seconds later, scratching at a rash on her hand, but before Angus could ask her if she'd also had a letter, Catcher Sparks appeared in the hallway. Her long black hair was pulled back into a tight bun. She was dressed in a brown leather jerkin, fastened up the front with ten buckles. It looked strong enough to stop a vicious icicle storm in its tracks.

"I wonder what she wants," Angus mumbled quietly.

As their master lightning catcher Catcher Sparks regularly sent them to complete some of the most revolting tasks at Perilous.

"Silence!" she bellowed, and a swift hush fell in the curved hallway. "I am here this morning to assign each of you to your new departments and lessons. May I remind everyone that this latest stage in your training should be treated with the utmost seriousness." She glared at Nicholas Grubb, Clifford Fugg, and Theodore Twill, the three lightning cubs who were most likely to start a spur-of-the-moment food fight or throw water bombs at

one another in the bathrooms. "When I have called your name, you may proceed up to the kitchens for breakfast. Grubb, Strumble, Follifoot, Cambrun," she said, consulting a long list. "You will be attending weather observations lessons in one of the weather bubbles with Catcher Greasley first thing this morning."

"But, miss, I can't!" Nicholas wailed loudly, causing several younger lightning cubs to snicker.

"What on earth are you talking about, Grubb?" Catcher Sparks sounded irritated.

"Catcher Greasley banned me from the weather bubbles after I accidentally filled one with soapsuds, miss."

"Stop telling ridiculous stories, Grubb." Catcher Sparks rolled her eyes at him. "And you might try filling your brains with some useful knowledge this term, instead of larking about and playing the fool."

Nicholas grinned at Angus as he hurried past Catcher Sparks and up the spiral stairs with the rest of his friends.

"Jessop, Croxley, Pope, you have now been assigned to Catcher Vellum in the Lightnarium for advanced lightning identification lessons." Catcher Sparks continued. "You will need to collect lightning deflector suits and tinted safety goggles from the supplies department first. MacDonald, Whitte, Silverdale, Shirra, please report to Catcher Grimble in the research department."

Angus let his attention wander around the hallway as Catcher Sparks made slow progress down her list. He smiled at Georgina Fox and Millicent Nichols, who were standing next to the lightning catcher. Directly behind them, skulking in a dark corner and looking uglier than ever were Pixie and Percival Vellum. The vile hairy twins bore a strong resemblance to a pair of gorillas.

Angus caught Percival's eye. The twin scowled, mouthing silently at him, "You're dead, Munchfungus!"

At the end of the previous term, Percival had threatened to spread false rumors that Angus's mum and dad had been kicked out of Perilous for causing a deadly accident on a fog field trip. In return, Angus had warned that he'd tell everyone that the twins' dad had been big friends with Adrik Swarfe, Dankhart's chief monsoon mongrel.

It was obvious that Percival's loathing for him had only deepened over the holidays.

"What's his problem?" Dougal whispered as Catcher

Sparks continued reading out names and Percival continued glaring in their direction.

"You mean apart from being an irritating idiot?"

"McFangus!"

Angus spun around and felt his stomach sink like a stone. Everyone in the corridor, including Catcher Sparks, was now staring in his direction.

"Er, yes, miss?"

"If you had been listening properly, you would now know that you, Dewsnap, and Midnight have been assigned to Catcher Wrascal in the forecasting department," she informed him with nostrils flaring dangerously. "I suggest you pay more attention in the future or you'll find yourself heading straight up to Doctor Fleagal for an earwax scraping. Do I make myself clear?"

Angus nodded swiftly. "Yes, miss."

The Vellums sniggered as he darted up the spiral stairs, his face shining with embarrassment.

After a hurried breakfast in the noisy kitchens Angus, Indigo, and Dougal made their way straight up to the Octagon, an eight-sided marbled hall with doors leading directly to each of the main departments at Perilous.

They were met outside the forecasting department by an unfamiliar lightning catcher with short auburn hair and a round face.

"Hello! My name's Catcher Wrascal, but you can call me Winnie when there's no one else around," she announced, bounding toward them with a friendly wink. "No need to be all stuffy and formal when it's just the four of us."

Catcher Wrascal had a bright, cheery sort of voice. She was also the youngest lightning catcher Angus had ever seen. Her leather jerkin was far too long, reaching well below her skinny knees. It was also extremely shiny, with none of the usual rips, tears, and scorch marks. Angus suddenly understood. Catcher Wrascal had only just qualified.

"The forecasting department is one of the busiest at Perilous," she said, leading them through the door and into a short corridor, her leather jerkin squeaking as she walked. "We issue daily, weekly, and monthly forecasts to the most senior lightning catchers at Perilous and a variety of other Exploratoriums around the world, which is why we operate twenty-four hours a day, in every time zone. We also work in close liaison with the London

office, which relies on us for weather warnings, blizzard alerts, and emergency weather flashes."

Angus stared around as they entered a large square hall, which he had officially visited only once before with Edmund Croxley. There was a collection of submarine-type periscopes, each manned by a lightning catcher on a swiveling chair, used for observing weather fronts as they approached Perilous. There were long strips of dangling seaweed, a bank of mechanical pinecones, and live hedgehogs, all used for predicting rainfall. The large vats that were normally filled with cold rice pudding for the purpose of measuring humidity had been drained for cleaning.

"We use a wide range of weather information for producing each forecast, including air temperatures, wind direction, humidity levels," Catcher Wrascal said, counting them off on her fingers as if trying to remember a shopping list. "We also consider different types of cloud, rainfall patterns, changes in air pressure, and the thermy-holine circle and its effects on the weather."

"Er, the thermy-what-thingy, miss?" Angus asked.

"I can't remember what it's called exactly," she told them

brightly, "but it's definitely got something to do with the oceans, the weather, and climate regulation, or so Catcher Killigrew claims anyway."

"I think she's talking about thermohaline circulation," Dougal whispered when Angus and Indigo still looked confused. "It all starts with the formation of sea ice in the North Atlantic; it involves some deep ocean currents that circulate the globe on a seventy-thousand-mile round trip that takes about a thousand years."

"A thousand years?" Indigo said, impressed.

"That's exactly what Catcher Killigrew keeps telling me," Catcher Wrascal said, smiling at them. "To be honest, forecasting isn't really my strong point. I failed the exam twice. I'd much rather work in the experimental division, but until a position comes up—"

"Where did you train, miss?" Angus asked. He was certain he'd never seen her among the older trainees at Perilous.

"Please, call me Winnie! And I trained at a tiny Exploratorium in Fort William, Scotland. Now, what else am I supposed to tell you?" she said, staring at them blankly. "Oh, yes, we also spend a great deal of our time monitoring the local weather here on Imbur, which, as you know, can be extremely unpredictable."

"Yeah, especially when your dear old uncle Scabby starts messing around with it," Dougal whispered.

"Don't!" Indigo warned, scratching her hand again. It now looked rather red and angry.

"What's wrong with your hand?" Angus asked her.

"Nothing." Indigo shoved it hastily into her pocket. "It's just a stupid rash. I've got some lotion for it in my room."

A telltale blush began to creep up both sides of Indigo's neck. But before Angus could ask why she was suddenly looking so flustered they were approached by an older lightning catcher with extremely bushy eyebrows and silvery hair. Angus recognized him from the kitchens.

"Catcher Wrascal, a word, if you please," he said, scowling down at them. "Are these three our new trainees?"

"Yes, Catcher Killigrew. I'm just giving them a tour."

"Good. Make sure they understand the evacuation procedures in the event of an emergency weather flash. And when you've finished, you will go straight to Valentine Vellum's office and apologize to him."

"Oh. Yes, sir." Catcher Wrascal hung her head, blushing furiously.

"It seems you have delivered the wrong forecast to him for the last five days in a row. He has absolutely no interest in wind speeds at the Arctic Circle or the likelihood of fog in Brussels."

"It won't happen again, Catcher Killigrew, I promise," Winnie Wrascal mumbled.

"Just make sure it doesn't. And when you have finished apologizing to Catcher Vellum, you will spend some time learning the correct procedures for delivering daily forecasts." He walked away from them briskly, shaking his head in apparent exasperation.

Catcher Wrascal continued to blush as she led them beyond the vats, through a door, and into an empty tunnel-like corridor with no natural light.

"Now, let me see." She opened a door on the right. Angus caught a brief glimpse of some changing room lockers and someone wearing long stripy underpants.

"I say! Shut that door!" an irate voice shouted.

"Oops! Sorry!" Catcher Wrascal closed it hurriedly. "Oh, dear, that's the third time this week I've barged in on Catcher Clavinger."

Angus tried to hide a grin. Indigo stared at the floor, her shoulders shaking with silent giggles. Catcher Wrascal hurried them farther down the corridor.

"Ah, at last," she said cheerfully, opening another door. "This is where you'll be working for the next few weeks."

She shuffled them into a cramped hallway facing an inner door. Angus swallowed hard. The door was round and made of steel. It was the kind found only in the most dangerous parts of Perilous, including the Lightnarium, the Rotundra, and the weather tunnel.

"Behind this door is the weather archive," Catcher Wrascal announced. "It was started by the earliest lightning catchers in order to catalog and collect daily weather samples here on Imbur. Many charts and written forecasts are also kept, of course, but a physical record of the weather itself is invaluable when predicting long-term weather patterns, or so Catcher Killigrew keeps telling me anyway," she added with a shrug.

"Ph-physical?" Dougal asked, starting to sound worried.

With a twist and a tug Catcher Wrascal led the way through the safety door. It took Angus's eyes several seconds to adjust to the gloom inside. They had entered another long, windowless corridor with craggy walls and an impressive collection of stalactites hanging from the ceiling. There were a further twelve steel safety doors set deep into the walls before them, six on the left-hand side, six on the right. Angus gulped. It reminded him of the testing tunnels where the experimental division assessed its most dangerous inventions, far away from the rest of the Exploratorium.

"All the rooms on the left side of the corridor contain storm jars from different eras and written records of the weather," Catcher Wrascal explained. "The doors on the right, however, are specially fortified and store much larger samples, collected from some of the biggest and most violent storms in the history of Imbur. There's a cold store for all the worst of the wintry weather, including icicle storms and ice-diamond storms." She pointed to a door that was covered in a thick layer of sparkling ice crystals and looked frozen solid. "We have a separate archive for all the weather

that comes spilling out of Castle Dankhart, of course."

The door to the Dankhart archive was much smaller than any of the others, with an extra wheel lock on the front.

Angus glanced swiftly at Dougal and Indigo. It was exactly the kind of archive that might help them uncover the truth about the weather vortex.

"C-can we have a look inside it, miss?" Angus asked hopefully.

"Catcher Killigrew would kill me if I let you anywhere near it! It's far too dangerous for lightning cubs. Only senior lightning catchers are allowed to enter without an escort. But we also receive daily weather reports for Castle Dankhart from our mountain observation post, and they're a lot safer."

"Where are those kept, miss?" Dougal asked, clearly trying not to sound too interested.

"All weather reports are kept in the paper archive." Catcher Wrascal pointed vaguely to one of the other doors. "Right, I'd better show you three where you'll be working."

She led them straight over to the first door on the left

and began to heave it open. Angus held his breath, hoping they weren't about to be thrust into a raging storm.

"I think I'm going to be sick!" Dougal whimpered beside him.

Light fissures flicked on as Catcher Wrascal stepped through the door and—

"Oh," Angus said, almost feeling disappointed.

Behind the door was a vast, cavernous room. It was filled from top to bottom with thousands of glass containers.

"Wow! Storm jars!" Dougal gasped, looking relieved that the room contained nothing more dangerous. "Dad uses those to store his pickled walnuts."

Some of the jars had been arranged neatly along stone shelves cut directly into the walls. Others sat higgledy-piggledy on the floor. A number of the smaller jars hung from the ceiling on hooks. Some lightning catchers had clearly been forced to collect their weather samples in empty pickle jars, vinegar bottles, and tin cans. Each one appeared to hold a sliver of snowstorm, a glimmer of sunlight, or a splinter of hailstone as if someone had tried to cut and preserve a single delicate shaving of storm.

"Imbur weather samples have been kept in storm jars from the time of the earliest lightning catchers," Catcher Wrascal explained. She picked up a jar and let them gaze at a wafer-thin slice of fog as it drifted and floated gently inside, nudging against the sides of the glass. "Unfortunately, some of the older jars were damaged recently by a number of strong tremors that occurred in the experimental division and have started to develop cracks. Your job is to transfer those weather samples into new jars, where they should be sealed and labeled."

She pointed behind them to where a collection of brand-new storm jars, a pile of rubber stoppers, and some funnels had been neatly arranged.

"Right, I think that's everything. I'll be back midmorning to see how you're getting on." Catcher Wrascal beamed at all three of them as she headed toward the door. "Oh, I almost forgot." She stopped abruptly. "I'm supposed to tell you not to enter any of the other parts of the archive."

Angus exchanged glances with Dougal.

"And don't let the different types of weather mix either. It causes dreadful problems. I'll see you three later. Happy labeling!"

"But, miss," Indigo said as the lightning catcher headed for the door once again, "we haven't got anything to label the jars with."

"Oops!" Catcher Wrascal hurried back. She extracted three pens and some smart-looking labels from her pocket and handed them to Indigo. "Catcher Killigrew says I'd forget my own buttocks if they weren't already attached. There's one last thing I should warn you about before I go. Stay away from the farthest corner." She pointed into the dark, where only the faintest gleam of glass was visible. "Heaven knows what some of those jars contain."

And she finally disappeared with a cheery wave.

"What else do you reckon she's forgotten to tell us?" Dougal mumbled, keeping his voice low in case Catcher Wrascal returned one last time.

"I dunno," Angus said, checking over his shoulder. "But I wouldn't mind finding out more about that Dankhart archive."

Dougal instantly turned pale.

"I mean, what if they've got a sample from the weather vortex in there?" Angus continued. "Gudgeon said they'd already collected some from the outer edges of the cloud, and maybe if we could just get a quick look at it—"

"We might be able to work out what's really going on inside that vortex and what Dark-Angel's not telling us about it," Indigo said, looking eager to try.

"In that case, one of us had better have a good rummage around inside that paper archive as well," Dougal said, swiftly volunteering for the job. "There's got to be something useful in those daily Castle Dankhart weather reports. Maybe there were some clues, you know, the day before the explosion."

Angus led the way back into the dim passageway outside, checking that the coast was still clear. He and Indigo hurried over to the small double-locked door that led to the Dankhart archive as Dougal peeled off to the left and disappeared into a far more friendly-looking room.

"I'll go first," Angus said, carefully twisting the first of the two wheel locks. "This was my idea, so if there's anything dangerous lurking inside . . ."

Indigo rolled up her sleeves, looking ready to tackle anything. Angus opened the door with a final twist and a tug and clambered through the small opening.

"Whoa!"

Inside, the archive was dimly lit and freezing cold, with the clammy atmosphere of a dungeon. Storms jars filled almost every inch of floor. The noise was overwhelming. A cacophony of howling winds, roaring rainstorms, and violent thunder surrounded them on all sides, making Angus's ears ache. They squeezed their way through the sea of glass, between towering samples of crimson snow and sneaking mists. Ice-diamond spores, desperate to break out and freeze their lungs solid, flung themselves against the glass as they passed.

"D-do you think this is what it feels like inside Castle Dankhart?" Indigo said over the noise, staring around at the dreadful storm samples.

Angus shuddered, hoping he'd never have to find out.

A collection of huge wide-necked jars lay empty on their sides, their stoppers missing.

"I wonder what used to be inside those." He stared anxiously up at the ceiling for signs of any escaped storms that might be lurking.

But Indigo had finally spotted what they'd been searching for.

"Over there!" A string of smaller storm jars had been

set aside from the others and lined up in a neat row. Indigo was already racing over to inspect the contents. "'Dankhart weather vortex,' " she said, bending down to read the labels. "This sample was collected just three days ago. It's the most recent one in here."

Angus crouched on his knees to study it more closely. Dark slivers of storm swirled around at a furious pace, filling every square inch of jar with dense cloud and tumbling debris.

"So, was this taken from a real storm or a fake?" Indigo asked, peering into the jar with a look of deep concentration.

Angus felt his hopes of finding an answer suddenly plunge. The samples taken from the vortex looked just as fierce, just as angry and malevolent as any of the others in the Dankhart archive. Tiny fragments of twig, snail shell, and short wiry-looking quills raced around inside it. But did the strange debris come from a real explosion at the castle? Or did it point to something even more sinister?

"Listen, Indigo, can't your mum find out what's really going on under that cloud?" Angus sat back on his heels, struck by a sudden thought. "Doesn't she know anyone at the castle she could contact, like an old housekeeper or someone? Or maybe there's a secret passageway she could sneak a message inside."

"I'm sorry, Angus, but it's no use." Indigo shook her head sadly. "She won't even mention the Dankharts."

Angus nodded, his hopes of finding an answer sinking even further. He was just about to suggest they make a quick exit from the archive when—

"It's just so horrible!" Indigo burst out suddenly, making him jump. "I can't believe the Dankharts have created such awful things!" She jerked her head toward the storm jar. "I mean, they're part of my family."

"Yeah, but the Midnights would never do that. And you're half Midnight, too," Angus reminded her.

"Maybe my mum was right. I should have gone to school on the mainland, where no one's ever heard of the Dankharts."

"But you love being at Perilous," Angus pointed out gently because Indigo was now on the verge of tears. "You've always wanted to be a lightning catcher."

"I know." Indigo sniffed sadly. "I just wish my uncle

wasn't the biggest villain on the entire planet. What if someone finds out who I really am?"

"Well, me and Dougal definitely won't tell anybody," Angus promised. "And Germ won't go blabbing it to anyone, will he?"

"But the Vellums!" Indigo said, holding her face in her hands. "They know all sorts of personal stuff about your parents. What if Valentine Vellum tells them about my uncle Scabious, too? They'll tell everyone!"

Angus shifted his balance uneasily. "Listen, if Vellum even hints that he knows anything about your family, we'll go straight to Gudgeon or Rogwood," he said.

Indigo smiled weakly and blew her nose. "Thanks."

"I think we'd better get out of here before Catcher Wrascal catches us snooping about," Angus said as soon as Indigo had stuffed her handkerchief back into her pocket.

He stood up and turned, accidentally nudging one of the older jars with his foot. The jar wobbled precariously. Before he could reach out and grab it, it toppled over and smashed across the floor.

"Angus! Look out!" Indigo warned.

He jumped out of the way as a sliver of toxic-looking storm oozed onto the floor and drifted in an aimless manner around his knees. "We've got to catch it and stuff it back into a storm jar! If anyone finds it drifting about in here . . ."

"Quickly, it's getting away!" Indigo pointed.

The storm sliver, freed from its glass prison, was now on the move. Indigo reached out, making several unsuccessful attempts to trap it between her hands.

"Gotcha!" Angus pounced on top of it, crashing straight through the cloud and hitting the floor underneath. "Oh, no! Where's it gone now?"

They chased the weather sample helter-skelter down to the far end of the archive, desperately trying to grab it.

"How are you supposed to trap this stuff?" Angus said, attempting to ambush it unawares.

It was Indigo who finally came to their rescue, tying their sweaters together to form a thick, spongy net. She flung it over the escaped weather, which soaked rapidly into the woolen fibers.

"Quickly, wring it out into this jar!" Angus said, grabbing an empty container.

He pushed a rubber stopper in the top before the storm could escape again, and the jar was finally sealed.

They left the archive swiftly and ran back to the much safer room where Catcher Wrascal had left them half an hour earlier. Dougal returned from the paper archive just a minute later, his sweater bulging with lumpy objects.

"What did you find?" asked Angus, eager to hear some good news.

But Dougal shook his head. "I'll tell you later." He hastily stuffed a number of mysterious items into his bag as Catcher Wrascal appeared in the doorway with a cheery wave.

They were forced to put all thoughts of Dankhart, archives and the weather vortex aside to tackle the storm jars after that. Transferring the weather samples wasn't nearly as easy as it sounded, even when they followed a sketchy list of handwritten instructions from Catcher Wrascal.

"Oops! Sorry, I should have given you those ages ago," she said, passing a scrunched-up sheet of paper over to Dougal with an apologetic smile.

"'Step one,'" Dougal said, reading the instructions

aloud when they finally got started a few minutes later. "'Identify the weather contained within the storm jar.'"

"The weather in this one's gone all runny," Angus said, examining the sticky-looking substance at the bottom. "How am I supposed to know what it is?"

"What does it say on the label?" Indigo asked.

"It looks like 'night owls with beastly wiz,'" Angus said, trying to decipher the faded words.

"Er, I think that's supposed to be 'light showers with easterly winds.'" Dougal grinned. "'Step two, remove the rubber stopper from the old storm jar.'"

Angus and Indigo wrestled with it for several minutes before the stopper eventually gave way with a loud pop, causing Angus to fall over backward.

"'Step three, fit a funnel in the neck of the new storm jar and transfer the weather sample by pouring slowly.'"

The jar was heavy and extremely difficult to maneuver into the correct position. It took all three of them just to lift it.

"Hold that funnel steady!" Dougal bellowed as the whole thing wobbled at a precarious angle.

"I can't!" Angus yelled. "It keeps sliding!"

"We've got weather trickling down the outside of the storm jar!" Indigo warned as a puddle began to form at their feet.

They left the weather archive at the end of the day feeling disheveled and ravenously hungry. Angus piled his plate high with extra spaghetti and meatballs at dinner, hoping that the next day would prove less exhausting. Indigo quickly filled Dougal in on their adventure in the Dankhart archive. Luckily, Dougal had had more success.

"I managed to find some weather reports from Castle Dankhart and some of those mechanical pigeon messengers." He extracted one of the feathered birds from his bag to show them. "But they both contain some really complicated weather symbols that I've never seen before. So I'll need a good book on advanced weather icons if I'm going to decipher them properly."

Instead of retiring to the lightning cubs' living quarters after dinner, therefore, Angus and Indigo followed Dougal straight up to the reference section of the library.

The library at Perilous was large, with a splendid spiral staircase leading to a balcony and an impressive glass-domed ceiling at the top. It was also one of Dougal's favorite places to linger.

He disappeared quickly into a corner, where he immersed himself in a pile of dusty books.

Indigo wandered down the next aisle. Angus inspected a row of highly technical-looking books about creating a storm archive. It was only when he drifted into a different section a few minutes later that he caught sight of a familiar figure sitting at a study table.

"Hey, Germ!" he called quietly.

Germ looked up and waved. It was the first time Angus had seen him since their return to Perilous. Normally the noisiest center of any crowd, Germ was sitting quietly on his own for once, surrounded by piles of books and scribbled notes, ink smudged across his nose.

"What are you doing here?" Angus asked, sitting in a chair opposite.

"St-st-studying." Germ stretched his arms high above his head, yawning. His brown hair looked as if it hadn't been brushed for days. There were dark circles under his eyes. "Old Fleagal reckons I'm ready to sit my first medical exams. I'm reading up on boils, blisters, and spotty bumps this evening." He showed Angus the front cover of a book with the same title. "Listen to this bit; it's really revolting," he said, opening the tome just as Indigo joined them. "'Belching blisters, thin gas-filled bubbles of skin, caused by rubber boot chafing, usually form in clusters on the soles of feet, emitting a loud burping noise when popped.'"

Germ grinned. Indigo rolled her eyes at her brother. Angus swallowed, wondering if simply hearing about the symptoms of belching blisters could cause them to spontaneously erupt all over his feet.

"'Secondary symptoms include—' Hey, what's wrong with your skin?" Germ flung his book aside and grabbed Indigo's hand before she could pull it away. "Whoa! That's definitely not normal," he said, inspecting her rash gleefully. "Five red spots in a triangle formation. There are signs of inflammation, possibly even infection. It's bound to be something incurable, or contagious, or both. It's also the perfect case study for my spotty bumps exam."

"No! It's just a stupid heat rash." Indigo pulled her hand away and hid it behind her back.

"Suit yourself, little sis," Germ said, shrugging, "but

don't be surprised if your fingers turn purple in the middle of the night and start dropping off."

Dougal appeared a second later, clutching several thick books. But before he could show them exactly what he'd found:

BOOOOOOM!

Everything inside the library shook, causing several startled mice to scuttle across the floor in front of them. The glass roof above their heads rattled. Small puffs of ancient dust rose from the shelves, forming tiny, grimy-looking clouds.

"It's a frost quake!" Dougal dropped his books all over Germ's study notes in a panic.

"But it's only September," Indigo pointed out as the library continued to shake and vibrate alarmingly. "There hasn't been any frost yet!"

"Then why in the name of Perilous is the whole library trembling?"

"Maybe Valentine Vellum's finally vaporized himself in the Lightnarium," Germ suggested with a hint of hopefulness.

The shaking slowly subsided and finally stopped less than a minute later. An eerie silence fell, broken only by the sound of whimpering coming from the next aisle.

"Come on, let's find out what's going on," Angus said, helping Germ stuff his books into his bag.

They hurried toward the staircase only to find the librarian, Miss Vulpine, racing toward them in a flap.

"Everyone must leave the library immediately! The ceiling could shatter at any second!" she said, rushing a group of frightened-looking first years toward the stairs.

"But, miss, what's going on?" Angus asked, standing his ground.

Miss Vulpine, however, was far too frantic to answer any questions and dashed off, herding more groups of lightning cubs toward the exit.

"Is it my imagination or has it suddenly got darker?" Germ said, gazing upward.

Angus stared at the glass-domed ceiling above their heads. The skies had darkened to a murky gray. A storm was about to break over Perilous. But this was no ordinary storm, Angus realized, hiccuping in surprise. Thick rain, giant snowflakes, and small silvery fish were suddenly raining down on the roof. Giant hailstones hammered against the glass panes, along with a smattering of garden snails.

"Oh, no," Dougal said, turning pale. "This is exactly the kind of stuff Gudgeon makes us tramp through with our weather watches for practice."

But for once Angus knew that Dougal was wrong. He felt the contents of his stomach lurch. Rogwood, Gudgeon, and Jeremius had described this exact weather to him the other day in Dark-Angel's office.

"Those snails and hailstones have come from the weather vortex," he said, suddenly feeling certain. "There's been another explosion at Castle Dankhart!"

6
THE STORM HOLLOW

Strange showers of garden worms and moss-colored rain continued to fall throughout the night, making it almost impossible to sleep. Angus, wrapped up in his comforter, sat hunched beside his bedroom window, watching as the weather raged outside. Had there now been a genuine accident at Castle Dankhart? How was he supposed to find out what was really going on? He had no idea how to get in touch with Jeremius. Did his uncle even know about the second explosion?

Angus watched a cascade of goldfish fall past his window, feeling sick with fear and worry. Would he ever see his mum and dad again?

By the time he went up to the kitchens the following morning with Dougal, he'd already decided to find Gudgeon or Rogwood and ask him directly about the explosion, just as Jeremius had told him to. The weather had finally cleared, and a weak sun was hiding behind a high cloud. The snow, ice, and hailstones had melted long ago, but the strange storm had deposited piles of flotsam and jetsam across every inch of the courtyard outside the main entrance.

"Whoa!" Dougal gasped as they stared out through the open doors. "It looks like there's been a shipwreck."

There were metal cogs, long splinters of wood, balls of knotted string, and something that looked like a rusty old bicycle pump. Fragments of shattered glass, fish scales, and acorns were being swept up and collected in large buckets by a dozen or more lightning catchers.

"McFangus! Dewsnap!" Catcher Sparks marched toward them through the wreckage, armed with a bucket and a broom. "Lightning cubs are forbidden from entering the courtyard until this mess has been cleared away."

"But, miss—" Angus began, desperate for some answers.

Catcher Sparks cut him short. "No buts, McFangus. Unless you two are volunteering to sweep up this rubbish, I suggest you make your way into the kitchens for breakfast immediately."

Angus scoured the courtyard, looking for any signs of Rogwood or Gudgeon, but as Catcher Sparks was now flaring her nostrils angrily at him, he decided it was safer to leave.

"Have you found anything in those weather reports from Castle Dankhart yet?" he asked Dougal as they hurried away from the courtyard.

Dougal shook his head. "Catcher Plymstock wrote all the reports in the two weeks before the first explosion. She mentions some abominable snowstorms and a brief scattering of pale pink snow, but there's no unusual activity, no dangerous weather experiments or machines, and most of the mechanical pigeons have had their messages removed. I haven't given up yet, though," Dougal said, plucking a stray pigeon feather from his hair. It was obvious he'd fallen asleep using one of the messengers as a pillow.

They hurried on into the crowded kitchens where new

"Coming Soon!" posters had appeared overnight. Nobody was showing the slightest interest in the mysterious notices, however. Instead, all talk centered on the weather explosion, and a nervous buzz filled the air like the distant humming of bees. Indigo was already sitting at their usual table with a stack of toast lying half forgotten in front of her, her head bent over the pages of a glossy magazine.

"What are you reading?" Angus asked as he and Dougal both sat down.

Indigo flinched, looking up in surprise. "Thank goodness it's only you two."

"Were you expecting somebody else?" Dougal asked, his eyebrows raised in surprise.

"Germ keeps pestering me about the rash on my hand," Indigo said with a sigh, scratching it absently. "I've been avoiding him."

"So what are you reading?" Angus asked, helping himself to a slice of Indigo's toast.

"It's the latest copy of the *Weathervane*."

The *Weekly Weathervane* had proved an invaluable source of information last term, when it had revealed interesting details about Adrik Swarfe and the Lightning

Catcher of the Year award. Most lightning cubs had never read a copy because of the general belief that it was rather boring and nerdy. But Dougal devoured each edition with relish.

"How come you've got a copy?" he asked, frowning.

"When I came up to breakfast this morning, everyone was talking about it, so I ran up to the research department and grabbed one before they all disappeared and—Oh! You'd better take a look at it for yourselves!" Indigo pushed the magazine across the table.

In the center pages was a picture of the weather vortex hanging over Castle Dankhart. Angus felt his stomach clench. Even seen from a safe distance it was a deeply shocking sight. The vortex was monstrous, far larger than he'd imagined. It engulfed the castle in a whirling shroud of lightning bolts, fognadoes, black rain, and collections of far more solid-looking objects.

"It's like someone's smashed a thousand storm globes and let them run riot," Dougal said, looking pale and shaken. "I can see giant snowflakes, thunderclouds, and icicle storms."

"This must have been taken before yesterday's

explosion," Angus said, studying the photograph in detail.

"I wonder what it looks like now," Indigo said, biting her lip anxiously.

No part of Castle Dankhart was visible through the weather vortex, but it was clear that the castle was vast. It was flanked on either side by impressively large snow-capped mountains. It was the first time Angus had seen any image of it. He stared at the picture hard. Somewhere beneath the violent layers of weather his mum and dad were trapped in a dungeon.

"What if there really has been an accident this time?" Angus said, voicing the concerns that had kept him awake long into the night. "I mean, what type of experiment could have caused such a huge explosion?"

Dougal shook his head. "And if it wasn't an accident, if Indigo's dear old uncle Scabby really is doing this on purpose," he added, lowering his voice, "what's he doing it for? It doesn't make any sense."

Before anyone could come up with any answers, Angus spotted a familiar figure striding across the kitchen toward them. Gudgeon was dressed in a battered leather jerkin that appeared to be made entirely out of repaired rips and scars. He was also wearing a deep scowl.

"I thought you three might have your heads buried in the *Weathervane*," he said, nodding toward the magazine, still spread out on the table before them. "I've just come to tell you what we know about this latest explosion so you don't go skipping off after monsoon mongrels or dangerous lightning hearts. Besides, I promised Jeremius I'd keep a special eye on you three."

"What's going on? Has the vortex disappeared?" Angus asked, unable to contain himself. "Is Castle Dankhart visible now?"

"Does it look like there's been a real explosion?" Dougal chipped in.

"Or a horrible weather catastrophe?" Indigo added, looking just as anxious for news as her friends.

"If you shut up for a minute and let me get a word in edgewise, I'll tell you!" the gruff lightning catcher said, trying to keep his voice low. "It was impossible to see anything until first light this morning, but it looks like the weather vortex is still hanging over Castle Dankhart."

"But what about all the stuff that fell over Perilous last night?" Angus asked.

"The force of last night's blast blew a small portion of the debris over to this side of the island. The rest of it's still swirling around the castle and looking more violent than ever. In fact that blowout seems to have stirred things up a bit."

"Do you think it was a real explosion this time?" Dougal asked.

"It wouldn't surprise me if those monsoon mongrels blew themselves to smithereens one day. But I reckon this is all part of Dankhart's plan. He's got something big going on, and no mistake, so you three had better keep your wits about you."

"But what about my mum and dad?" Angus asked, swallowing a lump in his throat. "How can anyone be sure they're still safe?"

"Now you three listen to me." Gudgeon folded his arms across his chest and fixed each of them with a stern glare. "That leaky old castle's got more secret passageways and tunnels than Perilous. If there had been a real weather catastrophe, those monsoon mongrels would be fleeing in all directions like a bunch of stinking water rats abandoning ship. And there's been no sign of any fleeing yet. If there's been a real accident at that castle, I'll eat my own vest."

Angus stared at Gudgeon, startled, not sure if the gruff lightning catcher was simply trying to stop him from worrying about his mum and dad or if he was telling the truth.

"Oh, no!" Indigo jumped up suddenly. She stared around the kitchen, which had almost emptied out while they'd been talking to Gudgeon. "We'll be late for Catcher Wrascal."

"Sit down, you three. You're not going anywhere."

Indigo frowned. "But we've got to get up to the weather archive."

"You're not doing anything with archives today. You're coming with me."

"But what for?" Angus asked warily.

Gudgeon checked his weather watch. "Meet me in the Octagon in ten minutes in your full wet-weather gear, and you'll find out." And he marched out of the kitchen without explaining any further.

"I definitely don't like the sound of that." Dougal gulped. "The last time Gudgeon took us for a lesson we ended up in the Rotundra, and look how well that turned out.

I mean, we almost got killed by ice-diamond spores and snowbombs."

"I wonder what he's got planned for us this time," Indigo said, looking eager to find out.

Angus crossed his fingers under the table, hoping that just this once it wouldn't involve something treacherous or life threatening.

Ten minutes later they reached the marbled Octagon to find the rest of the second years waiting anxiously. Millicent Nichols, who was already allergic to fog, snow, and heavy rain showers, was biting her fingernails in a state of advanced nervousness. Jonathon Hake and Nigel Ridgely were talking with serious expressions. Pixie and Percival Vellum were standing to one side, separate from the rest of the group.

"Those two look more like a pair of gargoyles every time we see them," Dougal said as they hovered behind Georgina Fox.

Angus grinned. "Maybe Dark-Angel will throw them out of Perilous this year for being extra thick."

"Yeah, or extra ugly!"

Gudgeon appeared a few moments later, and a tense

hush fell around the marbled hall.

"Right, you lot. Due to recent weather events here on Imbur, Principal Dark-Angel has decided that all lightning cubs, from the second year and up, need some special additional training."

Angus glanced sideways at Indigo.

"Training will take place with me inside the storm hollow, which you won't have heard anyone talking about, even though it's one of the oldest parts of Perilous."

"What on earth's a storm hollow?" Dougal whispered as a low murmur swept around the Octagon. "And why isn't anyone allowed to talk about it?"

"Before we go any further," Gudgeon continued, "I'm supposed to warn you lot that weatherproof clothes must be worn at all times in the storm hollow. Random checks for rubber boot leaks will also be carried out. So you've been warned!"

Angus glanced down at his own boots, which hadn't been cleaned since the previous term. They were starting to pinch his toes, and he had a sneaking suspicion they no longer kept the rain out. What would they have to protect his feet from in the storm hollow?

"I also need everyone's signature on the sheet at the bottom of this declaration," Gudgeon said.

"I *knew* it!" Dougal whispered as Gudgeon shoved a clipboard at a worried-looking Violet Quinn and told her to pass it around. "I knew there'd be another declaration to sign. If this storm hollow turns out to be even more dangerous than the Lightnarium or the Rotundra . . ."

Angus took the clipboard from a pale Nigel Ridgely when it was his turn. The declaration attached to it had clearly been read many times before and was smeared with sticky fingerprints and something that smelled like regurgitated carrots. It was also the shortest declaration he'd signed so far. It said:

We, the undersigned, promise never to mention the storm hollow or anything that happens inside it. Anyone caught whispering about the storm hollow in the kitchens, bathrooms, other communal areas of the Exploratorium will be expelled immediately. Anyone caught drawing pictures, passing secret notes, or frightening first year lightning cubs with tales of the storm hollow will also be expelled. There will be NO second chances!

Angus added his signature to the bottom of the page and passed it onto a quaking Dougal. He still had absolutely no idea what they were about to face in the storm hollow, but if they had to promise not to frighten the firstyears with any of the details . . .

"Right then, you lot, follow me," Gudgeon barked as soon as everyone had signed the declaration, "and no dawdling at the back!"

He turned on his heel and headed straight toward the Lightnarium. Jonathon Hake and Violet Quinn both gasped in unison.

"There's no need to get your rubber boots in a twist," Gudgeon said, opening the door. "This is the only way to reach the storm hollow."

Angus felt his heartbeat quicken as they filed through the door, his eyes finding the faded fire dragon that had been etched upon it long ago. Instead of taking them into the Lightnarium, however, Gudgeon veered off to the left, leading them down a steep set of spiral stairs just inside the door.

The steps continued downward for what felt like hours.

When they finally reached the bottom, feeling hot and sweaty, they were met by a steel safety door.

"Stay close to me once we're inside the storm hollow," Gudgeon warned. "Don't go wandering off, and don't touch anything unless I give my permission, understand?"

Angus held his breath as the gruff lightning catcher opened the door with a twist and tug and shuffled them inside. For a moment, he could see nothing but the back of Georgina Fox's head; then:

"Angus! Look!" Indigo was tugging urgently on the sleeve of his coat.

Angus saw it a split second later and almost choked. At the far end of the storm hollow a huge dark castle bulged out from the rocky wall behind it.

"It's Castle Dankhart!" Indigo whispered. "I know it is!"

"I don't believe it!" Dougal said, standing wideeyed beside them. "What's it doing in here?"

The castle, complete with turrets, windows, and an eerie, foreboding silence, loomed over them in a very sinister fashion. An extremely realistic mountain range with snowcapped peaks emerged from the bare rock on either side of it, just as they'd seen in the *Weathervane* less than an hour ago. Up close, grotesque gargoyles protruded from the crumbling walls and turrets.

Georgina Fox gave a small sob and clung to Violet Quinn's arm. Even the Vellum twins looked uncomfortable, and they shuffled about at the back of the group. Indigo, however, was rigid. This was the castle where part of her family still lived. She looked appalled by its very existence.

"Calm down, you lot. That castle isn't real. It's just a projectogram used for senior lightning catcher training," Gudgeon told them. "That's not what you're here for today."

He reached down into the shadows where a small box with two lenses sat half hidden. He removed a plate from the back with a clunk. The castle instantly disappeared. Angus felt his fists unclench. Indigo let out a long, quivering breath as Gudgeon gathered them together before him.

"No lightning cub has ever set foot inside this hollow before," he announced, "but Principal Dark-Angel's decided you need to know the worst of it. As fully qualified lightning catchers you'll spend plenty of time in cold countries fighting blizzards and trekking through invisible fog, but the weather coming out of Castle Dankhart gives us more trouble than all the hurricanes, typhoons, and snowstorms put together. You've already had a taste of it. You've seen the damage ice-diamond storms can cause, and Dankhart and his monsoon mongrels are capable of worse."

Angus could now feel Indigo trembling beside him.

"The storm hollow is used to study and understand any new weather that emerges from Castle Dankhart. The extra-high ceiling allows the storm to rise, unfold, and develop to its full potential. That way we can learn how to tackle any dangers those mongrels can throw at us."

Angus looked up for the first time since entering the hollow. Even with his head thrown back he couldn't see all the way to the top.

"You've all seen the pictures in the *Weathervane*," Gudgeon said, sounding extremely serious. "There's a vortex hovering over Castle Dankhart. It's volatile, unpredictable, and capable of showering Perilous with all kinds of dangerous weather. If it were just a matter of dodging a few flying fish and some hailstones, we would have sent you into the weather tunnel or the Rotundra, and you'd be none the wiser about the storm hollow. But this vortex contains traces of something far more lethal."

Gudgeon led them over to the far side of the hollow, where seven enormous storm jars stood in a row; each contained a different sample of violent-looking weather. Angus checked his weather watch, which had now gone completely haywire, showing him blizzard cautions, fog alerts, and rubber boot overload warnings all at the same time.

"The samples inside these jars were taken from the seven most severe and deadly storms ever to have occurred on the planet. Every single one of them happened right here on Imbur."

A shocked hissing sound like a slowly boiling kettle swept around the storm hollow.

"And every single one of them was created by the Dankharts and their monsoon mongrels as a weapon, to turn against those they wish to control and destroy."

Indigo gave a small involuntary sob, looking deathly pale.

"Normally only fully qualified lightning catchers learn how to tackle the deadly seven, but as traces of all these storms have been found within the vortex hanging over Castle Dankhart, Principal Dark-Angel has decided you need to see what damage they can cause with your own eyes. You need to experience just how deadly they can be."

"You mean you're going to set those storms on us, sir?" Georgina Fox asked, her voice rising in alarm.

"There's no need to panic, Fox. All you're doing today is learning more about what's in these jars."

A thick silence pressed in all around. The fact that Gudgeon had made no promises to keep them safe from the contents of the jars the *next* time they entered the storm hollow had not been lost on anyone.

"Right, let's get a better look at these jars. I'll explain more about the contents as we're going around, so pay attention," he barked, making Millicent Nichols yelp. "I'll also be asking questions at the end of this lesson, and anyone who gives the wrong answer will be scrubbing out storm drains for the rest of the week."

Gudgeon marched over to the first jar. It was taller than the gruff lightning catcher by several feet. Angus glanced guiltily at Indigo. They'd seen several jars just like it when they'd sneaked into the Dankhart archive.

"Scarlet sleeping snow," Gudgeon said, tapping the first jar with his knuckles. Angus peered over Jonathon Hake's shoulder, trying to get a better look at the bloodred flakes of snow falling inside the jar. "Not to be confused with red snow, which is colored by the presence of minute algae called *Protococcus nivalis,* or with blood rain, which is created when dust particles, blown in from the Sahara, combine with normal drops of rain. As the name suggests, scarlet sleeping snow can induce an overwhelming sense of sleepiness, causing its victims to lose consciousness in dangerously cold conditions and putting them at serious risk of hypothermia, frostbite, and eventually death. This particular sample was collected after a party of lightning catchers was rescued from Mount Maccrindell, where they'd been sent to study a troop of fog yetis. The lightning catchers in question were found only just in time, having been buried by the stuff for several hours. Scarlet sleeping snow is one of the monsoon mongrels' nastiest inventions. Make sure each of you gets a good look at it before we move on to the next jar."

Angus shivered as he pressed closer to the glass, which felt extremely cold to touch. The snow had a strangely hypnotic effect, making his eyelids feel exceptionally droopy, his thoughts muddled and slow.

"You wouldn't last five minutes in a shower of scarlet sleeping snow, Munchfungus," Percival Vellum hissed, pushing past Indigo and elbowing Dougal out of the way. He stood squarely in front of Angus with a very smug look on his face. Pixie followed, pigtails swinging. "You and Dewsnap would be blubbing like a couple of first years before the first flake fell."

"Shut up, Vellum, nobody asked you!" Angus took a step closer, his fists clenched. Up close, the twins looked even uglier than usual.

"There's no need to be so touchy." Percival sneered. "I'm just pointing out the basic facts."

"Yeah, well here's another fact," Dougal said, standing shoulder to shoulder with Angus. "You two wouldn't know what to do with a pair of gum boots in a puddle of rain."

Angus grinned at Indigo, who only managed a weak smile in return. Percival Vellum's face, however, darkened.

"You and your pathetic little friends had better watch it this year," he said, looming over them. "Me and Pixie are sick of getting into trouble because of you three."

"It's not our fault you act like brainless idiots the whole time," Angus said angrily. "You can't blame us for that."

"We can blame you for anything we want," Pixie said. "We're sick of doing rubber boot cleaning duty, so this year we're going to make sure you get all the detentions instead."

Angus frowned at the twins. "How are you going to manage that?"

"We're not telling you, Munchfungus. But me and Pix have got big plans."

"Yeah." Pixie nodded earnestly. "We *know* things, big important things."

"Good," Dougal said folding his arms across his chest. "It's about time somebody taught you two how to spell your own names properly. Now stop bugging us and go away."

"You're really starting to irritate me, Dewsnap." Percival lunged forward, pushing Dougal hard.

"Hey!" Dougal staggered backward and collided with Angus.

"Stop it, you idiot! You're making the storm jar wobble!"

Angus warned. But Percival ignored him, taking a reckless dive at him instead.

Angus ducked out of the way at the last minute. Percival skidded, but it was too late!

Smash!

The tall storm jar toppled over and shattered into a thousand pieces. Big scarlet flakes of snow spilled out over the wreckage and quickly began to disperse throughout the storm hollow.

"Argh!" Percival turned and ran, trampling over anyone who got in his way. "Scarlet sleeping snow! Scarlet sleeping snow!"

Pixie, looking thoroughly alarmed, followed in his wake.

Angus scrambled, frantically brushing flakes of snow off his arms, face, and hands where they had already started to settle, giving his skin an odd feeling of numbness. Indigo stumbled clumsily over the broken glass and collided with Jonathon Hake. Dougal stood petrified as the snow swirled inches from the tip of his nose.

"Everyone, out of this storm hollow now, unless you want to spend the rest of the afternoon unconscious!" Gudgeon came striding toward them. He grabbed Dougal

by the coat and propelled him away from the shattered storm jar. Angus followed, quickly joining the stampede of lightning cubs now hurtling toward the steel door at the far side of the hollow.

"Jonathon Hake's been hit!" Violet Quinn wailed as soon as everyone was safely on the other side of the door.

"Did anyone see him fall?" Nigel Ridgely asked.

Dougal nodded, still trying to catch his breath. "He went down like a sack of potatoes."

"It's all my fault!" Indigo whispered, looking thoroughly wretched. "I bumped into him by accident, and he must have lost his balance."

"But he'll be all right, won't he?" Georgina Fox put a comforting arm around Violet, who looked very tearful and shaken. "I mean, he's not, he's not—"

"Calm down, everyone!" Gudgeon barged through the door a moment later, making them all jump. He was carrying a limp Jonathon Hake in his arms. "There wasn't enough snow in that jar to kill anyone."

"But, sir, will Jonathon be all right?" Nigel Ridgely asked as Gudgeon set the sleeping lightning cub down carefully on the floor.

"Doctor Fleagal will need to treat him. Then he'll have to sleep it off for a few hours up in the sanatorium, but he's in no immediate danger, unlike you two!" Gudgeon swung around, pointing angrily at the Vellum twins. "Deliberately smashing a storm jar full of highly dangerous weather is enough to get you two idiots expelled if I've got anything to do with it. Stand there until I decide what to do with you."

The Vellum twins glared at Angus, shuffling their feet.

"The rest of you had better head straight up to the supplies department and get your coats washed down and thoroughly decontaminated." Gudgeon continued. "And not a word to anyone about what you've just seen, understand? You've signed a declaration. You know the consequences."

One by one the remaining lightning cubs began to trudge their way back up the spiral stairs, leaving a trail of melting snow behind them. Angus followed, feeling he'd had quite enough of the storm hollow for one day. His feet were squelching inside his socks. The bare skin on his hands and face now felt prickly and peculiar. He turned to see if Indigo and Dougal

were experiencing the same unsettling symptoms and stopped mid-stride.

Dougal had come to a halt several steps behind him. He was now lying slumped against the wall, snoring soundly, with flakes of scarlet snow melting in his hair.

7
SECRETS OF
THE INNER SANCTUM

Both Dougal and Jonathon Hake were hurried up to the sanatorium for urgent treatment after their brush with the deadly scarlet snow. Angus and Indigo waited anxiously in the kitchens for news. By the time Dougal finally reappeared, looking extremely grumpy and groggy, it was already dark.

"I'm going to kill Percival Vellum for knocking that storm jar over!" Dougal declared, slouching into a chair at the table. "Doctor Fleagal's just forced me and Jonathon to drink this disgusting tonic," he added with a shudder. "It tasted like swamp water. And we've got to go up to the sanatorium twice a day for the next week so he can check for side effects."

"What kind of side effects?" Angus asked, concerned.

"Fleagal says it takes time for the snow to work its way through your system. He says we might start falling asleep mid—"

Dougal suddenly slumped across the table and started snoring loudly. Indigo quickly managed to revive him, however, by pinching his arm. After eating a large plateful of cheese on toast, Dougal retreated to his room in a thoroughly bad mood to work on his puzzle competition and to let Norman, his pet lightning moth, stretch its wings. Indigo disappeared shortly after, still looking traumatized by the dramatic events in the storm hollow.

Angus therefore spent the rest of the evening alone in the Pigsty, huddled close to the fire. He grabbed his scare-me-not puzzle and his bag of magnetic marbles from a drawer in his bedside cabinet, trying not to let his thoughts stray back to the deadly seven . . . or his parents . . . or the massive cloud that was sitting over Castle Dankhart . . . or the fact that the Vellums, the two people he hated most in the entire Exploratorium, were busy hatching another plan to get him expelled or get him put on sock-washing duty for the rest of the term at the very least.

When he could no longer keep his eyes open, he fell into

his bed, his dreams instantly filled with violent weather explosions and hair-raising escapades through the depths of a dark castle. It felt so terrifyingly real that he woke up with his heart pounding inside his chest, his palms clammy with sweat.

It was only when he stumbled out of bed, a few hours later, deciding on an early breakfast, that he discovered a note had been slipped under his door.

He stared at the neat writing on the envelope and opened it warily. The note inside said:

> Dear Angus,
> Please meet me in the kitchens before breakfast. Wet-weather clothing will not be necessary, but I would advise you to wear something warm.
>
> Yours sincerely,
> Aramanthus Rogwood

Angus felt his stomach churn with nerves. Events in the storm hollow had driven all thoughts of the Inner Sanctum and storm prophet lessons temporarily out of his head. But it was clear that today he would finally discover what lay behind the mysterious door. Would there be more projectograms of Castle Dankhart? Or strange storms that nobody had ever heard of?

He got dressed hastily, accidentally pulling his pants on the wrong way round, and slipped out of his room. He hovered outside Dougal's door for several seconds, toying with the idea of waking his friend up but finally decided against it.

The kitchens were practically deserted, apart from a few weary-looking lightning catchers who had clearly been on night duty. Angus was already halfway through a hot bacon roll when Rogwood found him at his usual table.

"Ah, Angus." Rogwood sat down and smiled at him. "I hope you have recovered from your first visit to the storm hollow. Gudgeon has just been filling me in on the thrilling details. I hear Mr. Dewsnap got rather more sleep than he bargained for?" he added, tawny eyes twinkling.

"Yes, sir." Angus swallowed a large mouthful of bacon.

"Luckily, the snow has no lasting side effects. He will be as right as rain after a hearty breakfast and some short afternoon naps." Rogwood stood up, tucking his braided beard inside his leather jerkin to keep it out of the way. "If you are ready then, Angus, we will make a start before questions can be asked."

Suddenly losing his appetite, Angus left the rest of his breakfast on his plate and followed Rogwood out of the kitchens. When they reached the Octagon a few minutes later, he realized he'd never seen it so utterly deserted before. Something that sounded like a rusty gate-hinge was squeaking loudly inside the experimental division. A small puff of smoke drifted from under the door to the sanatorium, but it quickly dissipated, and a deep silence fell.

"Before we enter the Inner Sanctum, Angus, Principal Dark-Angel has asked me to remind you of your promise to reveal none of its secrets to any of your fellow lightning cubs," Rogwood said, taking a large bunch of keys from a pocket in his leather jerkin. "I, however, would encourage you to share every possible detail with Mr. Dewsnap and Miss Midnight. I believe it is extremely important for your most trusted friends to understand what it means to be a storm prophet."

"Er, yes, sir," Angus said, taken aback. "I've already told Dougal and Indigo everything."

"Excellent." Rogwood smiled kindly at him. "There is one more thing before we begin. If anyone other than your friends should see you entering or leaving the Inner Sanctum, I believe it might be necessary to tell them you have been volunteered by Principal Dark-Angel to clear up an infestation of pustular mold, and that should deter anyone who is overly curious."

"Yes, sir." Angus agreed, hoping there was no real mold.

"Good. I must also ask you not to touch anything unless I give my permission."

Rogwood fitted a different key into each of the eight locks on the door and then disappeared through it. Angus took a deep breath and followed him down a long, narrow stone tunnel. At the end of the tunnel they stopped before a round steel safety door. Rogwood opened it with a twist and a tug before Angus could worry about what might lie behind it and clambered through into another eight-sided hall. Angus gulped. It was almost an exact replica of the Octagon they'd just left behind, only this one had no marbled pillars or domed ceilings, and the eight doors were set deep into bare rock. Two large buckets had been deposited outside one of the doors. They were filled with piles of tangled rubbish.

"Ah, I believe that is some of the flotsam and jetsam collected from the courtyard after the latest weather explosion," Rogwood told him before he could ask. "It is being thoroughly inspected for any clues it might offer about the weather vortex over Castle Dankhart. Principal Dark-Angel has asked that—"

"ARGHHH! OOOOO!"

Angus flinched as sounds of a scuffle reached them from behind one of the eight doors.

"What's happening, sir?" he asked urgently, but his words were drowned by another strangled yelp.

"ARGHHH!"

A door burst open suddenly, and a short lightning catcher whom Angus had never seen before came tumbling through it. He slammed the door behind him and slumped against it, breathing heavily.

"Ah, Catcher Donall, good morning," Rogwood said calmly ignoring the sound of weighty footsteps now thundering toward them from the depths of the room beyond. Angus shrank back, wondering if he should make a run for it. Something monstrous was about to come bursting into the Octagon.

"Aramanthus," the man said, finally catching his breath, "we haven't seen you in the Inner Sanctum for some time."

"I'm afraid my duties have been keeping me rather busy of late."

Bang!

"Grrrrrrrrr!"

Angus took another hurried step backward, pressing his whole body into the wall as what sounded like a gigantic creature threw itself against the door, causing the rusty hinges to groan and bulge. Was Rogwood taking him to see some real fire dragons?

"It seems you have your hands rather full this morning," Rogwood said, his eyebrows raised. "Perhaps I could locate Catcher Roxbee for you and send her along with some assistance."

The man nodded gratefully, wiping his forehead with a handkerchief. "If you could also ask her to bring a strong rope and some pink marshmallows . . ."

The man's leather jerkin had been savagely ripped and torn. Angus noticed, as Rogwood steered him away, that there were also several sets of enormous teeth marks clearly imprinted upon the hemline.

"But, sir, what was that thing behind the door?" Angus asked, desperately trying to look back over his shoulder as Rogwood took him through another of the eight doors.

"We need not concern ourselves with that particular section of the Inner Sanctum on this occasion," Rogwood said mysteriously, without answering his question.

They had now entered a long, high-ceilinged room. The contrast with the bare rock of the Octagon was startling. Soft light fissures gave the wood paneling all around them a warm, comforting glow. Tall glass display cases towered over them from both sides of the room, stuffed with interesting-looking objects and ancient dust. It was like stepping into the depths of a grand old museum.

"This is one of our artifact rooms," Rogwood explained, leading him quickly past a display of archaic measuring instruments. "Everything contained in this room has great historical significance to the lightning catchers. These spectacles, for example, belonged to Philip Starling." Rogwood stopped suddenly and removed a spindly-looking pair of glasses from the cabinet beside them. Smudged fingerprints covered both lenses. Angus couldn't help wondering if they, too, had belonged to Philip Starling. "This is the first photograph ever taken of a storm," Rogwood continued, returning the glasses to their case and pointing to a very blurry black-and-white picture that looked as if it had been taken through a dark fog.

"But why not put everything on display inside Perilous, sir?" Angus asked. He was positive Dougal and Indigo would love to see such amazing artifacts.

"Unfortunately, many valuable items have been lost in the past, our most potent ideas stolen and used against us by the monsoon mongrels. In the Inner Sanctum we can protect our precious weather secrets and preserve that vital knowledge for future generations of lightning catchers. This weather suit, for instance, was worn by Veronica Stickleback when she discovered the existence of glizzards, or glacial blizzards," Rogwood said, standing beside a display case containing a battered-looking leather jerkin and saggy woolen pants. "It is an essential part of our heritage."

They meandered past a striking assortment of early waterproof pantaloons and some impressive fossilized snowflakes. There was also a vast collection of fulgurites (formed when a bolt of lightning struck sand, leaving a perfect cast of the lightning bolt behind) that had been found in various locations around the world.

"I believe this is where we will find Catcher Roxbee," Rogwood said as they reached the end of the artifact room and ducked through a low wooden door. The other side of it resembled a junkyard. Large collections of dangerous-looking inventions, similar to the ones Angus had seen in the experimental division, littered the floor. Some had shiny metal wheels and cogs; others were vibrating. Angus was certain that Uncle Max would trade his top-secret recipe for mashed potato and gravy muffins just to spend one glorious hour investigating such hidden treasures.

"These machines and inventions have been placed in the Inner Sanctum to protect everyone from their potential dangers," Rogwood explained as they ducked under swags of dangling chains and ropes. "Some are hundreds of years old and were discovered in the stone tunnels and passageways beneath Perilous." He pointed to what looked like a mountain of rust-covered scrap metal. "We still have no idea what many of them were used for, and it's far too dangerous to investigate."

Angus dived to the left suddenly as a large copper machine, which appeared to be covered in mechanical ears, coughed, belching out a long stream of black smoke.

"Although a few of the less dangerous specimens have been kept in working order," Rogwood said, brushing soot off his leather jerkin.

As they rounded a corner, they found a small group of lightning catchers, armed with wrenches and pots of grease, gathered around another machine.

"Ah, Catcher Roxbee." Rogwood shook her oily hand. "I come with a request from Catcher Donall. He is in urgent need of an extra pair of hands, a sturdy rope, and some pink marshmallows."

Catcher Roxbee nodded. She turned quietly to another member of her team, who grabbed a pair of thick protective gloves and darted off, looking mildly anxious.

"I hear the weather vortex is keeping you rather busy here in the Inner Sanctum," Rogwood said.

Catcher Roxbee nodded, scratching her nose and smearing it with dirt. "The weather station has collected some fresh samples just this morning."

Angus listened carefully to their conversation. Any

information he could gather about the weather vortex might be vital to his own search for answers with Dougal and Indigo.

"There are signs that the deadly seven are beginning to mix with fragments from some of the other storms in the swirling cloud," Catcher Roxbee said, "which could see them mutate into entirely new weather forms, so we must be prepared for anything."

"Indeed." Rogwood's face was suddenly serious. "That may have been Dankhart's real intention from the start."

"That is precisely why Delphinia wants us to resurrect this old experimental cloudpuller. If there is another explosion at Castle Dankhart, it will help us deal with any magnetic storm particles that drift over Perilous."

Angus stared at the machine properly for the first time. It resembled a giant octopus with eight long tentacle like attachments, each with a magnet fixed to the end.

"Unfortunately, it hasn't been activated since the great iron raindrop showers of 1919, and it's taking quite a bit of coaxing."

At that moment, however, the machine finally spluttered into life, causing several lightning catchers to dive for cover. Angus scuttled backward as the machine suddenly lurched.

"The cloudpuller must be reacting to something nearby!" Catcher Roxbee called above the scraping noise it was now making. "Everyone, search the area for magnetic materials!"

But Angus had a sudden horrible thought. He thrust his hands into his pockets and retrieved his bag of magnetic marbles.

"Er, e-excuse me, Catcher Roxbee!" he said, holding them out at arm's length.

The cloudpuller turned, adjusting its position, and headed straight for him, tentacles waving wildly.

"Quickly, boy, throw the marbles away from you!" Catcher Roxbee ordered as the machine began to close the gap between them with alarming speed.

Angus lobbed the bag and ducked as a wrench flew over his head. Small oil cans, screwdrivers, and rusty nails were being drawn toward the octopus arms like silver lightning moths to a flame.

Rogwood yanked him aside as the machine hurtled past them hungrily, in search of the marbles. It was now on a direct collision course with what looked like a giant snow shovel on a spinning wheel.

SMASH!

The collision rocked the Inner Sanctum with the force of a small earthquake. Angus threw his arms over his head for protection as coils, springs, magnets, and tentacles flew in every direction. A heavy shower of iron filings pooled at his feet, forming a glimmering metallic puddle.

"And that, Angus, is why I have sworn never to keep a Cradget's product about my person," Rogwood declared, brushing iron filings out of his beard. "I believe the time has come for us to leave Catcher Roxbee and her team to it."

Angus followed the lightning catcher in a daze, his ears ringing. They retraced their steps through the artifact room and back to the rough stone chamber, where Angus stood a few minutes later, facing the eight closed doors once again. Catcher Donall had now disappeared. All was quiet behind the door with the rusty hinges.

"If you are feeling up to it, Angus, we will begin our first lesson properly," Rogwood said.

Angus nodded, hoping his legs weren't about to give way beneath him. The incident with the cloudpuller had left him feeling distinctly shaken. Rogwood led him through a different door this time, decorated with swooping fire dragons. The room inside was completely dragon free. It was also empty. Puzzled, Angus twisted around in every direction, staring into the dark corners. There were no pictures, bookshelves, display cabinets, or rusty weather machines. As he followed Rogwood across the room, however, his eyes were drawn to a small round trapdoor in the floor.

"Oh!" Angus stopped in his tracks as he felt a sudden stirring in his chest. It was the same unsettling sensation that he'd experienced after his trip to the Storm Science Museum.

"Er, sir?"

Something beneath the trapdoor was connected to the storm prophets. He was sure of it.

"Ah." Rogwood smiled behind his beard. "I see your extraordinary senses have drawn you straight to one of the most significant parts of the Inner Sanctum. I was planning to take you through that particular door on a different occasion, but as your curiosity has clearly been piqued . . ."

Rogwood lifted the trapdoor, revealing a long set of stone steps heading downward. The air grew steadily colder as they descended. When they finally reached the bottom—

Angus gasped. Stretching far into the distance was what looked like a large underground graveyard, packed tightly with an assortment of creepy tombs and stone coffins. There were Egyptian-style obelisks, sunken stairs leading down to mysteriously inscribed doors, and great mausoleums protected by marble lions and tigers. The air inside the crypt was bitingly cold and filled with the dank smell of decay. The only light came from a few flickering lamps that hung from the vaulted ceiling, casting grotesque shadows in every direction.

"Welcome, Angus, to the Perilous crypt."

"C-crypt?" Angus had a sudden vision of wailing ghosts and vampires and shivered. What did any of this have to do with the storm prophets? He followed Rogwood through a whole avenue of lofty stone mausoleums. The lightning catcher appeared to be heading for one of the larger tombs with pillars and fancy engravings on the front. As they drew closer, Angus was surprised to see a half-open door leading inside the tomb, where he could clearly make out an unmade bed and a small kitchenette.

Rogwood knocked on the door, and a few seconds later another lightning catcher appeared in tartan pajamas, with a matching bathrobe and slippers.

"My apologies for intruding upon you at such an early hour, Rufus," Rogwood said. "Please allow me to introduce Angus McFangus. Angus, this is Catcher Coriolis."

Angus did his best to smile, but his face was already frozen with cold.

"I am showing Angus some of his storm prophet history, and I thought we might take a quick look in the crypt if you have no objections."

"I'm afraid you'll have to keep it short," Catcher Coriolis said, glancing at his watch. "Some of the older tombs are riddled with crypt fungus and are beginning to crumble in the damp conditions, and I have someone coming shortly to inspect the damage."

"Then we will waste no more of your time."

Without another word Rogwood turned on his heel and led Angus into the very depths of the crypt, only stopping when they reached a long row of impressive tombs. Each one was the size of a small shed and had been decorated with intricate carvings of Perilous, thunderstorms, hailstones, and lightning towers.

"It was decided long ago by the earliest lightning catchers that Perilous should provide a final resting place for those who wished to remain within the walls of this magnificent Exploratorium," Rogwood explained. "Many had themselves mummified in the early years, of course, as was the fashion of the time."

"Mummified?" Angus said, startled. He thought back to the bone merchant's in Little Frog's Bottom, and the long hook that Creepy Crevice had drawn from his pocket, and shivered.

"This area of the crypt has been reserved for the most senior and important lightning catchers, such as Eliza Tippins or Hortence Heliotrope, the famous lightning catcher who first discovered the existence of double-ended lightning bolts, and, of course, for Philip Starling and Edgar Perilous."

Rogwood pointed to a matching pair of massive stone confections. Two marble lightning bolts guarded each entrance. Angus edged closer, feeling equally fascinated and revolted by the thought of what lay inside.

"And now we must go in search of the storm prophets," Rogwood said, turning briskly and disappearing into the gloom again.

"The storm prophets were buried here, in the crypt?" Angus asked.

Rogwood smiled kindly at the shocked look on his face. "Principal Dark-Angel thought you should see the coffins for yourself, Angus. She wants you to understand as much about your own history as possible, and this is an important part."

He led them straight over to a spectacular collection of coffins. Angus stared, his jaw dropping in wonder. The tombs were nothing like the cold stone monuments that the other lightning catchers were buried in. Made from smooth, ancient-looking wood, they were shaped like fire dragons, with powerful wings extended, talons clawing at the sky, bodies rippling with long streaks of fearsome flame. Each scale had been decorated with iridescent blues, greens, reds, and gleaming gold. Each dragon was different from the next in size, shape, color, and expression. It was the presence of these tombs, he realized, that had drawn him toward the trapdoor.

"According to written accounts from the age of the early lightning catchers, the only time a fire dragon can ever be seen by another living soul is when a storm prophet dies," Rogwood announced, leaving Angus so startled he almost tripped over a stone griffin. "It has been reported that the fiery creature blazes in the air above the storm prophet at the precise moment of his or her death, shedding its scales as golden droplets of light, which then fall onto the body and harden around it like armor or a toughened shroud." In the spooky gloom of the crypt, it was easy to imagine the dazzling display.

"As you can see, each of the storm prophet tombs was then carved in the likeness of his or her own unique fire dragon, and the shrouded body placed inside. A fitting final resting place for such magnificence, I think you will agree."

"But, sir," Angus said, "when you first told me about the storm prophets, you said the fire dragon was just a warning of dangerous weather."

Rogwood nodded. "I did indeed."

"So how can it suddenly be visible to everyone else

when a storm prophet dies? I mean, how can a fire drag-on's scales turn into armor if they're not even real?"

"I'm afraid there are many things about the storm proph-ets that we are yet to understand," Rogwood said. "One possible theory, however, is that at the end of a storm prophet's life, his or her fire dragon somehow transcends its own ethereal boundaries and joins with the body of its storm prophet in the physical world."

Angus stared at the lightning catcher, feeling utterly overwhelmed. The strange knot in his chest tightened.

"Naturally, such powerful stories about dragon scales have given rise to many myths and legends," a different voice said.

Angus spun around. Catcher Coriolis had joined them. He was now fully dressed.

"Dragon scale pendants and amulets have made regularly appearances in the markets of Little Frog's Bottom," he continued with obvious disdain, "allegedly stolen from the body of a storm prophet before it was entombed, supposedly able to boost brainpower, cure dim-wittedness, scurvy, bunions, and pimples. These are nothing more than common lizard scales, however, dipped in a golden tincture and with no greater power than a painted fingernail."

Angus blinked at the lightning catcher.

"One tomb you may find particularly interesting, Angus, is that of the great Moray McFangus." Rogwood pointed to one of the largest dragons of all. "As you already know, Moray McFangus fled from the Great Fire in 1666 and came to Imbur with Starling and Perilous," he said, watching Angus closely. "It is from him that you appear to have inherited your own storm prophet skills."

Angus rocked back on his heels. He'd somehow forgotten that the tomb of his own ancestor would be among those of the other storm prophets. It was also the first time anyone had said his full name out loud in Angus's hearing.

The fire dragon tomb was impressively fierce with shimmering gold and red flames, which glowed like hot embers even in the gloom of the crypt. Angus hesitated for a second, then reached out and traced the line of its wing with his fingers, almost expecting to feel a scorching heat.

"But, sir, this looks exactly like my fire dragon, only bigger," he said.

Rogwood exchanged surprised glances with Catcher Coriolis.

"There is another theory, Angus, that the features and appearance of a fire dragon can be passed down from one generation to the next, much the way the color of your hair and the shape of your ears have been inherited from your own parents."

Angus, awestruck, stared at the tomb again. He couldn't wait to tell Dougal and Indigo about everything he'd seen in the Inner Sanctum, although he wasn't sure they'd believe a word of it.

"Does my dad know about Moray McFangus?" he asked.

Rogwood nodded. "Although I believe he has never visited the actual tomb."

"The entrance to the crypt is usually locked at all times," Catcher Coriolis said, looking determined to keep it that way. "Visits to the tombs are strictly forbidden without express permission from Principal Dark-Angel." He glanced at his watch pointedly.

"Ah, yes, that is quite enough for one morning," Rogwood said, checking his own watch. "Angus, we must return to the kitchens before you are missed by your fellow lightning cubs and leave Catcher Coriolis to his duties. Thank you for your time and expert knowledge, Rufus."

The lightning catcher returned to his own tomb hurriedly and closed the door. Seconds later, Angus could hear sounds of a kettle's being boiled inside. Rogwood led the way back through the grand mausoleums. Angus tried to read some of the names and inscriptions as they swept past. But the most unusual tomb of all was set well apart from the others. With no marbled lightning bolts, dates, or names it was strikingly simple and mysterious.

It was only when Angus turned his attention back to the stairs they were now climbing that he saw a figure descending toward them. He recognized the man immediately and felt his stomach lurch. It was his least favorite lightning catcher in the whole of Perilous—Valentine Vellum, Pixie and Percival's dad. Over the course of the previous term, Angus, Dougal, and Indigo had developed a growing suspicion that Vellum was in cahoots with Scabious Dankhart, that he had helped Swarfe execute his plan to revive the dormant lightning heart and kidnap Angus. As they had no proof that Vellum was a devious traitor, however, they hadn't shared their inklings with anyone else . . . yet.

"Aramanthus, I see you have drawn the short straw," Vellum said, looking down his nose at Angus as they stopped beside each other on the stairs. "Delphinia informs me that the McFangus boy is to learn more about the storm prophets. Personally, I'm not convinced it's worth the effort. He has shown remarkably little promise so far. I think you may be in for a very disappointing time."

"On the contrary, Valentine, I believe Angus has a vast deal of potential as a lightning cub and a storm prophet."

A muscle twitched in Vellum's forehead as he shot a scornful glance at Angus. "Then I'm afraid we shall have to agree to differ on the subject."

"As we have done so many times before, Valentine," Rogwood said, smiling.

"If you will excuse me," Vellum said, briskly. "Catcher Coriolis is expecting us."

He stepped to one side, and Angus froze. Lurking on the stairs behind Vellum was Creepy Crevice, the bone merchant. Crevice nodded briefly at Rogwood as they passed each other. He glared at Angus, a faint sneer curling the corners of his lips. It was clear that he had not forgotten the incident in his shop in Little Frog's Bottom.

"What's Mr. Crevice doing down in the Perilous crypt, sir?" Angus asked as soon as he and Rogwood emerged into the empty room at the top of the stairs.

"As you have just seen for yourself, Angus, some of the older tombs containing mummified remains are beginning to crumble and need some attention before they deteriorate any further. Mr. Crevice is an expert in that area. I understand from Catcher Coriolis that there is nobody else on the island qualified to perform such work. Am I correct in assuming that you and Mr. Crevice may have crossed paths before?"

"Er, me and Dougal sort of wandered into his shop by accident," Angus said, trying to make it sound like an honest mistake.

"Indeed?" A hint of a smile crossed Rogwood's lips. "Do not trouble yourself about Mr. Crevice. He is here for the tombs only. His presence will not interfere with our work."

But the sudden appearance of the bone merchant made

Angus feel instantly uneasy. Had Creepy Crevice been sworn to secrecy before entering the Inner Sanctum? Would he guess why Angus had been visiting the crypt? Would he soon discover that Angus had a secret he did not want the rest of Perilous to discover? Or would Valentine Vellum simply tell him everything?

8

"COMING SOON!"

That evening in the Pigsty, Angus told Dougal and Indigo everything he could remember about his first memorable trip into the Inner Sanctum. Dougal hid behind a cushion as Angus described the teeth marks in Catcher Donall's leather jerkin.

"M-maybe they've got some sort of extra-vicious fog phantom in there," he suggested, gulping. "But what's it doing in the Inner Sanctum? I mean, if the hinges on that door really are rusty and it somehow escaped into the Exploratorium . . ."

Pencils, papers, and library books lay abandoned at Dougal's feet. He'd been planning to work on his Tri-Hard competition entry that evening but had dropped everything as soon as Angus started talking.

Indigo chewed her lip, looking extremely worried, as he told them what Catcher Roxbee had said about the most recent storm sample from Castle Dankhart and the strange particles it contained.

"And she actually said the deadly seven could be mixing with the other types of weather?" Indigo asked.

"Yeah, Rogwood sounded pretty concerned about it, too. We could end up with something really weird, like scarlet ice-diamond storms."

"Or icicle lightning," Indigo said.

"Not to mention frozen thunderbolts," Dougal said, shuddering at the thought.

When Angus described what he'd found down in the Perilous crypt, however, both his friends listened in stunned silence.

"And then Rogwood showed me the tomb of Moray McFangus," he said, finally finishing his tale. "Rogwood thinks that's who I get the storm prophet stuff from."

"Wow!" Dougal gasped, sounding seriously impressed. "I wish some of my ancestors were that cool. All we've got in our family are boring historians and peasants."

"At least none of them have ever been notorious weather villains," Indigo pointed out.

"Oh, yeah, sorry, I forgot," Dougal said sheepishly. "But those dragon tombs sound amazing!"

Angus grinned, grateful that neither Dougal nor Indigo had been put off by the startling news that one day his fire dragon would cover his entire body in golden scales, like a suit of extra-tough armor.

"W-what does *your* fire dragon look like, Angus?" Indigo asked shyly.

It was the first time either one of them had dared to ask. Angus tried to describe the fiery creature that appeared before him in his moments of most desperate need, feeling his face grow hotter the more he revealed.

"I still can't believe they've got an actual crypt in the Inner Sanctum," Dougal said, shaking his head in wonder once Angus had told them everything he could.

"Do you think Rogwood will show you what's behind the rest of the doors?" Indigo asked.

"Yeah, when's your next lesson?"

Angus shrugged. "Rogwood didn't say. There's something

else," he added, suddenly remembering about the bone merchant. "I met Creepy Crevice in the Inner Sanctum. Vellum was taking him down into the crypt as we were leaving."

"You're kidding!" Dougal almost choked.

"Rogwood says he's here to repair some of the older tombs."

"I don't care," Dougal said. "I wouldn't trust that old goat near anything important. What's Dark-Angel doing letting him roam around Perilous?"

"Did he recognize you?" Indigo asked.

Angus nodded. "What if he knows everything about me now? Vellum said something about my having storm prophet lessons right in front of him."

Dougal and Indigo exchanged worried glances, but as none of them had any answers to such a tricky question, they eventually dropped the subject and returned to Angus's other startling revelations.

Angus spent the next few days wandering around Perilous in the same sort of daze he'd experienced after his visit to the Starling Museum of Storm Science in London. Images of the storm prophet tombs and golden fire dragon scales burned through his dreams. The uncomfortable feeling of indigestion now grew ten times worse, as if he'd tried to swallow a whole cow. Had all storm prophets experienced such strange sensations? Or had he accidentally gulped down some crypt fungus spores that were now making him feel extremely peculiar?

He was very glad when Dougal gave him something else to think about.

"I've been looking through the rest of those weather reports and mechanical pigeon messengers from Castle Dankhart," he told Angus and Indigo the next Saturday morning as they caught up with their homework in the library.

Dougal reached into his bag and dragged out one of the dusty tomes and a scrawny-looking bird.

"There's some really interesting stuff in here about unusual cloud formations and sudden temperature spikes, but I can't find anything that explains the explosions, or the weather vortex, or what Dark-Angel isn't telling us about it all."

Angus picked up the mechanical pigeon, feeling his spirits sink, and extracted a message from under the wing. It was short and extremely unhelpful. "No change in weather vortex. Catcher Azolla Plymstock."

"But we've got to find out somehow," he said, frustration suddenly spilling over. "My mum and dad are trapped inside that castle, and if there's another explosion, or Dankhart's planning something even more dangerous . . . Dark-Angel's never going to give us any real answers. There's got to be somewhere else we can look!"

Dougal nodded. "There is. I reckon I might find something useful in the research department. Dark-Angel, Rogwood, and Gudgeon are obviously getting their information from somewhere. Plus there could be something old or obscure in there about storm science and weather vortices that everyone else has forgotten about. It might help explain what Dankhart's really up to."

"Can't me and Indigo help you look?" Angus asked, desperate to do something useful.

But Dougal shook his head. "It's easier if I do the sneaking about on my own. That's one advantage of being a known bookworm," he added, suddenly looking embarrassed. "Nobody ever questions why I'm surrounded by books."

Angus and Dougal went up to the kitchens on Monday

morning still discussing the mysteries of the weather vortex. They were met in the entrance hall by a large group of lightning cubs who were gathered excitedly around a notice pinned to the wall.

"What's going on?" Angus asked Violet Quinn as they joined the others a moment later.

"Catcher Sparks put up a new poster, and now Theodore Twill won't let anyone look at it unless they pay him two silver starlings!"

Angus bobbed up and down on his toes, trying to see over the head of Edmund Croxley, who was standing directly in front of him.

"I said get out of the way, Twill, or I'll report you to Principal Dark-Angel for obstructing important lightning catcher information!" Edmund said angrily.

"The price just went up to three silver starlings, Croxley. Come on, hand it over," Theodore Twill said, holding out his hand.

"I'll do no such thing!"

Angus and Dougal edged their way around the side of the crowd for a better look as the two lightning cubs continued to argue.

"I can see it! Oh," Dougal added, sounding disappointed, "it's just another 'Coming Soon!' poster."

"Hang on a minute; there's something different about this one." Angus grabbed Dougal by the sleeve before he could disappear, and they sneaked in behind Theodore Twill. Underneath the usual "Coming Soon!" pronouncement were several fresh lines of information that Twill had tried to cover up clumsily with some sticky tape and paper. Angus ripped it off quietly, so Twill, who was still arguing with Croxley, wouldn't hear what he was doing. "It says, 'Lightning Catcher of the Year award: the winners' tour,'" he said in hushed tones.

"You're joking!" Dougal's glasses steamed up instantly with excitement. "They're coming to Perilous to demonstrate their winning entries?"

The Lightning Catcher of the Year award was an extremely popular annual event that every Exploratorium on the planet could enter. Rogwood had won it more than once. Adrik Swarfe had been awarded the top prize for his work with extra-strong lightning before he'd betrayed the lightning catchers and fled to join the monsoon mongrels. Even Angus's own mum and dad had won the large lightning-shaped trophy, and a lifetime's supply of luxury, all-weather, lightning-proof leather jerkins, for writing the *McFangus Fog Guide*. Dougal had shown him a picture last term.

"Does it say when they're coming here?" Dougal asked.

Angus shook his head. "But it looks like their first stop is the London office; then they're traveling on to Paris, Washington, D.C., Wellington, in New Zealand, and somewhere in Finland I can't even pronounce before they come anywhere near Perilous," he said, tracing the printed line of destinations with his finger. "So it could be ages yet."

Angus carefully replaced Twill's slip of paper so the older lightning cub wouldn't track him down and demand payment for sneaking a look at the poster. They entered the kitchens a few moments later, grabbed some toast, and headed for their usual table under one of the fake palm trees.

"Who were last year's winners, anyway?" Angus asked as they sat down. Indigo was already waiting for them. A steaming bowl of porridge lay forgotten in front of her; her head was buried in the pages of a magazine.

"I can't remember exactly," Dougal said. "But there was definitely someone called Herbert Hoffenmier, or it could have been Herman Buckleswamp. Hey, why are you reading the *Weathervane* again?" Dougal frowned across the table at Indigo.

"It came out first thing this morning," Indigo said, showing them the cover of the latest issue. "So I ran straight up to the research department to grab one. There's a six-page special about the winners' tour. Here."

She turned the magazine around and slid it across the table so they could both see it. Staring up at them was the headline "Winners' Tour Comes to Perilous!" with a photo of a small, slightly nervous-looking lightning catcher with mousy-colored hair. Her fingernails were bitten down to the quick, Angus noticed.

"That's Edna Smithwyck," Dougal said excitedly. "I remember now; she came third in last year's competition."

"It says here she trained for seven years at the Canadian Exploratorium before continuing her work in Iceland. I wonder if she knows Jeremius," Angus said, wishing his uncle were here to tell them more.

He read the next paragraph quickly. According to the

Weathervane, Catcher Smithwyck was an expert in cold-weather climates. She had taken part in a daring escapade through the very same Canadian ice maze that Dougal's dad had spun them a story about at Feaver Street. And she had carried out many solo research projects into frost quakes.

"Why would anybody want to do more research into frost quakes?" Dougal said, reaching the end of the same paragraph and instantly turning pale.

"Does it say what she won third prize for?" Angus asked thickly, through a mouthful of toast.

Dougal scanned the rest of the page. "No, but I think it involved something inflatable. This is going to be brilliant!"

Indigo left them a few minutes later to return a book to the library, giving Angus and Dougal just enough time to read the rest of the article before they were due up in the forecasting department.

Angus munched on a slice of toast, scanning the words quickly. According to the *Weathervane,* Catcher Smithwyck enjoyed playing the trombone, growing carnivorous water lilies, and— Angus allowed his eyes to jump to the top of the next page, but the magazine had leaped straight to an article about emergency sock-darning procedures instead.

"I don't believe it. Pages thirteen and fourteen are missing," he said, flicking back through the magazine to check.

"But they can't be. Have a look on the floor."

There was no sign that the missing pages had fallen around their feet or under the table, and a few minutes later they were forced to abandon the search and head up to the weather archive.

News of the winners' tour spread swiftly around Perilous, causing great pockets of excitement to bubble up in the kitchens and the lightning cubs' living quarters. A wild rumor also began to circulate that Catcher Smithwyck would be performing dangerous experiments on a number of lightning cubs as part of her demonstration.

"Don't tell anyone, but I made the whole thing up!" Germ confided in Angus one evening as they bumped into each other outside the boys' bathrooms. "You should have seen Percival Vellum's face when I told him she experiments only on the hairiest and ugliest lightning cubs in the audience."

Germ was still studying hard for his upcoming exams

and asked Angus, Dougal, and Indigo to test him on random topics, such as belching blisters, crumble fungus, and snow boot boils, whenever they passed him in the library. He also continued to interrogate Indigo about the rash on her hand, pouncing on her unexpectedly in the stone tunnels and passageways with long lists of questions.

"Have you eaten any rotten turnips in the last seven days, little sis?" Germ asked on one such occasion, taking a small notebook and a pencil from his pocket.

"What? No. Go away and leave me alone," Indigo whispered.

"Have you been exposed to any toxic miasmas or oily fumes in the experimental division?"

"Of course I haven't," Indigo said, starting to sound annoyed. She folded her arms across her chest and glared at her brother. Angus caught a quick glance of the rash as she did so and was surprised to see how red and angry it now looked.

"Have you accidentally put your hand in a stinking bowl of—"

But Indigo had finally had enough and stomped off before Germ could finish.

"Now we're finally getting somewhere!" He scribbled hurriedly on his notepad with a mischievous grin. "Symptoms include sudden outbreaks of extreme grumpiness."

In the forecasting department they were now tackling some of the oldest and most fragile storm jars in the weather archive. The tiny jars had been placed on the topmost shelves and had to be lifted down with great care on the end of a long hook. Unfortunately, several jars smashed to the ground during this process, releasing the weather inside, and they spent a number of extremely wet and windy afternoons trying to sweep up the evidence. Luckily, Catcher Wrascal was only too happy to help.

"I'm already in enough trouble with Catcher Killigrew as it is," she told them when this happened for the third time in one hour. "I accidentally flooded his office the other day with cold rice pudding from the vats. And if he hears about broken jars in the weather archive, he'll be sending me straight back to the Scottish mountains for a month on snow-shoveling duty."

In the evenings Dougal was now splitting his time between searching for information about the weather vortex in the research department and working on phase two of his Cradget's puzzle competition entry.

"What does phase two involve, exactly?" Angus asked as they sat in the comfy chairs before the fire in the Pigsty.

"It's called a word splice, and it's absolutely brilliant!" Dougal explained, looking thoroughly overexcited. "You've got to merge all these random words together in the right order so they become a whole string of different words, and then they form the next clue."

Two weeks later the second-year lightning cubs finally returned to the storm hollow for another lesson on the deadly seven.

Gudgeon led them straight over to a single storm jar placed at the far end of the hollow. It had been covered with a tarpaulin, hiding its contents from view.

"Right, you lot, settle down," Gudgeon barked as a nervous silence fell. "And let me remind everyone that any larking about in this lesson will not be tolerated." He glared at the Vellum twins, who had just finished a long stint on rubber boot repairs as punishment for releasing the scarlet sleeping snow.

"Before we get started, everyone should grab a copy

of *The Dankhart Handbook*, by Gretchen Grimoire." Gudgeon pointed to a heap of books on the floor beside the storm jar.

Angus, who hovered at the back of the throng as a disorderly queue formed, took the last book on the pile. It was jet black, with a rough, knobbly texture like stone. It was also shaped exactly like Castle Dankhart, Angus realized, tracing the outline of a turret with his thumb. He turned to the first page. It issued a stark warning in thick black gothic-style letters: "Caution! The information contained in this book may cause shortness of breath, nervous headaches, dizziness, and night terrors. Read with extreme care!"

"Have you seen the section in the middle?" Dougal whispered beside him.

Angus flicked warily past the first chapter, which was titled "Rise of the Dankhart Family." The following pages appeared to provide a detailed floor plan of the castle itself, which he definitely wanted to study in more detail. And then . . . Angus swallowed hard. The middle section of the book was entirely devoted to Dankhart and the monsoon mongrels. He instantly recognized the picture of Adrik Swarfe. With his inquisitive, clever gaze, his shoulder-length hair and goatee flecked with gray, he still looked more like a kindly teacher than a weather scoundrel. There was also someone called Victus Bile, who came from a long line of monsoon mongrels. His shaggy brown hair and narrow eyes gave him the look of a ferret. But it was the picture of Scabious Dankhart that disturbed Angus the most. It was an exact replica of the real Dankhart whom he'd come face-to-face with in the lightning vaults, with a large black glittering diamond protruding from his right eye socket, dark tangled hair, shriveled stumpy teeth, and deep pocks and scars on his face. It was the same Dankhart who had threatened to "deal with" Indigo in a very spine-chilling manner.

For Indigo, however, it was the first time she'd ever seen a recent portrait of her uncle. The malicious figure bore little resemblance to the only photo she had of him, which showed a young boy with short hair and an innocent-looking smile. Angus suddenly wished he'd prepared her for the repulsive transformation that had since taken place.

"Um, Indigo, are you all right?" Angus asked, turning toward her.

Indigo nodded, giving an involuntary shiver as she stared at the picture of her uncle. "I'm fine," she said, covering the rash on her hand with her sweater sleeve.

But before Angus could ask any more . . . "This must be right up your alley, Munchfungus," Percival Vellum said, barging roughly past Indigo and Dougal and looming over Angus.

"Nobody wants to talk to you, Vellum." Angus turned away from the twin.

"But isn't this what you're supposed to be good at, saving lightning cubs from the deadly seven?"

"Our dad's told us everything about you," Pixie said, a gleam in her eyes. "You're the first storm prophet at Perilous for hundreds of years."

Thump!

Dougal dropped his book on the floor in shock. Indigo glared at the twins. Angus felt his chest tighten, as if something big and heavy were trying to squash his lungs.

"But . . . how did you—"

"I always knew there was something weird about you, Munchfungus." Percival continued, looking at him shrewdly. "Dark-Angel's always calling you up to her office. Rogwood sends you mysterious notes and messages."

"Doctor Obsidian's been testing your brain, too," Pixie added.

Percival grinned. "Personally, I'm surprised he could find anything there to test."

Pixie sniggered. It was clear that both twins were enjoying their moment of triumph immensely.

"How do you two know about those tests?" Angus demanded, still reeling with shock.

"Dark-Angel tells our dad everything," Percival said. "And he saw you being tricked by a fake ice-diamond storm down in the testing tunnels."

"He says you're a rubbish storm prophet," Pixie added.

"He says you fainted like a girl as soon as the ice-diamond spores got anywhere near you. You couldn't save a fog mite from a fake fog, Munchfungus."

"Don't say that!" Indigo burst out suddenly. "Angus saved you from being killed by a fognado on the Imbur marshes!"

"Yeah, and I didn't hear you complaining about it at the time, you ungrateful toad," Dougal added.

Percival's face darkened. "Shut up, Dewsnap, nobody asked you."

"And nobody asked you to poke your big nose into my business either," Angus said, growing more annoyed by the second.

"Oooo, I'm really scared now, storm boy. What are you going to do, send a load of scary snow chasing after us? Oh, save us from the teeny-tiny snowflakes, Munchfungus!" Percival jeered, causing several other lightning cubs to turn and stare. "Is that what Rogwood's teaching you to do in the Inner Sanctum?"

Dougal called Percival some extremely insulting names under his breath. Angus clenched his fists, seething with instant anger. Yet again Percival Vellum seemed to know something highly personal about him, something so sensitive and supposedly secret he didn't even understand it himself yet. Did the Vellum twins also know what his fire dragon looked like or that his ancestor Moray McFangus was buried beneath the Exploratorium?

"Pixie and me know more about your grubby little secrets than you do, Munchfungus," Percival said, seizing his opportunity. "We reckon you ought to be locked in the crypt with the rest of those fire dragon freaks and—"

He stopped talking abruptly and stared across the top of Angus's head. Gudgeon was now watching all five of them closely. "Never mind," he sneered. "It'll keep. See you later, storm boy."

"Just ignore him," Indigo whispered under her breath as the twins slouched away. "He's trying to make you angry on purpose."

"Well, it's working!" Angus snapped, his face now burning with rage. "Why do those two have to know *every-thing* important about my life? They'll be telling everyone how many times a day I pick my nose next!"

Dougal grinned.

"This isn't funny!"

"Sorry," Dougal said, trying to control his face.

"Why are those two so determined to make my life a misery?"

"Obvious, isn't it?" Dougal said wisely. "You stand up to them; you're not scared of them."

"And Percival doesn't like it," Indigo added.

"Plus you're ten times more intelligent and a hundred times less ugly than any member of the Vellum family," Dougal pointed out truthfully.

Gudgeon started the lesson in earnest a few moments later, forcing Angus to continue seething in silence.

"This book will tell you everything you need to know about Dankhart and his monsoon mongrels and give you a step-by-step guide on how to deal with the deadly seven. So study it well. It might save your life one day," the gruff lightning catcher said, holding up a copy of *The Dankhart Handbook*. "What it won't teach you is how to recognize the stench of a sulfur storm when it's coming straight at you or how to escape from a cloud of ice-diamond spores without quaking in your snow boots. That's what we'll be tackling in the storm hollow."

Gudgeon shuffled each of them closer to the storm jar, which rattled ominously. Millicent Nichols whimpered, hiding behind Georgina Fox as Gudgeon ripped off the tarpaulin, revealing the contents of the jar underneath. It looked as if a large angry rainstorm had been scooped up and bottled in a jar. Heavy drops of black rain clung to the sides of the glass without falling.

"This is rancid rain," Gudgeon told them. "This particular storm was caught trying to rain on a group of lightning catchers who were on the roof at Perilous observing some unusual cloud formations. Principal Dark-Angel has given her special permission to release a small quantity of the storm. It's not enough to inflict serious injury on anyone in this hollow, but traces of it have been found in the cloud over Castle Dankhart, so you need to know the worst of it!"

Angus swallowed hard; his heart was still beating much faster than normal after his argument with the Vellum twins. From the corner of his eye, he could see them whispering and shaking with silent giggles.

"But before you lot get anywhere near the contents of this jar, you need to understand some basic stuff about rain first. Everyone, turn to page thirty-four of your handbooks," Gudgeon said.

Angus flicked clumsily to the correct page. At the top was the heading "The Water Cycle."

"Dewsnap."

Dougal jumped several inches in the air.

"Read the first section out loud."

Dougal pushed his glasses up his nose. "'R-rain is formed during the water cycle,'" he began, with a quiver

in his voice. "'The sun heats oceans, lakes, and rivers, causing water to evaporate and rise into the sky, where it forms clouds. As the water vapor cools, or condenses, it becomes water once again. If the cloud is big enough and contains enough water droplets, these will collide together, becoming heavier, and eventually gravity causes them to fall back as rain to the earth, where they collect in oceans, lakes, and rivers, and the water cycle begins once again.'"

"Carry on, boy, read the next bit," Gudgeon barked as Dougal paused.

"'The same water that exists on our planet today has been here since the early earth was formed. It has been recycled again and again, completing the water cycle millions of times over,'" Dougal read, sounding startled.

"Which means that the same water that Percival Vellum brushed his teeth with this morning might one day fall across the Himalayas as snow," Gudgeon informed them.

"That's if he even bothers brushing his teeth," Angus whispered to Indigo, staring at the twin's mossy-looking molars.

"It also means that in 1666, Philip Starling could have

washed his socks in the very water that is now used to boil your eggs for breakfast."

"Ew! Gross!" Georgina Fox grimaced.

Angus quickly decided to have toast in the mornings from now on.

"Read the rest of it, Dewsnap," Gudgeon said.

"'It can take thousands of years for a single drop of rain to complete its journey around the planet,'" Dougal continued, "'as it can be frozen at the polar ice caps, become part of slow-moving glaciers, or be stored as groundwater in aquifers before continuing its journey through the water cycle once again.'"

"There's only one type of rain that gives you a glimpse of the endless journey water takes around our planet, and it's called ancient rain," Gudgeon said. "It's rare. You won't ever see it here on Imbur, so I've brought a sample with me that was collected some years ago."

He took a familiar glass sphere from his pocket. Dougal nudged Angus in the ribs. It was a long time since either of them had seen a storm globe. The last time they'd tried to use one it had almost flooded the Pigsty.

"Right, stand back!" Gudgeon warned.

Angus jumped out of the way as Gudgeon smashed the storm globe on the ground. Broken glass skittered across the floor, releasing gray wisps of mist.

"Each drop of ancient rain contains a fleeting image of the last thing it fell on," Gudgeon explained as a cloud quickly began to form above their heads. "It can be seen only for a fraction of a second from the corner of the eye. But it's one of the most amazing spectacles a lightning catcher will ever witness, and you lot are extremely lucky to see it."

Angus stared up as the first drops began to fall, but he was still too angry with the Vellums to see anything except a soggy blur of rain. His eyes flitted from left to right, his head twisting in every direction in short, jerky movements.

"What are you trying to do, boy, give yourself a stiff neck?" Gudgeon asked as he moved around the storm hollow. "Stand still and let your eyes slip out of focus. That's when you'll see it."

Angus concentrated hard, trying to put all thoughts of the Vellum twins out of his mind. His eyes went blurry for a fraction of a second and . . . "Wow!"

The ancient rain was astonishing. He caught a quick, breathtaking glimpse of lush forests, gargantuan trees, deep valleys, and spectacular river-filled gorges. There were swaying meadows full of delicate flowers and buzzing bees, crashing waves on rocky shorelines, and even the shifting sands of a desert. Angus felt his head spin. It was like taking a whirlwind tour of the planet before people even existed, before pollution, highways, cars, and cities.

The shower stopped just as suddenly as it had started, leaving the ground glistening and wet. Angus turned and grinned at Indigo. Dougal wiped a smattering of opalescent raindrops off his glasses.

"Right, now you know all about ancient rain and the water cycle, it's time to tell you more about this stuff," Gudgeon said, drawing their attention back to the storm jar. After the wonders of the ancient rain, it looked even gloomier than before. "Instead of traveling freely through the oceans of the world, falling over mountains, forests, and valleys, rancid rain is deliberately captured and sealed inside a series of dark tunnels underneath Castle Dankhart by the monsoon mongrels. It then gets filtered through a range of bleak and sinister projectograms showing images of terrible storms, deadly lightning strikes, desolate landscapes, and horrors such as fog phantoms."

"I knew it!" Dougal gasped. "I knew they were real!"

"Rancid rain is tremendously potent; some say it's the most terrifying of the deadly seven. It acts upon the brain, via the optical nerve, causing fearful delusions, anxiety, and disorientation. It probably won't kill you," Gudgeon added. "But it can cripple even the best lightning catchers with feelings of overwhelming fear and panic, leaving them extremely vulnerable. Closing your eyes won't help," he said, pointing at Georgina Fox, who was swaying on the spot, both her eyes screwed tightly shut. "Your best defense against it is to get undercover as quickly as possible. These guardian glasses will provide some protection for a short period of time," he said, taking a pair from his leather jerkin and holding them up so everyone could see. "A special silvery coating on the lens filters out some of the more terrifying images, but they won't be much use in prolonged showers or torrential downpours. And you won't be using them today. You'll be facing this shower alone. Right, spread out so you're not standing too close to anyone else."

Angus glanced swiftly at Dougal, who had turned a shocking shade of white. Indigo looked determined to face the rain bravely. The rest of the lightning cubs moved reluctantly away from one another. Gudgeon waited until Pixie and Percival Vellum finally separated; then he pulled the stopper from the top of the storm jar, releasing the rancid rain.

A small cloud drifted upward, slowly expanding into the full height of the storm hollow. Angus felt his skin prickle almost instantly. An odd taste like salted peanuts filled his mouth, making his tongue stick to the back of his teeth. The cloud grew darker and darker until—

Flash!

Long chains of dazzling lightning streaked past him to the left. He swung around just in time to catch a momentary glimpse of a gnarled forest full of twisted, tortured-looking trees. Within seconds, everyone around him had disappeared behind a curtain of black rain. The sound was deafening. Disturbing images of violent, bone-chilling blizzards cascaded past him. There were vicious typhoons that flattened houses, trees, and everything that stood in their path like flimsy cardboard. Great fognadoes

whirled past him, each one tugging at his senses, caus-
ing an instant tide of panic to rise up inside him, just as
Gudgeon had warned.

He closed his eyes, trying to shake off the unsettling
nightmarish visions. If he could just make them stop for a
fraction of a second . . .

"What's the matter, Munchfungus, scared of the rain?"
His eyes shot open. Percival Vellum had somehow muscled
his way through the weather, wearing a pair of guardian
glasses that he'd clearly sneaked into the storm hollow. He
was also wearing the smuggest smile Angus had ever seen.

"Where's your fire dragon now, storm boy?" he jeered.
"Has the rancid rain drowned it?"

It happened in the blink of an eye. Angus felt a violent
jolt inside his chest that threatened to crack his ribs wide
open and then—

BANG!

The fire dragon leaped before his eyes, its wings unfolded
and stretched wide through the rancid rain. The creature
dived swiftly toward Percival Vellum, dragging the storm
with it, herding heavy black raindrops with each flap of
its great wings.

"W-what's happening?" Percival staggered backward in a sudden panic. "No! Munchfungus, you—you're doing this! I know you are! You freak! Make the rain stop!"

He turned and charged helter-skelter across the storm hollow, desperately trying to escape the rancid rain.

"Arghhhh!"

But large swaths of the storm were now following his every move.

"No!" Angus yelled, racing after the blazing tail of the dragon, feeling just as shocked as the fleeing twin.

For a fraction of a second he'd wanted to scare the pants off Percival Vellum, to make the vile twin think twice before taunting him again, to punish him for knowing everything most secret and personal about his life, and in that second the dragon had appeared. But it wasn't here this time to warn him of imminent danger. The creature had burst into the storm hollow with one purpose, to control the weather, to drive the rancid rain after Percival Vellum and bombard the twin with terrible images of hurricanes, tornadoes, and deadly wisps of poisonous fog, almost as if Angus had ordered it to do so. He had to make it stop! He raced through the dense rain and crashed into someone's shoulder, knocking him sideways.

"Stop! Please . . . stop!" he shouted hopelessly, chasing the flash of golden flames up ahead. But the dragon had now herded Percival into a dark corner. The storm hovered ominously over the snivelling twin's head as he pulled his legs and arms up into a tight ball.

"Make way! Stand back there!" Gudgeon came tearing across the storm hollow.

The fire dragon vanished in an instant. The painful throb in Angus's chest subsided. Lightning cubs all around emerged from the gloom soaked through and shivering as the storm fizzled and died.

Gudgeon crouched down beside Percival, who was now shaking uncontrollably. Angus kept his distance in case the fire dragon appeared again and inflicted even more damage.

"What's wrong with him?" Pixie ran to her brother's side.

"He's had a nasty shock to the system, nothing more. Doctor Fleagal will give him something to calm his nerves," Gudgeon said, helping Percival onto his feet again. "You lot had better get yourselves back to the Octagon, and remember, no talking about anything that's happened in this storm hollow!"

And he led Percival Vellum to the door without looking back.

9

SHIMMER SHARK SURPRISE

"**H**a! This is brilliant!" Dougal guffawed with laughter as Angus related the whole horrible incident to him and Indigo later that evening in the Pigsty. "It serves him right for bugging you about fire dragons and storm prophets. No wonder he was looking so sorry for himself!"

"But I turned the weather against him!" Angus said as Dougal continued to laugh, holding his sides. "Storm prophets are supposed to predict dangerous weather, not send their fire dragons chasing after people. What if— what if none of the other storm prophets ever did that?"

"They would have done if they'd known Percival Vellum," Dougal said with conviction.

"But what if I'm the only one?" Angus persisted. "What if this makes me just as bad as the monsoon mongrels?"

"Of course it doesn't!" Indigo said earnestly. "You didn't do it on purpose."

"Yeah," Dougal said, removing his glasses and wiping the tears from his eyes. "Dankhart and his monsoon mongrels do everything on purpose. I mean, Dankhart's seriously twisted when it comes to the weather, er, no offense," he added as an afterthought, turning toward Indigo.

Indigo rolled her eyes. "And it's not like you went into the storm hollow planning to scare Percival. It was an accident," she added.

Angus hoped Indigo was right. But how could he be sure? For the first time ever he'd made the fire dragon appear without anyone's being in a life-threatening situation. He'd used it to turn the rancid rain against Percival Vellum. Like a weapon. And there'd been nothing he could do to stop it from happening. He wasn't even sure *how* it had happened. What if he did the same thing again with something more dangerous next time, or he lost his temper with Dougal and accidentally set a thunderstorm loose on him?

"Do you think Vellum will tell anyone what really happened?" he asked.

Dougal shook his head. "Even if he did, he's got no chance of proving it; you're the only one who can see the fire dragon."

Percival Vellum appeared in the kitchens the next morning pale and subdued and avoiding all eye contact with Angus, Dougal, and Indigo. In the days that followed, Angus replayed the terrible events over and over inside his head like a ghastly movie that wouldn't end. Each time the tight knot in his chest throbbed painfully, threatening to crack his ribs wide open, just as it had done in the storm hollow, leaving him afterward with a dull, empty ache.

To make matters worse, they were now spending every evening in the Pigsty studying *The Dankhart Handbook.* The highly informative guide contained detailed descriptions of each of the deadly seven, with photographs and eyewitness accounts. Some, such as ice-diamond spores that floated through the air, freezing lungs, blood cells, and hearts, they'd already encountered. Others, including giant exploding hailstones, sounded so terrifyingly deadly that Dougal turned green and sat with his head between his knees for several minutes before they could continue reading. After that, he retreated to the far corner of the Pigsty, where he immersed himself in documents about weather explosions and the science of vortices.

Angus, however, sat glued to the guide each evening, poring over every detail of the Castle Dankhart floor plans, most of which had been drawn by Jeremius McFangus, he discovered, spotting the familiar name at the bottom of each page. He tried to imagine every inch of the grand hall, Dankhart's private rooms, and the monsoon mongrels' living quarters, which, according to the neatly drawn plans, were situated in the turrets. The lower reaches of the castle contained storerooms, experimentation chambers, and the dungeons. Night after night he stared at the drawings until his brain ached with the effort of picturing which dungeon his parents had been imprisoned in for the last year. Did Jeremius know? Had he completed the drawings during his mysterious adventures at Castle Dankhart?

A few mornings later they were met by the delicious smell of hot cinnamon toast coming from the kitchens and the thrilling news that the Lightning Catcher of the Year award winners would be arriving at Perilous in seven days.

"Catcher Sparks made an announcement a few minutes ago," Jonathon Hake informed them as they passed his table. "They'll be staying here at the Exploratorium, eating in the kitchens and everything. Sparks told us not to bug them for autographs and stuff, though," he added, frowning.

Fresh copies of the *Weathervane* had been placed next to the serving tables. Dougal grabbed one and raced over to their usual table, flicking to a special report in the center pages as he munched on a slice of cinnamon toast.

"There's a picture of all the winners together," he said, excitedly turning it around so Angus could see. "There's Catcher Smithwyck; we already know she came third."

Next to Catcher Smithwyck stood someone called Herman Hornbuckle, with crooked teeth, sideburns, and a long beard; and the first-place winners, Lettice and Leonard Galipot, clutched a lightning-shaped trophy.

Indigo joined them a moment later. Before she could speak, however, she caught sight of Germ, who had just entered the kitchens and was now helping himself to double bacon and eggs at the serving tables. Germ glanced in their direction and waved.

"Oh, no, not again!" Indigo jumped up out of her seat, a folded piece of paper fluttering out of her pocket as she darted off in the opposite direction.

"Hey, Indigo, wait! You've dropped something!" Angus called after her, but it was already too late. She dashed out of the kitchens without looking back.

"What's up with her?" Dougal asked, mystified.

"Germ's still bugging her about the rash on her hand," Angus explained. "He cornered her in the library yesterday at lunchtime and wouldn't let her go until she'd let him take a skin rubbing and some photos."

Instead of coming to sit at their table, however, Germ joined a group of his own friends. Angus scooped up the sheet of paper that Indigo had dropped and unfolded it.

"Hey, these are the missing pages from the *Weathervane*," he said, surprised. "It's got the last bit of that interview with Catcher Smithwyck." The rest of the pages were covered in garish ads for Cradget's crazy half-price sale, sticky sausage doughnuts at the Frog's Bottom Bakery, and a book signing at the Horrible Endings Bookshop by someone called Demelza Slype.

"I don't get it." Dougal scratched his head, peering over Angus's shoulder. "Why did she rip that out of the magazine? Hang on a minute; she's circled something." He pointed to a colorful promotion at the bottom of the page for Fawcett Family Tree Hunters:

"Tired of trying to fill the empty spaces on your family tree? Bamboozled by endless names on birth certificates, gravestones, and census records? Fawcett Family Tree Hunters can complete your family tree for you!"

Underneath the ad another small paragraph had been added in tiny letters:

"Fawcett's takes no responsibility for uncovering any of the following undesirable ancestors during our research: criminals, confidence tricksters, bossy ancient aunts, and swamp dwellers. Fee must be paid in full in advance. Terms and conditions apply."

"Why on earth would Indigo want to know more about her ancestors?" Dougal said, sounding mystified.

Angus frowned at the ad. "It doesn't make any sense. She spends most of her time pretending they don't exist."

"So how is ordering a Dankhart family tree going to make her feel any better? I mean, after everything she's said about them. Do you think we should tell Germ?" Dougal added.

Angus glanced across the kitchens. Indigo's brother was laughing and joking with Kelvin Strumble and Joshua Follifoot. She definitely wouldn't thank them for involving him in her private affairs.

"She'll go ballistic if we tell *anyone*," he said.

"Maybe we should talk to Indigo then?" Dougal suggested. "Get her to see some sense before she does something really brainless?"

But Indigo was notoriously private when it came to her family. It had taken her months to tell them Dankhart was her uncle in the first place. If they tackled her directly, she was likely to clam up and reveal nothing.

Angus folded the page from the *Weathervane* and stuffed it deep into his pocket, hoping that Indigo wasn't setting herself up for another big family disappointment.

Meanwhile, excitement levels over the winners' tour had reached fever pitch. Large, noisy groups of lightning cubs gathered in the living quarters each evening to discuss the latest rumor, started by Germ, that Catcher Smithwyck would be carrying out her demonstration in the Lightnarium in the middle of a thunderstorm. Several heated arguments on the subject followed. Things quickly got out of hand, however, when Theodore Twill's lightning moth ripped Nicholas Grubb's homework to shreds, then chased Clifford Fugg in circles around his own bedroom. Several minor scuffles and water fights instantly broke out before Catcher Mint intervened, sending everyone to bed in a huff.

"It's no use. I can't even concentrate on my puzzle competition," Dougal said, shoving it aside one evening as they sat in the Pigsty. "I just can't stop thinking about the winners' tour."

Dougal had now progressed to phase three of the competition, which involved something called a wiggly-word trail. It came on a long, narrow strip of paper the length of a swimming pool and brought Dougal out in a cold sweat every time it was mentioned.

The award winners finally arrived on a misty afternoon to a great round of applause along with much pointing and staring. Lightning catchers and cubs lined the entrance hall, all jostling for a better position as the winners swept past and headed straight up to Principal Dark-Angel's office.

"I can't see anything except Herman Hornbuckle's beard!" Dougal shouted, jumping up and down and trying to see past a tall sixth year with bushy hair. Angus attempted to push his way in between Catcher Mint and Catcher Wrascal for a better view, catching nothing but a glimpse of Catcher Smithwyck's sensible shoes.

The first of the demonstrations took place the following evening in one of the weather bubbles, which had been scrubbed clean and decorated with hundreds of extra lamps for the occasion. Darkness pressed in all around the ornate steel and glass structure. A faint twinkling of stars was already visible through the windows above, and a cool, clear night threatened the first frost of the season. Angus, Dougal, and Indigo squeezed into three empty seats near the back, next to Edmund Croxley and Juliana Jessop. Germ turned and waved at them from several rows in front. The best seats were already packed with the most senior lightning catchers, including Principal

Dark-Angel, Catcher Sparks, Rogwood, and Gudgeon. Even the strange owl-eyed Doctor Obsidian had made an appearance. It was the first time Angus had seen him since the storm prophet tests with the projectograms. He shrank back in his seat just in case the doctor caught sight of him and felt prompted to carry out a quick experiment on his brain.

"Look out." Indigo nudged him in the ribs a moment later as Pixie and Percival Vellum took the last two empty seats close by. Percival glanced over at Angus, with a distinctly wary look. He mumbled something to Pixie, and they both turned to face the front without a single snide remark.

"Is it my imagination," Dougal said quietly, "or do those two gargoyles look a bit . . . scared of you?"

Angus stared at the back of Percival Vellum's head. A familiar knot tightened in his chest as images of rancid rain and fire dragons flashed before his eyes once again. He was glad when the lights began to dim and Principal Dark-Angel stepped to the front of the weather bubble. She turned to face the audience as an expectant hush fell all around.

"Good evening to you all, and welcome to our first demonstration by the winners of the Lightning Catcher of the Year award."

There was a smattering of polite applause.

"We are very honored to have with us this evening a lightning catcher whose research into frost quakes has helped many of us on our expeditions into cold climates. She is here tonight to talk to you about Arctic shimmer sharks. So please welcome Catcher Edna Smithwyck."

"Shimmer sharks?" Angus raised his voice above the applause. "Didn't Jeremius mention those in the Rotundra once?"

Indigo nodded, and Dougal suddenly looked apprehensive. Catcher Smithwyck entered the weather bubble and stood behind a large table, her mousy-colored hair illuminated under the light fissures. There were several large lumpy-looking objects before her, covered with a cloth.

"For lightning catchers, the weather holds many hidden dangers." She began as soon as the clapping died down. She shuffled her notes nervously. "There are fog yetis, piranha mist fish, and fog mites, to name just a few. But many of you here tonight have yet to encounter shimmer sharks in your travels. First spotted by a party of lightning catchers in the Arctic, they were initially thought to be nothing more than an optical illusion caused by the severe polar winds and the unhappy intestinal consequences of eating an undercooked beef stew. It was ten years later, in 1929, when Bartholomew Basildon accidentally captured some of the minuscule creatures in a pair of socks he was drying outside on a tent pole, that he realized he'd discovered an entirely new species of weather pest. Bartholomew brought his socks back to Perilous, where the shimmer sharks were studied extensively and their characteristic teeth, fins, and sharklike shape were documented. It is much easier, however, to show what they look like with some large-scale models. So let's have a big round of applause for my shimmer shark volunteers!"

She turned to nod at someone who was hovering by the door at the back of the bubble. A moment later half a dozen figures filed into the room awkwardly; they were dressed in colorful shark-shaped foam suits. They stopped beside the table, trying not to make eye contact with anyone in the front row.

A roar went up around the weather bubble as the

audience slowly began to recognize the lightning cubs inside the fishy costumes.

"Hey, I don't believe it, that big one's Clifford Fugg!" Dougal laughed, pointing.

"Look at his face!" Indigo said.

Clifford Fugg stood with his head hung low, looking mortified. Next to him, Theodore Twill was squirming with embarrassment, his cheeks hotter than a boiled beet. Nicholas Grubb, Kelvin Strumble, and Joshua Follifoot, however, looked as if they were having the time of their lives. They beamed at the audience, waving.

"Catcher Mint must have volunteered them for shimmer shark duty after they had those water fights the other night," Angus said, grinning widely. The pointing and sniggering finally died away, and Catcher Smithwyck continued with her presentation.

"Now, if our volunteers would kindly give us a twirl, you can see clearly that shimmer shark teeth and fins are disproportionately large, compared to the size of their bodies, which explains why they have long been a hazard for lightning catchers. And if we observe the way a shoal moves through the Arctic winds . . ."

The volunteers began to weave their way between and around one another, elbows and fins clashing. Clifford Fugg barged into the other volunteers, knocking them over in a very surly fashion. Theodore Twill stood completely motionless, refusing to budge. But Nicholas Grubb, Kelvin Strumble, and Joshua Follifoot threw themselves into the demonstration with gusto, darting left and right, wiggling their fins vigorously at the audience, crashing into one another on purpose, and then rolling around the floor with uncontrollable hysterics.

"Yes, well, that's not strictly shimmer shark behavior, of course," Catcher Smithwyck said as they staggered to their feet again and scuttled off to one side, still grinning.

"Now to show you what real shimmer sharks look like in the wild . . ." She pulled a cloth off one of the lumpy objects on the table, revealing a large glass jar underneath. The contents glittered with a pearly iridescence, shifting direction slowly at first as if the sharks had been snoozing in the darkness under the cloth. "This batch was caught on an ice core expedition a few weeks ago." She continued as the entire audience leaned forward in their seats for a closer look. "Hidden in the depths of a blizzard, they sweep across the ice and snow on fierce Arctic winds, causing serious damage to weather equipment, clogging up storm vacuums, and ripping tents and clothing to shreds with their razor-sharp teeth." The shimmer sharks began flitting about with nervous flicks and darts. "One tiny shimmer shark would cause absolutely no damage, of course, but because they occur in such large numbers, they can sweep through a research site with devastating consequences. This is what happened to the ice core team as they tried to collect some samples."

She whipped the cloth off another of the lumpy objects and slotted a plate into the back of a projectogram box, then—

"Whoa!" Angus said, through the sudden hiss of astonished gasps and whispers. He stared at the three-dimensional scene, shocked. There was nothing left of the campsite. Tents, equipment, and snow boots had all been reduced to piles of dust by the plague of chewing pests.

"Unfortunately, shimmer shark attacks are on the increase." Catcher Smithwyck continued. "As lightning catchers explore some of the most remote places on the planet . . ."

Somebody sneezed directly behind Angus, breaking his concentration. He turned automatically to see who it was and froze. Several rows behind the sneezer, Catcher Coriolis, the keeper of the crypt, was locked in an intense private conversation with Creepy Crevice. Angus nudged Dougal gently and jerked his head in their direction. Indigo turned to see what they were both looking at.

"I wonder what those two are talking about," she said quietly.

"I dunno," Angus whispered, "but I'd bet my weather watch it's got nothing to do with shimmer sharks."

At that moment the keeper of the crypt shot to his feet.

"No, I'm sorry, but it's simply out of the question," he said in firm but hushed tones. "I absolutely refuse to share my tomb with anyone, even in the name of restoration. Principal Dark-Angel has already allocated you some very comfortable living quarters in another part of the Exploratorium, and I'm afraid you will have to be content with those!"

The conversation had come to an abrupt end. Catcher Coriolis swept down the stairs, his forehead creased with indignation. Angus twisted in his seat to face the front again, before Catcher Coriolis caught him staring. Dougal hastily pretended to clean his glasses on his sweater. Indigo hid her face behind a curtain of hair as he hurried past them and disappeared out of the weather bubble. Creepy Crevice followed a few moments later.

"What was that all about?" Angus whispered as soon as the coast was clear.

"Only a bone merchant would want to share somebody else's tomb," Dougal said, looking revolted by the very idea.

"I wonder what's wrong with the rooms he's been given," Indigo said.

Angus grinned. "Not enough bats at midnight? Or maybe he prefers sleeping in a coffin."

Indigo giggled quietly. Dougal shivered. "It wouldn't surprise me if he sprouted wings and did a few laps of the crypt while he was down there."

It took Angus several moments to remember that they were still sitting in the middle of a shimmer shark presentation. He turned his attention back to Catcher Smithwyck.

". . . to tackle the problem, therefore, I have designed a portable, breathable, transparent, pop-up net that can be

thrown over any area the lightning catchers are working in to preserve their campsite and any important research from a sudden shimmer shark attack."

Angus tried to concentrate. Catcher Smithwyck was about to demonstrate her invention and the very reason she'd been invited to Perilous with the other winning lightning catchers.

"Inspired by the emergency instant weather shelter, it can be deployed in under ten seconds, providing complete and instant protection."

She had already placed the device at the feet of the audience in the front-row seats. It looked like a neatly folded paddling pool, the kind that Uncle Max liked to dip his feet into on a hot summer's day at the Windmill.

"The net should be deployed only after a verbal warning has been issued. So, three, two, one, firing!" she shouted.

The net exploded with a blast like the weather cannon. One of the smallest volunteers yelped and staggered sideways, colliding with Clifford Fugg, who lurched across the table, accidentally smashing the jar of real shimmer sharks with his flailing fins. The jar crashed to the floor, instantly setting the tiny iridescent creatures free.

Dougal leaped out of his seat. "Oh, no! This is bad!"

Several foam-clad volunteers dived under the protective net, along with Catcher Smithwyck and half the front row of the audience. The shimmer sharks rose swiftly to the ceiling, pearly white against the night sky above, and then descended upon the table beneath, reducing it to dust in a matter of seconds.

Churrr-ruga-ruga-ruga-ruga!

The noise they made was dreadful, like a thousand tiny grinding chainsaws cutting through tree trunks.

"We've got to get out of here!" Indigo grabbed Dougal by the wrist and steered him clear of the stampede now heading for the exit. Angus followed as she climbed awkwardly over the scattered seats instead.

"Angus! Look out!" Indigo suddenly shrieked, and pointed. A small group of shimmer sharks had detached itself from the main body and was now speeding toward him like a glittering arrow.

Angus dived beneath the empty seats and tucked his body into a tight curl as the sharks struck.

Churrr-ruga-ruga-ruga-ruga!

The hungry sharks demolished his shelter in seconds,

like a plate of tantalizing fish food. Angus scrambled to his feet again. The door was still twenty feet away. The shimmer sharks would turn them to dust before they made it halfway. Indigo, however, had other ideas.

"Quickly, give me Norman!" She turned to Dougal, holding out her hand.

"But . . . what do you want him for?"

"Does this look like a good time to ask me questions?" she said, glancing up at the shimmer sharks, which were already gathering for another attack.

Dougal hesitated for a second, then grabbed the lightning moth from his pocket.

"Just don't break him, okay?"

But Indigo wasn't listening. She lobbed Norman high above their heads. The lightning moth took flight instantly, stretching its wings, zooming straight up to the glass ceiling. It hovered for a second, glinting in the moonlight, before plummeting toward the shimmer sharks at lightning speed in a daring death dive.

Smash!

Several shimmer sharks were instantly knocked unconscious and began to drift aimlessly across the weather bubble. The rest scattered far and wide, desperate to avoid another attack. Indigo caught the lightning moth as it did a victory roll overhead and handed it back to Dougal unharmed.

"Wow! Norman was brilliant! I mean, he saved us," Dougal said, cradling the moth with deep affection.

"Er, I think Indigo might have had something to do with it as well," Angus pointed out.

Indigo's cheeks burned with embarrassment, but there was no time to marvel at it now. The rest of the creatures were still rampaging around the weather bubble in a very destructive manner.

Indigo hurried them toward the exit. Angus ducked as another cloud of tiny shimmer sharks swooped overhead, causing a fresh wave of panic and screaming.

"Dewsnap, Midnight, McFangus! Quickly!" Catcher Sparks shouted, hurrying them through the door along with Georgina Fox and Nigel Ridgely, who were carrying a limp Millicent Nichols between them.

"That was the most dangerous lecture I've ever been to in my life!" Dougal said as they were rushed away from the weather bubble at top speed.

10
THE CRYPTIC STRANGER

An excited buzz filled the boys' end of the corridor the following morning. Clifford Fugg was keeping a very low profile after his star appearance as a shimmer shark, his bedroom door remaining firmly shut with no signs of life within. Several of the other volunteers, however, wore their costumes proudly and were instantly swamped by crowds of admiring lightning cubs.

"Catcher Smithwyck said we could keep the shark suits since this is the last stop on the winners' tour," Nicholas Grubb explained as Angus and Dougal bumped into him outside the bathrooms. He gave them a quick twirl, showing off his fins, which up close looked rather floppy. "We all got herded up to the sanatorium after the real shimmer sharks escaped," Nicholas said, grinning from ear to ear. "It was absolutely pandemonium. The weather bubble had to be sealed off. Catcher Smithwyck had to be rescued from her own shelter. Dark-Angel was yelling at anyone who tried to sneak back in for a look."

"Wow! I can't wait for the next demonstration. If that was only the third-place winner, imagine what's coming next," Dougal said, sounding keen, despite the fact it had taken two mugs of hot chocolate in front of a warm fire in the Pigsty to calm his nerves after the frightening incident.

Due to the excitement of the winners' tour, all talk of the weather vortex had slowly faded into the background. No new pictures had appeared in the *Weathervane* for some time. Angus was very relieved, therefore, when Dougal announced that he had news. For once all three of them were sitting in the library. Catcher Wrascal had suddenly remembered that as part of their training in the forecasting department, they were supposed to complete a difficult homework assignment on the proper procedure for pickling the contents of a storm jar. It was complicated, dull work involving a number of mathematical equations that Angus had no hope of solving.

"I found something in the research department last night," Dougal said, lowering his voice and checking the tables close by for eavesdroppers, "and I think it might be important."

"Go on," Angus said, swiftly closing his workbook so he could concentrate.

"They've got a whole section up there about memorable weather events and accidents, and quite a few of them have caused the same kind of vortex that's now hanging over Castle Dankhart. But the biggest one I found happened right here at Perilous in 1777."

"At Perilous?" Indigo looked up from behind a pile of books, shocked.

"I know. I couldn't believe it either," Dougal said. "But according to this one paper, it sat over Perilous for three weeks before it finally blew itself out. It was full of rain, snow, fog, and lightning, but it also contained splinters of wood, snails, and all kinds of other rubbish. It sounds exactly like the stuff swirling around Castle Dankhart."

"But what caused the explosion?" Angus asked.

"Was it an accident?" Indigo added.

Dougal shrugged. "It didn't say, and I got chucked out of the research department before I could find anything else that mentioned it. But it must have been something major. I'm going straight back after dinner tonight to find some answers. I'll look up everything that happened at Perilous in 1777 if I have to."

"What do you three know about 1777?"

Indigo jumped as a large shadow suddenly fell across the table. Gudgeon was towering over them, his arms folded across his chest.

"Er, nothing," Angus said, quickly trying to cover their tracks. "D-Dougal was just doing some reading . . . about weather vortices."

"It's part of our homework for Catcher Wrascal in the weather archive," Indigo added, indicating the books on the table in front of them with a nervous twitch.

"Hmm." Gudgeon studied all three of them shrewdly, looking unconvinced.

"Is there any news on the weather vortex over Castle Dankhart?" Angus asked before the lightning catcher could ask them any more questions.

"Principal Dark-Angel's sent me to give you an update," Gudgeon said, still eyeing them suspiciously. There were dark smudges under his eyes; the rest of his face was pale and drawn; even his bald head somehow looked more tired than usual. "The weather station has been forced to retreat to a safer distance to avoid being sucked into the swirl and torn to pieces, so we've stopped taking samples for the time being. The only thing we know for sure is that in the last few days the cloud has grown bigger."

"B-bigger?" Angus exchanged worried glances with Dougal and Indigo.

"We've also detected two new types of weather we've never seen before, razor rain and tumblewind, both as nasty and vicious as any of the deadly seven," Gudgeon said. "I'd still bet my best pair of self-cleaning socks there's been no real weather catastrophe. But Dankhart and his blasted monsoon mongrels are up to something, and until we find out what, you three had better watch it!" He glared at each of them in turn. "Don't go poking your noses into stuff that doesn't concern you. This is lightning catcher business, understand?"

Dougal nodded vigorously. Gudgeon hesitated for a

second, looking as if he might say more; then he turned and marched away, shaking his head.

"That settles it; there's definitely something funny going on!" Angus said quietly as soon as Gudgeon was safely out of earshot. "Did you see Gudgeon's face when he heard us talking about 1777?"

"We've got to find what caused that explosion," Indigo said eagerly.

"Yeah, because whatever it was, I bet it's got something to do with what's happening at Castle Dankhart now. I mean, why else would Gudgeon get all angry about it?"

Dougal nodded. "I'll go straight up to the research department after dinner tonight, and with any luck we'll have some real answers by the end of the day!"

Angus found it extremely difficult to concentrate on anything else for the rest of the afternoon. After dinner he paced up and down the Pigsty, checking the clock every few minutes, waiting eagerly for Dougal's return. When Dougal finally appeared, however, he brought bad news.

"Gudgeon must have gone straight up to the research department after he overheard us in the library," he said, chucking his bag onto the floor and slumping into the chair beside Indigo. "All the books about weather accidents and vortices have been removed."

"You're joking!" Angus said, stunned. "But what about the *Weathervane*? Doesn't it report on everything?"

"All the copies from 1777 have disappeared as well. There was nothing left on the shelf except a pile of old mouse droppings."

Angus stared at him, flabbergasted.

"So what do we do now?" asked Indigo.

"I don't know, but thanks to Gudgeon, we've got more chance of discovering what's at the end of a rainbow than of finding out what happened in 1777."

At the end of the week an announcement that the second winners' demonstration would take place in the cloud gardens appeared in the latest issue of the *Weathervane*, along with a brief biography of Herman Hornbuckle. And a sense of excitement began to build once again.

"It says here Catcher Hornbuckle trained at Perilous years ago and he's an expert in fog," Angus said. He, Dougal, and Indigo were sitting in the Pigsty after another long day in the weather archive. Angus turned the magazine around, showing Dougal a picture of a middle-aged lightning catcher with impressive sideburns, crooked teeth, and a long beard, whom they'd already spotted in the kitchens on a number of occasions.

"According to the *Weathervane,* he spends most of his free time reading books on droplet densities, vapor sickness, and fog disorientation."

"Brilliant!" Dougal grinned. "He's an even bigger nerd than me! Does it say what he's doing in his demonstration?"

"Um." Angus scanned the rest of the article. "No."

Indigo looked up from behind her copy of *The Dankhart Handbook.* "I heard a first year telling his friends this morning that Catcher Hornbuckle's going to make everyone rappel over the edge of the Exploratorium, so we can all study a top-secret killer rain cloud, from the inside."

Dougal's face fell. "You don't think it's true, do you?"

Angus continued to flick through the *Weathervane,* which was now running a series of features on recent developments in storm vacuums, until a more interesting article caught his eye.

"Hey, there's something in here about Edwin Larkspur, you know, the archaeologist who uncovered the lightning tower remains."

He turned the magazine around again so Dougal and Indigo could read the article:

ARCHAEOLOGIST MAKES FULL RECOVERY

Mr. Edwin Larkspur, thirty-five, from Clapham Common, London, appeared in a number of newspapers yesterday claiming to have regained his memory after the traumatic robbery at the Museum of Ancient Archaeology. He has now given the police a full description of the thief who broke into his office and stole valuable lightning tower remains, several rare Victorian toilet seats, a pair of ancient Roman nosehair clippers, and a special presentation set of gilded archaeology brushes, which were presented to Mr. Larkspur at a Ruin of the Year awards ceremony. Police have issued an artist's impression of the thief.

Angus stared at the picture underneath and almost choked. The man in the drawing was wearing a smartly tailored suit; his short, wavy curls had been styled to perfection.

"Er, is it my imagination or does that artist's impression look nothing like Adrik Swarfe?" Dougal said, squinting at it through his glasses.

Angus grinned. "That's because it's Catcher Tempest from the London office."

"You're joking!"

"Didn't Catcher Tempest visit Mr. Larkspur at the museum after the theft?" Indigo said.

"Yep." Angus nodded. "And it looks like Larkspur's still got some of his wires crossed if he thinks Catcher Tempest stole the lightning tower remains."

Angus was so wrapped up in thoughts of the weather vortex and the next demonstration that he was extremely surprised when a note from Rogwood appeared under his bedroom door, announcing his next early-morning storm prophet lesson. Less than twenty-four hours later he was back in the Inner Sanctum.

"I must apologize, Angus, for the long delay since our last adventure," Rogwood said as he led the way from one Octagon to its mirror image inside the mysterious department. "The winners' tour has made it extremely difficult to organize a quiet time for your lessons."

"Oh, um," Angus said, not sure if Rogwood was expecting a longer, more intelligent answer. With so many other distractions it had been hard to think about retrospectacles and storm prophet tombs. The throbbing sensation that he'd felt in his chest after the storm hollow had also faded, and he'd been keen not to think or do anything that might set it off again.

"Has there been any more news about the weather vortex, sir?" Angus asked, seizing the opportunity.

"I'm afraid not. We still don't know what's going on underneath the cloud. There has been no word about your parents either."

"But my uncle Jeremius . . ." Angus said hopefully.

"I cannot discuss what Jeremius is doing. I'm sure you understand, Angus, that it wouldn't be wise."

Rogwood ushered him straight into the dark room they'd already visited, with the trapdoor that led down to the crypt. Angus wondered if they were about to pay another visit to the storm prophet coffins. This time, however, Rogwood led him to the far side of the room and through another door, concealed in the shadows.

The room behind it was small, round, and exceedingly cozy. Bookshelves ran from floor to ceiling, with rickety-looking ladders reaching up to the highest tomes. Several comfy armchairs with footstools had been arranged around a crackling fire. Pens, pencils, and paper had been laid out neatly on a table.

Rogwood lowered himself into one of the armchairs. "Please take a seat, Angus."

Angus sat, feeling his tense muscles relaxing slightly. It was not the kind of room where old machines suddenly went berserk.

"Now that you have seen the Great Fire of London through the retrospectacles and have visited the Perilous crypt, it is time to learn more about each of the storm prophets and their extraordinary lives," Rogwood said, folding his hands together. "I will try to answer all your questions honestly and tell you the facts as they are known. All the information we have, however, is historical, and some of the accounts tend to glorify events, as was the fashion at the time, and must be taken with a pinch of salt," he warned. "There is no one left to ask directly, of course, for which I am truly sorry, Angus. It is a great shame that you have no one to share your thoughts and experiences with at this important time in your life."

Angus swallowed, finding it easier to stare at the braids in Rogwood's beard than to meet the searching gaze of the lightning catcher directly.

"To make things a little easier to understand, I will use a series of projectograms." Rogwood bent forward and reached under his chair. He took out a small box with two lenses on the front. "These are mere re-creations of the people and events that I am about to describe and nothing more."

He placed the projectogram box on the footstool in front of him and slid a small plate into the back.

"As you already know, Angus, it is believed that the talents of the storm prophets date back to the days when lightning towers pierced the skies of London, when the operators of those mighty towers were infused with the very forces they were trying to capture and control. Their abilities were only truly explored once Edgar Perilous and Philip Starling came to Imbur and founded this great Exploratorium."

Rogwood twiddled with the lenses on the box. *Click.*

Angus gasped as a three-dimensional projectogram suddenly filled the entire room. The books and ladders faded into the background, and he found himself sitting instead before a long line of fidgeting figures, leaning awkwardly against a rough stone wall.

"There were ten original storm prophets. Their names were Benedict Swarfe, whom you already know something about." Rogwood pointed to a tall, lanky figure on the far left who was dressed in an old-fashioned leather jerkin with woolen leggings. Swarfe scratched his nose and blinked, staring directly at Angus. "He was killed by the Great Fire in London before his talents could be explored, of course, his blood fusing with the lightning tower to form the very powerful lightning heart. I think it is fair to assume, therefore, that he would have gone on to perform a number of interesting deeds had his short life continued. What you are seeing here is a mere image of the boy as he might have been, if he'd had the good fortune to join the other storm prophets at Perilous. Please feel free to wander among your fellow storm prophets, Angus, should the urge arise."

Angus hesitated for a second, then stood up awkwardly. The projectogram was incredibly lifelike. Each of the storm prophets looked as real and solid as any living lightning catcher at the Exploratorium. Some turned to watch him with interest as he made his way down the line.

Benedict Swarfe had the same intelligent features as the only other Swarfe he'd ever met. Angus poked the projected image, just to make sure it wasn't real. It wobbled gently, like the ripples on a pond.

"Next we have Gideon Stumps and Jasper Flinch," Rogwood said as Angus continued down the line to where two young-looking storm prophets stood with their arms folded. "Both went on to become experts in cold-climate dangers and made many important discoveries about blizzards and ice storms. Ah, now we come to the Bodfish brothers, Zebedee, Zachary, and Zephyrus."

The Bodfish brothers were three inches taller than anyone else around them, with striking features and long black hair; they were shoving one another playfully and generally larking about. Angus couldn't help smiling as he stood among the charismatic brothers. He had a strong feeling he would have liked all three of them a great deal.

"The Bodfish brothers used their unique connection as siblings to great effect and developed a storm prophet sixth sense that allowed them to work as a formidable team. They used it once to rescue a party of new lightning cubs who got separated and lost on the Imbur marshes in a thick fog.

"Then we have Moray McFangus, whom you have inherited your own storm prophet skills from."

Angus felt his heart leap. The family resemblance was striking. Moray was unmistakably a McFangus, with the same gray eyes and small bear-shaped ears that he, his dad, and Uncle Jeremius all shared. Moray McFangus also had a strong, proud face, masses of brown hair, and a twinkle in his eye. Close up, he smelled like candle wax. He watched Angus intently, scratching the stubble on his chin, as they stood face-to-face.

"Is—is that what he really looked like, sir?" Angus asked.

Rogwood nodded. "As far as we can tell, according to eyewitness accounts, letters, diaries, and portraits painted at the time."

Angus walked all the way around his ancestor, trying to take in every detail.

"Who are the others at the end, sir?" he asked when he finally managed to tear his gaze away from Moray McFangus. The last three storm prophets stood with their backs turned to the rest of the group, talking quietly among themselves.

"Their names are Nathaniel Fitch, Tobias Twinge, and Nicholas Blacktin." Angus kept his distance, feeling no desire to approach them for a closer look. Tobias Twinge was breathing loudly through his mouth, as if he had a head cold. "I would prefer to deal with those particular storm prophets at another time, Angus. I do not wish to confuse you with too many names at once," Rogwood said, looking slightly uncomfortable.

Before he could ask any more, Rogwood had removed the projectogram and slipped another one in the back of the box.

Click.

Angus was now surrounded by a group of six children, roughly the same age as he was, with two standing separately from the rest.

"Eventually the ten original storm prophets each married and had children of their own, and a second generation was born. Only six of those children showed any storm-spotting skills, but of a much watered-down variety. There were no storm prophets in the generation that followed theirs. And nobody knows why exactly, although I would guess that it has something to do with the fact that after the Great Fire nobody at Perilous was allowed to capture lightning bolts from live thunderstorms. It is possible that these talents resurfaced in you, Angus, when you were presented with a potentially life-threatening situation in the Lightnarium."

"So there were only sixteen storm prophets in total, sir," Angus said, doing a quick mental calculation.

"Seventeen, including you, but only the ten originals had true storm prophet capabilities, until now."

Rogwood bent forward and slid another plate into the back of the box.

Click.

Angus had now been transported to a wild and windy moorland devoid of all trees and shrubs, with just a few rocky outcrops to shelter behind. Violent lightning storms were closing in from every direction, filling the air with the crackle of electricity. Angus felt the hairs on the back of his neck rise in warning, his instincts suddenly taking over. His heart leaped again as Moray McFangus and several people he didn't recognize appeared beside him.

"Moray McFangus came to Imbur after the Great Fire." Rogwood continued speaking from his armchair, which looked bizarre sitting among the barren tufts of moorland. "He was very young at the time, just seventeen years old, and it took some time for his skills to develop fully. He was particularly adept at predicting lightning strikes and was one of the most talented storm prophets. He headed several important expeditions to regions of the world famed for their extreme electrical storms, making many vital and dramatic discoveries about this dangerous force of nature that were essential after the disastrous events in London."

Angus flinched as several very real-looking bolts of lightning flashed around him. The weather was growing more frightening by the second. The knot in his chest tightened.

"It was during one such expedition, re-created here, that he saved many of his fellow lightning catchers from a very close encounter with a storm cluster filled with lightning tarantulatis."

CRASH!

Angus spun around. Another storm was approaching from behind, trapping him and the lightning catchers in a pincers movement that left very little hope of escape.

"Quickly! Everyone, take shelter!" The firm, clear voice of Moray McFangus sent the rest of the lightning catchers scurrying for cover under an overhanging crag. Angus felt himself being pushed and shunted toward it. He tripped and fell, staggering to his feet again only just in time as the storm finally broke overhead.

CRASH!

The lightning tarantulatis spun a dazzling web of light above their heads; it jumped aggressively from storm to storm, gathering power, striking the ground with deadly force.

BANG!

There was a sudden flash of flame. Angus toppled over backward as a fire dragon burst onto the scene with a magnificent roar. It soared above Moray McFangus, who stood alone before the gathering storm. Molten fire dripped from the creature's outstretched wings, cutting a fiery swath through every cloud.

For one exhilarating moment, Angus could almost feel the full force of the storm surge through every molecule of his own body. The flames of the fire dragon intensified; it twisted high above Moray McFangus, tangling itself through wisps and curls of tempest, forcing each of the storms to collide, to fight for space in the skies above; then—

BOOOOM!

Angus dived for cover as a huge explosion extinguished every lightning bolt, blasting every storm to smithereens. The fire dragon had destroyed every storm, leaving nothing behind but a few harmless puffs of gray cloud.

Thrilled by the exciting new development, Angus stared at the powerful creature. If Moray McFangus could use his fire dragon to *control* the weather then maybe he, Angus, wasn't quite such a freak after all? Maybe the events in the storm hollow weren't nearly as dreadful as he'd first feared? And one day, when he'd learned to perfect his own skills, he might even turn out to be a storm prophet hero, just like Moray McFangus? The projecto-gram faded suddenly. He was standing once again in the peaceful room among the bookshelves and comfy chairs. All signs of the moorland had gone, but fresh, tantalizing images now formed in his mind.

He could suddenly see himself older, taller, surrounded by vicious storms and fog yetis out on the barren Imbur marshes, defeating the weather, guiding Indigo, Dougal, Jeremius, and Gudgeon to safety. He could almost hear the grand tales that would be told of his glorious and heroic achievements for hundreds of years to come. He imagined another nervous lightning cub sitting in the same chair that he had occupied being told of the time that a famous storm prophet, called Angus McFangus, saved Indigo Midnight from some lethal lightning in the Lightnarium.

"But, sir, why didn't you tell me fire dragons could help predict the weather *and* control it?" he asked, finally lowering himself into his chair, his heart still beating far too quickly. "I mean, Moray McFangus and his fire dragon totally destroyed those lightning storms!"

"I was a little concerned that the idea would seem too strange and unsettling when you were still struggling to accept your incredible gift," Rogwood said, watching him closely. "It is a skill that must be treated with great seriousness if it is to be controlled properly. The early storm prophets formed a unique bond, Angus." Rogwood continued. "They became great friends over time and worked together for the good of the Exploratorium and all of humankind. Not only by predicting when catastrophic weather was about to strike but, as you have just seen, by guiding and controlling the very elemental forces of nature. You belong to a very rare breed of lightning catcher, Angus. You should be extremely proud of your heritage. It is a great gift, and there are many who would kill to have it."

Angus swallowed hard. It was a chilling thought. Adrik Swarfe had already threatened to drain his blood in order to restore the lightning heart and his own storm prophet powers. He was also positive that Dankhart wouldn't hesitate to kill him if Angus ever stood in the way of his ambitions.

Before Rogwood could say anymore, however, they were interrupted by a knock at the door.

"Aramanthus." A lightning catcher stuck her head inside the room. "I have a message from Felix Gudgeon."

"Ah. Perhaps that is enough for one day," Rogwood said, rising from his chair with a smile. "I will meet you in the Octagon in a few moments, Angus. Please feel free to watch any of the projectograms again." Rogwood followed the other lightning catcher through the door and closed it behind him.

Angus quickly played the projectogram of Moray McFangus and the lightning storm over again, still feeling utterly flabbergasted. But a new thought quickly began to nibble at the edge of his euphoria, the glorious feelings he'd been basking in starting to fade. Rogwood hadn't mentioned anything about storm prophets turning the weather against their fellow lightning cubs. There had been no projectograms showing Moray McFangus sending showers of rancid rain chasing across the storm hollow. What if he, Angus, was one of the lesser, weaker storm prophets, who couldn't control his powers? What if he was dangerous? Would there be stories one day of the great catastrophes he'd caused, of the lightning cubs he'd injured?

He stood up quickly and slipped the plate out from the back of the box, and the projectogram faded. He turned off the light fissures and opened the door, suddenly eager to leave the Inner Sanctum, but—

He stopped dead in his tracks. Hairs prickled on the back of his neck. His eyes caught a flicker of movement in the dense shadows.

"H-hello?" Angus said quietly, letting his eyes grow used to the dark.

Nobody answered. The trapdoor in the center of the room, the one that led down to the crypt, was standing wide open. Had the keeper of the crypt called Rogwood down for some sort of coffin emergency? He walked quietly over to the opening and peered down the stone steps.

A dim light flickered below. Angus watched it for several seconds and then followed. He held his breath as the first few spooky tombs came into view. A faint glow came from the crypt keeper's tomb in the distance. There was no sign of any other light unless— He stepped into the darkness and inched his way into the thick shadow, keeping his fingers crossed that the Perilous crypt was free from all ghosts, ghouls, and flesh-eating zombies. He dodged carefully between the tombs, following the long avenue of mausoleums until he saw it. A small light glimmered up ahead. There was a sudden blur of movement. Somebody had stopped beside the storm prophet coffins.

Angus bobbed down into the pitch-black shadows of a shed-size tomb and watched. He was almost certain the person carrying the light wasn't Catcher Coriolis or Rogwood, and yet there was something oddly familiar about the figure now leaning over the coffins. Angus crept closer, crouching low as he shuffled silently past the simple unmarked tomb that he'd noticed the last time he'd visited the crypt. If he could just get a better look, if he could just see the person's face . . .

"Hey! You there!" Catcher Coriolis emerged from his tomb. He hurried toward the stranger as fast as his bathrobe and slippers would allow.

The flickering light was extinguished immediately, and Angus was plunged into sudden darkness. Footsteps hurried across the floor, scuffling in the stranger's haste to escape.

"Ooof!"

Somebody barged past him, knocking his shoulder painfully into hard stone. The hem of a heavy coat brushed his knee; Angus caught a brief glimpse of three triangular buttons on a sleeve in the faint light now coming from Catcher Coriolis's tomb. He had seen the same coat once before, in the bone merchant's.

"Caught red-handed!" The keeper of the crypt grabbed Angus by the elbow and dragged him back onto his feet. "What were you doing to my storm prophet coffins?"

"N-nothing, sir!" Angus protested. He glanced over his

shoulder, desperately trying to catch one last glimpse of the stranger, but Catcher Coriolis was already dragging him over to the carved wooden fire dragons.

"I saw a light from the top of the stairs." Angus tried to explain as the lightning catcher lit another lamp and inspected every inch of the tombs for signs of damage. "I only came down to see who it was."

"A likely story! I warned Delphinia it was a mistake to let lightning cubs into the crypt, and here you are, skulking about the tombs without permission."

"But there was someone else down here!" Angus protested. "He ran away when he heard you."

But the keeper of the crypt wasn't listening. "I'm taking you straight up to Principal Dark-Angel, and we will see if she believes your ridiculous story. And I will be recommending that she expel you immediately!"

11

THE SECOND DEMONSTRATION

"I'm extremely disappointed in your behavior, McFangus." Principal Dark-Angel glared at him from behind her desk.

The keeper of the crypt had marched him up straight to her office, after he'd returned to his own tomb to get dressed. Rogwood, Gudgeon, and Valentine Vellum had appeared just moments later, and the shouting had begun. For once Dark-Angel was on Angus's side, refusing to believe that he had sneaked into the crypt with the intention of damaging any storm prophet tombs. After a short and rather heated conversation, therefore, Catcher Coriolis had stormed out of her office in a huff. But for some strange reason Principal Dark-Angel had continued to yell, and now she was yelling at Angus.

"You have been told repeatedly not to go wandering off by yourself while in the Inner Sanctum," she said, an angry vein throbbing in her neck. "I have placed you in a position of great trust. You cannot simply poke your nose into every dark corner and investigate things that do not concern you."

"I'm afraid this is my fault, Delphinia." Rogwood stepped forward, placing a hand on Angus's shoulder before he could speak. "I was called away from our lesson. I left Angus alone, and he is not the kind of lightning cub to ignore odd noises and shadowy figures."

Dark-Angel frowned. "Nevertheless, that is no excuse for such reckless behavior. I must have your solemn promise, Angus, that you will do exactly as you are told in the future, even if you discover a troop of wild fog yetis stampeding through the Inner Sanctum."

"Yes, Principal," Angus muttered.

"Now, this person that you *claim* to have seen in the crypt." The principal leaned back in her chair, her fingers locked tightly together in a thoughtful pose. "Can you give us a description?"

Angus thought hard, trying to remember any details, but in the darkness of the crypt he had seen nothing new. "All I saw was someone in a long dark coat, miss, with three triangular buttons on his sleeves," he said. "But the same person was in the bone merchant's in Little Frog's Bottom a few weeks ago, talking to Creepy—er, I mean, Mr. Crevice."

"Was he, indeed?" Dark-Angel said, her eyebrows raised in surprise. "And you are certain it was the same person?"

Angus nodded.

"But you saw nothing of the person's face? You did not hear them speak?"

Angus shook his head.

"Well, I will be having serious words with Mr. Crevice about the company he keeps and his activities in the crypt."

Gudgeon nodded. "That weasel's got his fingers in more rotten pies than anyone else on this island. He's up to no good, you mark my words."

"Is it possible that Mr. Crevice has heard the tantalizing

rumors that fire dragon scales can boost brainpower, cure dim-wittedness, scurvy, bunions, and pimples?" Rogwood asked.

Gudgeon grunted. "It wouldn't be the first time he'd tried to flog some ridiculous cure in that flea-bitten shop of his. He once tried to sell me a shark's tooth amulet that was supposed to give me great wisdom and knowledge."

"I'm no expert, Felix, but perhaps you should have tried it," Valentine Vellum said, sneering.

Gudgeon glared at him. Angus glanced at Valentine Vellum as he continued to smirk. He was clutching what looked like a battered old copy of the *Weathervane*. A large headline on the front cover declared it contained an "Annual Review of 1777!" Angus felt his insides suddenly squirm.

"What we must decide is how to deal with Mr. Crevice," Dark-Angel said with a sigh. "Unfortunately, there is no one else on this island who can repair our damaged tombs, and if we allow them to deteriorate any further . . ."

"Perhaps if a lightning catcher accompanies Mr. Crevice into the crypt to keep an eye on his work in the future," Rogwood said as Angus slowly inched his way toward Valentine Vellum, trying to get a better look at the *Weathervane*. "I will also warn Catcher Coriolis that he may need to tighten security."

Dark-Angel nodded. "Those storm prophet tombs are extremely valuable. I will not have them damaged by a thieving bone merchant."

"Sorry to interrupt, Principal." All heads turned toward the open door, where Mrs. Stobbs stood holding a tray of tea and hot buttered crumpets. "Catcher Sparks asked me to tell you the latest report on the weather vortex has just been delivered from the weather station. And I thought you might like a hot pot of tea."

"Thank you, Mrs. Stobbs." Dark-Angel smiled weakly as the housekeeper placed the tray on her desk. "That will be all for now, McFangus," she added, turning to Angus. "Rogwood will inform you when your next lesson will take place. And remember, not a word of this to anyone."

Angus raced down to the kitchen as soon as he left Dark-Angel's office to find Dougal and Indigo already halfway through breakfast. He was now ravenously hungry after everything that had happened in the Inner Sanctum, and he wolfed down a bowl of porridge and two blueberry pancakes before describing the surprising events of the morning.

"You're kidding!" Dougal spluttered.

"And you're sure the person in the crypt was the same one you saw leaving the bone merchant's?" Indigo asked, buttering a thick slice of toast.

Angus nodded. "Positive."

"I bet it's Valentine Vellum!" Dougal whispered, leaning across the table. "Maybe he and Creepy Crevice have been plotting to break into the crypt together using Vellum's keys! You've already seen him taking Crevice down into the crypt."

"Yeah, and then Vellum could have hidden under that coat," Angus said, warming to the idea. "It could have been him in the bone merchant's that day in Little Frog's Bottom, too."

"Either that or Vellum's got an evil twin." Dougal grinned. "We already know they run in the Vellum family. Look at Pixie and Percival."

"Valentine and Valerina Vellum?" Angus suggested, picturing Vellum's fictitious twin sister, complete with a low, thuggish brow and a beard.

Indigo snorted with giggles, but she was already shaking her head. "It just doesn't make any sense. Why would Vellum help Crevice steal some fire dragon scales?"

"Obvious, isn't it?" Dougal said. "He's planning to give some to Pixie and Percival. I mean, if those scales can actually cure dim-wittedness . . ."

"Maybe that's the real reason Crevice was trying to persuade Catcher Coriolis to share his tomb with him at the shimmer shark demonstration," Indigo said thoughtfully. "So he could sneak into the crypt anytime he wanted."

"There's something else," Angus told them quickly. "Vellum was carrying a copy of the *Weathervane* . . . from 1777."

Dougal sat bolt upright in his chair. "But didn't Gudgeon remove all of those from the research department? I mean, if he didn't, somebody else did."

"Yeah, well, it looks like Vellum got his hands on them somehow."

"But why would Vellum want them?" Indigo asked, puzzled.

"I'd bet my scare-me-not puzzle it's got something to do with that weather vortex over Perilous," Angus said quietly. "First Gudgeon goes all funny when he hears us mentioning 1777, and now Valentine Vellum's looking at a *Weathervane* from the same year. It's got to be more than coincidence!"

"Angus is right," Dougal said with a familiar look of determination on his face. "That Perilous vortex must be important. And for some reason Rogwood, Gudgeon, and Dark-Angel don't want us knowing anything about it."

"Then there's only one place we're going to find any answers," Angus said, checking over his shoulder for eavesdroppers. "Valentine Vellum's office."

Angus now had so many worrying things to think about that his head was in a permanent state of fogginess. At night his dreams were filled with dramatic scenes from the projectograms, with visions of Moray McFangus and his fire dragon. He woke each morning with the uncomfortable feeling that he would never match up to their epic deeds.

The problem of how to sneak into Valentine Vellum's office without being caught was also far trickier than he'd first thought. For a start, none of them had the faintest idea where the office actually was, and they quickly resorted to following the lightning catcher around Perilous in the hope that he might lead them to it himself.

"McFangus, explain why you and your friends have decided to trail me around this Exploratorium like a pack of lost dogs!" he demanded when Angus accidentally crashed into him outside the library for the third time in one week.

"Oh, er," Angus said, trying to convey that the whole thing had somehow been a coincidence.

"If I find you, Dewsnap, and Midnight are planning some elaborate prank, or if I catch any of you skulking within ten feet of me again, I will see to it that Catcher Sparks buries you under a mountain of snot-repelling handkerchiefs!" And he stomped off, checking over his shoulder once.

Angus turned and marched in the opposite direction, wondering how they were going to find Vellum's office now.

Meanwhile, Germ had finally taken his first exam and was now frantically studying for the next.

"It's scabs, pus, and sores next, my favorite subject!" he told them, cheerfully dragging several large books out of his bag one lunchtime. "Who wants to test me on oozing and seepage?"

Indigo was still avoiding her brother and his relentless questions about the rash on her hand. Dougal was frantically trying to finish the third phase of his puzzle competition as the closing date for all entries was now only days away. He spent most evenings in the Pigsty hunched in one of the armchairs, shushing anyone who interrupted him.

Excitement about the second winners' demonstration was steadily building, with an eager buzz now filling the kitchens at every mealtime. Nicholas Grubb and his friends had begun wearing false beards exactly like Catcher Hornbuckle's, and had somehow got their picture in the *Weathervane*. Indigo, however, showed remarkably little interest in this hilarious story. She was now spending unhealthy amounts of her free time staring at the picture of her uncle Scabious in *The Dankhart Handbook*, her sweater sleeve pulled down over the rash on her hand. She had also borrowed half a dozen books on the Dankhart family from the library. Angus, who had been trying to follow Valentine Vellum through the lightning reference section at the time, had by chance seen Indigo hiding them in her bag.

"There's a whole section on the Dankhart family in the library," Dougal confirmed when Angus told him later that same day in the Pigsty. Indigo had gone to bed early, so each of them had bagged one of the comfy armchairs by the fire. "Anyone can borrow the books."

"But why is Indigo so keen to read up about the Dankharts all of a sudden?" Angus said. "You don't think it's got something to do with that ad she dropped from the *Weathervane*, do you?" He removed the page from his pocket and unfolded it for another look.

"Fawcett Family Tree Hunters?" Dougal frowned. "I dunno. But she must be taking this family tree stuff really seriously."

The day of the second demonstration brought a fresh crop of false beards, with Juliana Jessop wearing a particularly fine example that fell well below her sweater. Sounds of last-minute preparations filled the entrance hall. But it wasn't until late that afternoon that—dressed in hats, scarves, and coats—they were finally allowed down to the chilly cloud gardens, where the demonstration was to take

place. Set hundreds of feet below the main Exploratorium, the gardens were cut deep into the rock with tall grass, ferns, and long trails of ivy tumbling over a wide lip like another fine beard.

"Wow!" Angus gasped as they reached the bottom of the stone steps.

The cloud gardens had been specially decorated for the occasion with hundreds of glowing lamps and candles, which had attracted a large number of twilight bugs and early winter moths. Rows of chairs had been placed around a podium in the center. The views across the island were spectacular as the sun slowly began to set.

"McFangus, Dewsnap, Midnight! Hurry up and sit down," Catcher Sparks said. She pointed toward three empty seats in the row behind Germ and a group of his friends, who were all sporting long, curly beards. "And, Midnight, for goodness' sake, tell your brother to remove that ridiculous facial hair he's wearing before I remove it for him."

Indigo's face shone with embarrassment as she shuffled into a seat behind Germ and whispered furiously in his ear.

Angus walked quickly past Pixie and Percival Vellum, who had somehow managed to snag seats in the front row next to their dad.

"What are you looking at, freak?" Percival mumbled, glaring at him.

"Charming," Dougal whispered. "The whole Vellum family's about as friendly as a box of scorpions."

A few minutes later, after a short introduction by Principal Dark-Angel, Catcher Hornbuckle took to the podium with a thunderous round of applause. Several twilight bugs buzzed around his head.

"In 1739," he began nervously, "a lightning catcher named Neville Loxley took a wrong turning on the far side of Little Frog's Bottom and changed the history of fog forever. Loxley inadvertently found himself stumbling about the Imbur marshes, where he discovered some of the most rare and fascinating fogs known to man, including howling fog, spooky fog, and the ever-elusive invisible fog."

"He forgot to mention poisonous and contagious fogs," Dougal whispered, shivering.

"Such was the importance of his discovery that we still celebrate his work on Neville Loxley Day."

Every face in the crowd was turned toward Catcher Hornbuckle expectantly. Miss DeWinkle, the Perilous fog expert, was scribbling notes at a frenzied pace, her cheeks pink with excitement.

"Following in the footsteps of the great Neville Loxley, I spent four weeks on the Imbur marshes last year and discovered three entirely new types of fog, the first in over a hundred years."

A gasp swept around the audience, followed by a swift outbreak of mumbling and pointing.

"Didn't Neville Loxley go around the twist after three days out in the fog?" Dougal whispered.

"Yeah, and Catcher Hornbuckle spent a whole four whole weeks surrounded by the stuff," Angus said as a muscle in the lightning catcher's face twitched. On closer inspection, he had a slightly jittery look about him.

"I have since had my discoveries classified and verified by a panel of experienced fog experts, and I can now present my findings," Catcher Hornbuckle said proudly. "First, I would like to introduce stinging fog. Stinging fog lurks around gorse bushes and thorn trees and leaves a slight tingling sensation on the skin, caused by the dense number of fog particles it contains. I will now release a small sample to demonstrate, as twilight is the best time of day to observe fog in its natural state."

Catcher Hornbuckle opened a storm jar and shook the contents into the darkening skies around the podium. A strange fog drifted slowly over the audience, muffling some surprised squeals from the front row. Angus gripped his chair, waiting for the fog to reach him.

"Ow!" The fog nipped and stung his face, hands, and ears like a swarm of tiny insects. Beside him Dougal was attempting to waft it away with his hands. Indigo sat completely still, letting the fog drift past her.

"Well, that's really going to help mankind, that is!" Dougal said as the fog cleared a few moments later, leaving everyone covered in tiny red spots. "Why didn't he just leave it out on the marsh? It wasn't bothering anyone out there."

Angus grinned, wondering if his mum and dad would have to update their fog guide, if they ever escaped from Castle Dankhart. He braced himself for sample number two, which Catcher Hornbuckle was already getting ready to release.

"Lightning fog," he said, "appears to form after a thunderstorm, absorbing some of the electrically charged particles from the air around it. It is capable of delivering small lightning bolts of its own."

"What's the maniac doing?" Dougal said as the electrically charged fog rolled across the first few rows of audience. It fizzed and sparked, shooting miniature bolts of lightning in all directions like an out-of-control firecracker. Millicent Nichols squealed. Percival Vellum shot out of his seat and tried to hide behind his dad.

"Look out!" Indigo pushed Dougal's head down toward his knees as the fog finally reached them and began striking lightning cubs at random.

"I've been hit!" Dougal shrieked. "Oh," he added immediately, sounding surprised, "it didn't really hurt at all. Look." He showed Angus and Indigo the small burn in his sleeve where the lightning had struck. There was no other damage, however, and as the fog passed over the audience and dissipated into the evening air around them, a chatter of nervous excitement filled the gap it left behind.

"Lightning fog's cool," Angus said.

"That Hornbuckle guy could make a fortune if he just

bottled it and sold it," Dougal said, having a rapid change of heart now that any danger had passed.

Indigo shook her head at them both and smiled.

Angus turned to face the podium again, eager to experience the last of the new fogs. Catcher Hornbuckle was now looking distinctly nervous.

"The last of my discoveries came on the final night, when I was packing up my campsite. I must warn you that fearsome fog lives up to its name," he said, wiping his sweaty-looking face with a handkerchief. "Once released, it takes on the shape of monstrous creatures, feared phantoms, ghosts, and ghouls."

Dougal trembled beside Angus. Indigo, however, was leaning forward in her seat, looking more than ready to be frightened.

The fearsome fog rolled slowly toward them at first, rising like a column of smoke in the cool wintry air, and then—

"Argh!" Several screams came from the front row as the fearsome fog reared up, taking on the shape of an enormous bear, jagged teeth and claws ready to rip, shred, and maul.

"Stay in your seats!" Gudgeon yelled, trying to calm several hysterical first years. "There is no danger!"

The fog, however, was doing its best to prove Gudgeon wrong. The bear shape disappeared as the fog quickly rolled itself into the form of a giant phantom. Several lightning catchers leaped out of their seats and ran for cover. Dougal fainted and slithered down his seat onto the floor. A second later the fog surrounded Angus and Indigo, contorting itself into the monstrous spectral form of a ghost with blank, staring eyes and a wide, wailing maw. Angus held his breath, every muscle in his body clenched tight, until the fearsome fog finally dispersed on the evening breeze and suddenly the demonstration was over.

Catcher Hornbuckle took a bow to an uncertain round of applause.

"That was totally bonkers," Dougal said when Angus and Indigo had revived him and rescued him from under his seat.

"It was even better than the shimmer sharks," Indigo added, beaming.

Miss DeWinkle was on her feet, trying to start a standing ovation, high spots of color in her cheeks. Principal

Dark-Angel was already shaking hands with Catcher Hornbuckle when it happened.

BOOOOM!

The ground shook beneath their seats; the air seemed to quiver around them. Several people in the audience ducked, expecting more fog.

"I thought the demonstration was over," Indigo said as the sound of applause was swiftly replaced by an anxious buzz.

Angus stared around, wondering if the fearsome fog had returned. Beyond the cloud garden, beyond Little Frog's Bottom in the far distance, he finally saw it. Rising above Mount Maccrindell was a dark, menacing cloud.

"This has got nothing to do with Catcher Hornbuckle," he told Dougal and Indigo urgently. "Look!"

Dougal's face blanched. "There's been another explosion at Castle Dankhart!"

The cloud was moving rapidly on the wind, rising and stretching out across the evening sky with long rolls of threatening storm and flashes of ferocious lightning.

"Everyone, inside! Now!" Gudgeon bellowed, hurrying lightning cubs toward the stairs. He grabbed Angus by the

sleeve of his coat. "Stop gawping, you three, and shift it!"

"But—"

"No buts, McFangus! That cloud's going to hit Perilous like a tidal wave of weather. Anyone caught outside will get washed away by the deadly seven!"

Angus glanced back over his shoulder. The cloud had grown darker still, whirling toward Little Frog's Bottom and Perilous at a furious pace. He stumbled awkwardly up the steps after Dougal and Indigo as the first few flakes of black snow began to fall.

12

WINNIE WRASCAL STRIKES AGAIN

For the next few days, nobody was allowed outside as the debris cloud engulfed the entire Exploratorium in a howling storm of confused weather. Stubborn showers of hailstones, filled with black snow and crow's feathers, clung to the windows, making it almost impossible to see anything beyond the thick gray murk. The ornate glass-and-steel weather bubbles were quickly declared out of bounds after several panes of glass shattered under the impact of falling periwinkles. Lingering wisps of fearsome fog, given new life by the storm, now pressed themselves into frightening wolf-like shapes against the kitchen windows, causing two timid first years to lock themselves in the bathroom.

There was no news, however, about the cause of the latest weather explosion at Castle Dankhart. Angus caught only the briefest glimpse of Principal Dark-Angel, Gudgeon, Rogwood, and Catcher Sparks as they darted about the Exploratorium, looking worried, exhausted, and far too busy to answer questions. Of which Angus suddenly had dozens, like: What had happened to his parents? Was this explosion real? Was Castle Dankhart now lying in ruins under the dense cloud, blown apart by the force of the latest catastrophe?

The cloud over Perilous finally cleared a few days later. Large buckets of flotsam and jetsam were collected once again from the courtyard outside the main entrance to be sifted through for important clues. Angus was almost relieved when all second year lightning cubs were called down to the storm hollow for their next lesson with Gudgeon. He was determined to ask the gruff lightning catcher about the latest news on the weather vortex before the lesson ended.

Gudgeon stood waiting for them at the far side of the storm hollow, next to another large jar covered with a tarpaulin. He nodded as Angus, Indigo, Dougal, and the rest of the class gathered before him.

"You've all seen the weather hanging over this Exploratorium." Gudgeon began abruptly as silence fell. "You've heard the explosion, and you know that there's trouble hidden in that drizzle. Latest samples taken from the roof show that it contained large quantities of the weather I'm about to show you, so you need to know how to tackle it." He uncovered the storm jar standing beside him, revealing the foglike contents.

"Oh no! Not more fog!" Dougal whispered. "We've already had enough of that stuff with Catcher Hornbuckle."

"This isn't fog, Dewsnap; it's murderous mist," Gudgeon explained, causing Dougal's ears to turn pink with embarrassment. "Murderous mist encircles the body and tightens like a boa constrictor, squeezing the life out of anyone caught in its coils. It causes numbness and weakness in the limbs, and if it gets a strong enough hold, it will crush muscles, bones, and vital organs before you can squirm free. It can incapacitate even the most experienced lightning catchers unless you know how to handle it. That's what you're doing here today."

Angus gulped, staring at the mist as it swirled around the jar. Dougal had now turned whiter than a wet-dog fog. Even Indigo didn't seem quite as eager to tackle the sinister substance as she usually was. Percival Vellum was scowling at Angus from the back of the group.

"Even as fully qualified lightning catchers you will struggle to tell the difference between this stuff and a tropical fog at a first glance, so it's important that you know what to do if you ever run into any on the Imbur marshes."

"I don't know which is worse," Dougal mumbled under his breath, "having your vital organs crushed by some murderous mist or being nibbled to death by a load of piranha mist fish hidden inside a tropical fog."

Angus glanced at his weather watch, but all it could tell him about the murderous mist was that it should be avoided at all costs.

"Right, I'll give you lot a quick demonstration first." Gudgeon uncorked the storm jar, allowing a small portion of the murderous mist to escape.

Angus watched as the mist uncurled itself like an animal sniffing the air for its prey. Then it slowly began to drift toward Gudgeon, who allowed it to wrap itself around his torso in long, vaporous fingers.

"The longer you let the mist squeeze, the tougher it is to escape from," Gudgeon explained as the coils began to tighten. "It's no use struggling and thrashing about like a lunatic either. The mist will only grip harder. You can't slash your way out of it, as the mist re-forms too quickly for escape."

Angus could feel his heartbeat quicken as the curls of mist pulled in tight around Gudgeon's rib cage, constricting his breathing.

"The only way to break the mist's grip, once it's got a hold, is to perform a Maudling maneuver," Gudgeon said with some difficulty. "It was named after Montague Maudling, who accidentally discovered it after being trapped by the mist in a remote part of the Imbur marshes with no hope of rescue." Gudgeon tried to take another breath, but the mist had tightened once again. "It's tricky, but with a bit of practice, you should be able to do it well enough to save your own skin. Right, now watch me closely; I won't be demonstrating this twice."

Gudgeon managed to grasp one end of the mist, which

appeared to be more solid than the rest, and pulled, as if unraveling a thread. At the same moment, he twisted his shoulders rapidly to the left and right, forcing the coils apart. Then he slipped out backward, leaving an imprint of his own body hanging in midair.

"The mist won't be fooled for long, so don't stand around gawking at it after you've performed the Maudling maneuver. You'll need to make a run for it. I don't mean now, Nichols!"

Sounds of a scuffle broke out at the back of the group as Millicent Nichols attempted to sprint for the door. Georgina Fox grabbed her arm and dragged her back. Millicent gave a small sob and stared at the floor, looking mortified.

"Right, now it's your turn. Find an empty spot where you won't crash into one another."

Angus swallowed hard as the lightning cubs dispersed across the storm hollow, each looking just as anxious as he felt. Indigo turned to face the mist head-on, fists clenched tightly, as Gudgeon released the rest of it from the storm jar.

"Don't let the mist get a hold there!" Gudgeon warned

as Violet Quinn disappeared behind the misty coils and he was forced to pull her free.

Angus felt the mist wrap itself around his body, so lightly and delicately at first that it almost tickled. He waved his arms through the feathered wisps to try to disperse it, but just as Gudgeon had predicted, the swirls re-formed quickly, tightening their grip. A few seconds later his arms were pinned to his sides; the mist had him in a surprisingly strong hold. He managed to wiggle his fingers free, grabbed the thicker end, and pulled. Nothing happened. He tried again, grappling with the mist, which struggled against him like a wild animal. He shook his shoulders, forcing the coils apart and somehow squirmed his way to freedom, falling backward onto the floor of the storm hollow with a painful thump.

"Nice try, McFangus, but watch out for the mist after you've escaped." Gudgeon nodded toward the long fronds that were already reaching out, trying to recapture him.

Angus scrambled to his feet and moved away swiftly. Some of the other cubs hadn't fared so well. Georgina Fox had managed to escape the mist, but it had then chased her across the storm hollow, bound itself around her ankles, and brought her down with a crash. Nigel Ridgely had tried to punch his way through the mist, accidentally smashing Jonathon Hake in the nose at the same time. Indigo was far more skillful than everyone else at escaping the clutches of the murderous mist and performed the Maudling maneuver with ease. But Dougal was in big trouble.

"Ha! Look at the great lump!" Percival sniggered as Dougal suddenly toppled over. He was covered from head to toe in long, misty spirals and struggled like a caterpillar wrapped in a deadly cocoon.

"Hold your tongue, Vellum!" Gudgeon barked, marching over to free Dougal from the tightening fronds. "And the rest of you get back to your own mist." Percival Vellum continued to snigger quietly. Angus glared at the twin until he finally turned away.

"I suppose you three want to know what's going on over Castle Dankhart," Gudgeon said, helping Dougal back onto his feet again.

Angus breathed a sigh of relief. "Nobody's telling us anything!"

"Has there been a real explosion?" Indigo asked quickly, edging closer to listen.

Gudgeon shook his head. "The only thing we know for sure is that the cloud's becoming more volatile, more dangerous by the day; it's now sucking in all the weather from around it. And if you don't do something about the mist that's creeping up behind you, Dewsnap, it'll have you in a stranglehold again before you can say deadly seven."

"Oh no!" Dougal swung around and waved his arms at the long finger of mist that had been sneaking up on him, dispersing it temporarily.

"The weather vortex has already swallowed up several nasty electrical storms and some gale-force winds that were blowing around the mountaintops." Gudgeon continued. "There's also a fierce-looking storm front heading our way, so if it sucks that up as well, we could be looking at a hurricane vortex."

"But isn't there anything we can do to stop it?" Angus asked.

Gudgeon shook his head. "Not until we work out what's driving it. There's some evidence that this type of vortex might have occurred before."

"You mean, like the one that happened over Perilous in 1777?" Angus said without thinking.

A muscle twitched in Gudgeon's forehead. "I've already told you three, that's lightning catcher business. What happened in 1777 doesn't concern you."

"So something *did* happen in 1777?" Dougal said, seizing on the gruff lightning catcher's words.

"That's not what I'm saying, Dewsnap. Stop putting words in my mouth. And stop squirming, Quinn, you'll only make it ten times worse!" Gudgeon suddenly barked.

Angus swung around to see Violet desperately trying to escape the clutches of the murderous mist that had grabbed her by the wrists and was now dragging her along the floor. Georgina Fox hurried across to help her. "Right, I reckon that's enough mist for one day," Gudgeon added abruptly, checking his weather watch. "You two had better go and find Doctor Fleagal and ask him to come down here. Dewsnap's not going anywhere until he's been checked over. That mist can cause some nasty side effects."

"But I feel fine!" Dougal protested, looking shocked.

"I don't care how you feel, boy, I'm getting the doctor down here, and that's an end to it."

Dougal spent several uncomfortable hours in the

sanatorium having his ears, nose, and throat examined by Germ. He returned to the Pigsty, wincing.

"We've got to do *something*!" Angus said as soon as Dougal had lowered himself into an armchair. "That weather vortex is getting more violent with every explosion. Searching Valentine Vellum's office for those documents is still our best chance of finding out the truth. We've got to figure out if there's been a real catastrophe at Castle Dankhart!"

"But how?" Indigo asked, wrapping her sweater sleeve around her hand at the mention of her uncle's name. "We still haven't got a clue where it is."

"There is one thing we haven't tried," Angus said, a new plan suddenly forming in his mind. "We could ask Winnie Wrascal. I mean, she's always being sent to Vellum's office to apologize."

Dougal stared at him openmouthed. "That's a brilliant idea! I can't believe we didn't think of it sooner. I bet she knows it like the back of her hand by now."

The following morning, however, they hurried into the weather archive only to discover Catcher Wrascal sniffing loudly. There were dark circles under her eyes, and her usual cheery smile had been replaced by a trembling bottom lip.

"Er, is everything all right, miss?" Angus asked warily.

"No," she sobbed, shaking her head. "Catcher Killigrew's threatening to strip me of my lightning stripes and move me to the k-k-kitchens!"

"I hope Catcher Killigrew's only joking about the kitchens," Dougal mumbled as Catcher Wrascal blew her nose loudly into a pink handkerchief. "Can you imagine what would happen to the food in this place if Winnie Wrascal got her hands on it?"

"What happened, miss?" Indigo asked kindly, steering her over to a large glass jar that had been rolled onto its side so the catcher could sit down.

"It's Catcher Vellum," Winnie Wrascal sobbed. "I delivered two forecasts to him this week for blizzards in Albania that he didn't ask for."

"But you're always giving him the wrong forecasts," Angus pointed out as nicely as possible. Catcher Wrascal, however, hadn't finished yet.

"Catcher Killigrew sent me to apologize again," she

said, dabbing her eyes with her handkerchief. "But while I was waiting in his office, I-I accidentally smashed a storm globe that was sitting on his desk. I only picked it up for a quick look!" she wailed. "But it slipped through my fingers, and a horrible lightning s-s-storm appeared."

Angus stared at Dougal and Indigo horror-struck.

"I tried to waft it out through the door before it got too violent," Catcher Wrascal explained. "And that's when a bolt of lightning struck Catcher Vellum's desk! The whole thing went up in flames!"

"Flames?" Dougal said, alarmed. "You mean, you've incinerated Valentine Vellum's office?"

Catcher Wrascal nodded, looking utterly wretched. "It was an accident! I only went in to apologize."

"Did Catcher Vellum manage to rescue anything from the fire?" Angus asked hopefully.

Winnie Wrascal shook her head. "Everything was burned to a crisp! Catcher Killigrew says it'll take months to repair the damage. He says it's the worst fire at Perilous since a dozen storm vacuums backfired in 1908."

For several minutes they tried to console the distraught lightning catcher until she was finally forced to leave the weather archive in search of a fresh supply of tissues.

"What do we do now?" Angus said as soon as she was out of earshot. "I mean, if Vellum's office has been destroyed, if any documents from 1777 were in there at the time . . ."

"Then we're never going to find out what really happened," Dougal said, looking resigned.

Over the next few days an unpleasant smell of smoke drifted through the stone tunnels and passageways of Perilous, and more details emerged about the fire in Valentine Vellum's office.

"Edmund Croxley overheard Catcher Sparks telling Miss DeWinkle that the fire melted Vellum's entire collection of lightning-shaped belt buckles," Dougal reported in the library late one afternoon. The weather had taken a sudden turn for the wintry, and fresh flakes of snow were beginning to fall on the glass roof above. "Croxley said Vellum's been stomping about the Exploratorium, yelling at everyone and threatening to have Winnie Wrascal sent to the London office for a disciplinary hearing."

"Poor Winnie," Indigo said, biting her lip.

"Poor Winnie nothing!" Dougal said. "She's like a secret

deadly weapon. We should send her straight into Castle Dankhart. She'd have the monsoon mongrels fleeing for cover in seconds."

Angus couldn't help smiling.

"But that's just the tip of the iceberg," Dougal said, leaning in closer. "I think there's been more trouble in the Perilous crypt."

"What?" Angus said, startled. "How do you know?"

"Creepy Crevice got summoned to Dark-Angel's office yesterday evening, and they had a blazing row, according to Theodore Twill," Dougal told them both.

"How does Twill know about the crypt?" Indigo asked.

"He doesn't," Dougal said quickly. "He got sent up to Dark-Angel's office for starting another water fight, and he overheard Dark-Angel and Crevice shouting at each other. Twill says Dark-Angel was yelling something about a man in a long dark coat and about Catcher Coriolis's being kicked in the shins and tackled to the ground."

Angus stared at Dougal. It could mean only one thing. The Perilous crypt had been broken into once again.

"Then Crevice stormed out of Dark-Angel's office with Valentine Vellum following close behind. Twill says

Crevice isn't allowed to go anywhere in the Exploratorium now without someone watching him."

"Principal Dark-Angel's made Vellum his guard?" Indigo asked, surprised.

Angus frowned. "But if those two really are in it together, if Vellum is hiding under that coat, I mean, Dark-Angel might just as well hand Crevice her own keys to the crypt and tell him to help himself to dragon scales whenever he feels like it."

"I still don't understand why Vellum's so interested in stealing a bunion cure in the first place." Indigo frowned.

"That's easy. Valentine Vellum *is* a bunion." Dougal grinned.

Angus reluctantly returned to his homework after they'd discussed the latest crypt break-in thoroughly. By the time he finally closed his books half an hour later it was already growing dark outside. He was just about to pack away his pencils when Indigo's hand shot out to stop him.

"Don't! Wait!"

"What's wrong?"

"Your bag—it's shaking!" Indigo warned.

She edged her chair away warily as Angus's bag began to hop across the study table with a loud, clunking noise.

"Something must have crawled inside it," Indigo said, "or—"

"It's my scare-me-not puzzle!" Angus leaped up, suddenly remembering that he'd left the puzzle in his bag.

He grabbed the strap before the whole bag bounced off the edge of the table. He opened it carefully and rooted around under books, pens, and something sticky that felt like an apple core until his fingers closed around a familiar shape. He dragged the puzzle out of his bag before it could destroy his other possessions.

Ping!

Just as he'd feared, the puzzle was now shaking and vibrating.

Ping!

"It's about to self-destruct!" Angus said. There was no time to make a run for it. He looked around desperately for somewhere to throw it instead.

P-ting! P-ting! P-ting!

Angus lobbed the puzzle high over the top of the nearest bookshelf, hoping there was no one sitting on the table behind it. He ducked, sticking his fingers in his ears and scrunching his eyes tightly shut.

Bang!

Bookshelves swayed dangerously above their heads, causing several volumes about blizzard spotting to fall onto the floor around them. But there was no time to survey the damage. Thunderous footsteps were already closing in on them fast.

"Quickly!" Indigo dragged Angus and Dougal around the back of the nearest shelf. They crept silently along behind it, peering through small gaps in the books until they spotted the table where the puzzle had exploded. Miss Vulpine arrived on the scene two seconds later with a face that could wither poisonous stinkweed.

"What on earth is going on here?" she bellowed as two stunned-looking lightning cubs crawled out from under the scorched table where they'd clearly taken shelter.

"I don't believe it," Dougal whispered quietly. "You chucked the puzzle straight onto the Vellums! Excellent throw!"

Pixie emerged first, looking shocked and dazed. "We were just doing our homework, miss," she tried to explain.

"It wasn't our fault." Percival scrambled to his feet beside her. "Something landed on our study table."

But the librarian had clearly decided they'd been caught red-handed. "Cradget's self-destructing puzzles have been banned from this library since the great dictionary explosion of 1872! Who is your master lightning catcher? I will be recommending the most severe punishment!"

"What appears to be the trouble, Miss Vulpine?" Valentine Vellum appeared from the left.

Dougal nudged Angus in the ribs. "He must have been sitting close by. Maybe he's using the library now that his office has been Winnie Wrascaled."

Indigo stared at Dougal, her eyes suddenly bright. "Then this could be our best chance to search through Valentine Vellum's stuff!"

Dougal frowned. "Have you completely lost your marbles? Why on earth would we want to do that?"

"Because Vellum might have had some of those documents from 1777 with him when Winnie Wrascal set fire to his office. Some of them might have survived," Indigo whispered.

Before Angus or Dougal could point out the risks of riffling through Valentine Vellum's possessions, Indigo turned and began weaving her way in and out of the

bookshelves closest to the scene of the explosion. Most of the study tables were occupied by whispering lightning cubs, all of whom had heard the commotion and were now listening to the unfolding argument. There was one private study area, however, enclosed on three sides by towering shelves. A cup of half-drunk tea sat abandoned on the table along with a pair of tinted safety goggles, commonly worn in the Lightnarium.

"This must be it!" Indigo said, checking that the coast was clear before sneaking in between the shelves.

A heap of singed documents had been piled up on the table.

"Vellum must have rescued something from his office after all!" Angus said, feeling his hopes rise. "Quickly, see if any of those files mention explosions or vortices hanging over Perilous."

He grabbed a dog-eared copy of the *Weathervane*. The date on the front was the seventeenth of March 1777. His heart began to thud inside his rib cage. The stiff pages crackled with age as he thumbed swiftly through the magazine.

"I shall be speaking to Principal Dark-Angel about the

totally unacceptable behavior of your children, Catcher Vellum!" Miss Vulpine's irate voice suddenly rose above the bookshelves and echoed around the library. "They will clear this mess up before leaving my library, and if I ever catch them in here again with anything they've purchased from Cradget's . . ."

They had only a few moments at best before Valentine Vellum came back and caught them rummaging through his stuff.

"There's nothing in this *Weathervane*." Angus placed it carefully back where he'd found it.

"This one's had some of its pages ripped out, look!" Dougal showed them the jagged tears scattered throughout the magazine. Other long passages had been deliberately blacked out so nobody could read them. "All the *Weathervane*s are the same," Dougal said as he finished flicking through the last one on the table. "Anything interesting has been removed or blacked out."

"I think I've found something!" Indigo said suddenly.

Angus glanced back over his shoulder, his pulse beginning to race. He could now hear sounds of chairs scraping. They had seconds before Valentine Vellum returned.

"What does it say? Quickly!"

"It looks like an accident report . . . from 1777," Indigo said, urgently turning through the pages. "It talks about some investigations into an incident that occurred after some 'dangerous experiments caused a weather vortex to appear over Perilous.'"

"What sort of experiments?" asked Dougal, sounding shocked.

But there was not time to investigate any further. Footsteps were already heading in their direction.

Indigo stuffed the report into her bag, and they sneaked back out through the shelves. Angus had heaved his bag onto his shoulder, getting ready to make a quick getaway, when something grabbed him by the collar and yanked him backward.

"McFangus! I might have guessed." Valentine Vellum towered over all three of them, his face puce with rage from his encounter with Miss Vulpine. "Give me one good reason why I shouldn't throw you and your friends into the Lightnarium as storm bait?"

13

INDIGO'S CONFESSION

"**E**xplain yourselves! Why were you snooping around my papers?" Valentine Vellum demanded, his face now turning a violent shade of purple.

"We weren't snooping, sir," Indigo said quickly. "We were looking for books on storm pickling procedures. We didn't realize we'd wandered into your office."

Catcher Vellum folded his arms across his chest. "Are you trying to convince me, Miss Midnight, that while the rest of the library has been listening to exploding puzzles and the remonstrations of Miss Vulpine, you three have been diligently doing your homework?"

Indigo stood motionless, like a frightened rabbit caught

in the headlights. Dougal's ears turned pink with guilt. Angus stared at the lightning catcher, trying not to blink.

"Turn out your bag, McFangus!" Vellum instructed suddenly. "We'll soon see if you've been looking for books on pickling storms or stealing valuable papers that do not belong to you."

Angus unzipped his bag slowly, hoping there was nothing incriminating inside, like a receipt from Cradget's proving he'd recently bought a scare-me-not puzzle. He turned it upside down. Pencils, homework books, and apple cores scattered across the library floor. Valentine Vellum bent down to inspect the pile, his lip twitching with obvious disappointment.

"Empty your bag, Dewsnap." He stood up and turned on Dougal angrily. "You, too, Miss Midnight, unless you've got something to hide."

Angus felt his stomach lurch as neatly ordered notes, pencils, and *The Dankhart Handbook* tumbled out of Indigo's bag. There was no sign of the document she'd just taken. Indigo's face remained impassive, giving nothing away. Angus held his breath as Valentine Vellum rummaged through the notes. He stood up a moment later, scowling.

"Clear up this mess, and don't let me catch you three snooping around this section of the library again. And as for the rest of you!" He swung around abruptly, startling a small group of curious third years who had gathered to watch the latest commotion. "Return to your own tables, and get on with your homework!" And he disappeared back into his temporary office.

"Let's get out of here," Angus said, quietly scooping up the contents of his bag, "before Vellum changes his mind."

They left the library at a sprint and reached the Pigsty a few minutes later. Dougal dropped his bag on the floor, looking drained.

"That was way too close for comfort! I thought we'd had it. It's a good job Vellum didn't make us turn out our pockets as well." He pulled his last remaining scare-me-not puzzle from a pocket in his pants. "He would have blown a gasket if he'd seen this. Here." He chucked it across the Pigsty to Angus. "You'd better have a go at cracking it before that one self-destructs, too. I can't concentrate on anything until they announce the results of the Cradget's competition."

Angus stuffed it into his own pocket, wondering if they should have bought one of Cradget's less volatile puzzles.

There was a scraping sound from above a moment later, and Indigo descended the ladder from her room to join them.

"What happened to the accident report you took from Vellum's office?" Angus asked as soon as her foot touched the floor.

"Vellum made you turn your bag out first, so I slipped it up my sleeve when he wasn't looking," Indigo said, pulling a rolled-up document from her sweater with a grin.

"Wow!" Angus said, impressed by her sheer nerve. Dougal let out a long low whistle. Indigo quickly laid the paper out on the floor where they could all see it. But the rest of the report had been blacked out.

"You mean, we went through all that for nothing?" Dougal said, glaring at the thick black lines.

Indigo sighed, resting back on her heels. "It's like the whole of 1777 has been wiped out of Perilous records."

"At least we know what caused the weather vortex now," Angus said. "The lightning catchers were doing some dangerous experiments."

"Yeah, but experiments with what?" Dougal said,

frowning. "You don't get explosions and weather vortices from studying fluffy snowflakes."

Indigo nodded. "It must have been something really risky, something Gudgeon doesn't want us asking questions about."

"And I bet you anything it helps explain what's really going on at Castle Dankhart," Angus said, more certain of his theory than ever. "We've got to search through Vellum's stuff again. We've *got* to find out more about those experiments!"

"Have you completely lost your marbles?" Dougal said, looking thoroughly alarmed at the prospect. "You heard what Vellum said: If he catches us again, he'll have us catapulted straight into a storm full of lightning tarantulatis, or worse!"

"Then we'll have to make sure we don't get caught," Angus said, determined.

When they returned to the library the following day, however, it was clear that Valentine Vellum had moved his temporary office to a different location. There was no sign of him in the reference section on the balcony or at any of the other study tables in the library.

"I don't believe it. We're right back to square one again," Angus said as they left the library in a very despondent mood. "What are we going to do now?"

In the weather archive, Winnie Wrascal remained subdued, sniffing and blowing her nose at regular intervals. Catcher Killigrew was now checking up on her several times an hour, in an effort to prevent any more catastrophes from occurring. A few days later he also set Angus, Indigo, and Dougal to work ferrying some poorly pickled storm jars out into the Octagon. The contents of the jars had congealed and disintegrated over time and had now been earmarked for thorough decontamination.

"Ew! This one looks like it's got melted boogers at the bottom," Dougal said, inspecting a small jar where a lumpy green residue had stuck to the sides. "I'm glad *we're* not cleaning them out."

Some of the jars contained nothing but dried-up storm husks. Others had been contaminated by slivers of storm, dust particles, or cobwebs and looked fractured and worn out.

"I didn't realize weather could curdle." Indigo wrinkled her nose at a rancid-smelling specimen. She carried it at arm's length as they left the forecasting department for the tenth time that afternoon with the latest batch of jars. "I really don't think we should—"

She stopped suddenly as they entered the Octagon. The Vellum twins were blocking their path, with arms folded.

"I want a word with you, Munchfungus," Percival said, stepping forward and poking Angus hard in the chest with a thick finger.

Angus put his own jar down and, feeling his hackles rise, pushed the twin away. "What are you going on about now, Vellum?"

"You and Dewsnap have been messing around with those stupid Cradget's puzzles for weeks and then somebody threw one onto the table where me and Pixie were sitting and now Vulpine's making us dust the entire reference section, book by book!"

"You're barking up the wrong tree. My scare-me-not hasn't even exploded yet, see," Angus said, taking the last remaining puzzle from his pocket and holding it up as evidence. "And Dougal's went off weeks ago."

Percival scowled, momentarily confounded. "I don't care, Munchfungus. I know you, Dewsnap, and Midnight

had something to do with it, and now me and Pixie are going to make you pay."

Percival headed straight for a large collection of storm jars that Angus, Indigo, and Dougal had already carried into the Octagon and arranged neatly on the floor in order of height. He picked the largest one. It still contained visible traces of an angry storm.

"What would you do if I let this weather out, storm boy?" he said with a calculated look on his face. "Would you set a storm of fire dragons on us? Or start breathing fire? Or turn into an overgrown bat and flap around our heads?"

"Leave those jars alone, Vellum. Even you wouldn't be that stupid," Angus said.

"It might be worth it just to see how much of a freak you really are."

"Just ignore him!" Indigo said. "He's trying to get you into trouble, too."

"I know!" Angus snapped, wondering what he was supposed to do about it. He could feel the fire dragon stirring inside his chest. But he couldn't lose control this time. Not when they were surrounded by so many old and angry storms. He tried to shove Percival away from the storm jar, but the twin refused to budge.

"You're such a mutant, Munchfungus."

"Yeah, you don't belong here." Pixie snickered, nudging the jar with her foot until it wobbled dangerously.

"Is that why your parents haven't come home yet? Maybe they'd rather stay in their dungeon than admit their son's a freak."

"Shut up about my mum and dad!" Angus tried with all his might *not* to picture the fire dragon chasing the storm and Percival Vellum across the Octagon, *not* to imagine how satisfying it would feel to scare the pants off the sneering twin. But the fire dragon was now smoldering inside his rib cage, threatening to burst free at any second, overwhelming his self-control.

"It's about time everyone at this Exploratorium knew exactly *what* they've been sharing their living quarters with."

Percival glanced around the Octagon to check that they were alone. He stretched out an arm toward the storm jar.

"What is going on here?"

A door flew open behind them, and Catcher Sparks appeared from the experimental division.

"I've got some fourth years trying to reassemble some very tricky snow-shuffling machinery, which requires absolute silence, and all I can hear is you five arguing!"

Percival Vellum swiftly moved away from the jar and stood beside his sister. Angus felt the flames of the fire dragon slowly cooling inside him again.

"Midnight!" Catcher Sparks rounded on Indigo. "Explain what you're doing with these storm jars."

"Catcher Killigrew told us to bring them out here, miss," Indigo muttered.

"And did Catcher Killigrew also tell you to stand about arguing with these two idiots?"

Indigo shook her head.

"Then I suggest that you, Dewsnap, and McFangus continue with your duties. And as for you two," Catcher Sparks said, circling the twins slowly, "you're already skating on very thin ice. Do not give me a reason to follow Miss Vulpine's example and make you dust the entire experimental division as well."

Percival Vellum scowled over his shoulder at Angus as

he and Pixie slouched off, disappearing down the stairs.

"Vellum was bluffing," Dougal said as soon as Catcher Sparks had retreated to the experimental division again. "He never would have pushed that storm jar over in a million years."

But Angus wasn't so sure. What if the terrible twin really had smashed the storm jar? Would he, Angus, have sent the contents charging after him? What if he'd been unable to control the fire dragon or the powerful feelings that had once again been stirred up inside him? Percival Vellum would have felt the full force of the storm and would now be lying in the sanatorium with some very serious injuries.

To make matter worse, in the days that followed, Angus began to experience some tremendously unsettling sensations. They started with an odd bubbling feeling under his skin, like an itch that couldn't be scratched, and he wondered if he'd caught Indigo's rash. But soon they were impossible to ignore. He woke up each morning with an inferno burning inside his chest, as if the fire dragon were trying to incinerate his rib cage.

He was enormously relieved when Rogwood collected

him late one evening a few days later for his latest lesson in the Inner Sanctum. Angus quickly described the entire incident in the Octagon, leaving nothing out, as they entered the round room once again and sat in the comfy chairs.

Rogwood smiled kindly at him. "Yes, Catcher Sparks mentioned something about an altercation between you and the Vellum twins."

"I'm never going to be like Moray McFangus!" Angus said, staring at the floor. "I'm going to be a rubbish storm prophet!"

"Angus, you have already saved your fellow lightning cubs on a number of occasions. Miss Midnight might not be here today if it hadn't been for your bravery in the Lightnarium. And it will still be a very long time before Percival Vellum forgets he owes his life to you after an incident with a certain fognado."

"But I wanted the fire dragon to appear! I wanted it to chase Percival Vellum!" Angus admitted, still feeling wretched.

Rogwood chuckled deeply into his braided beard. "Do not be so quick to condemn yourself, Angus. I can assure you that your abilities are far too weak to inflict any real damage on your fellow lightning cubs, despite the intensity of any sensations you might be feeling. And I have no doubt that you were provoked. However, I would advise you to steer clear of Valentine Vellum for the time being. He seems to be rather annoyed with you, Miss Midnight, and Mr. Dewsnap for a variety of reasons." Angus gulped. "And if that does not calm your fears—" Rogwood stood up suddenly. "There is something I wish to show you, if you will come with me, please."

The lightning catcher took him swiftly through the dark room, back into the rough stone Octagon, and through one of the eight doors that they had never ventured through before.

"It is true that the storm prophets have performed many brave and noble deeds," Rogwood said, leading the way down a narrow stone tunnel. "Numerous books and projectograms have recorded their great achievements. But nobody can behave in a heroic manner the whole time. As you may already know, the trusty *Weathervane* records all events that occur at Perilous, including those of a less gallant nature," he said. "According to the *Weathervane,* there was an incident when a young storm prophet, Zachary Bodfish, who was showing off for his friends, managed to burn down an entire section of Perilous, which had only recently been completed. As you can imagine, he was very unpopular for some years afterward. I believe you can still see the scorch marks in the library behind Miss Vulpine's desk if you study the floorboards carefully."

Angus stared at Rogwood, hardly daring to believe his ears. He made a mental note to visit the library as soon as he left the Inner Sanctum. Rogwood stopped at the end of the stone tunnel, unlocked a plain wooden door, and allowed Angus to enter first. The room was completely dark. He could see nothing beyond the small pool of light in the doorway where they hovered.

"On another occasion," Rogwood continued, "two of the most hotheaded storm prophets, Zebedee Bodfish and Gideon Stumps, decided to settle their differences doing battle with a thunderstorm in the dead of night."

Rogwood flicked on the light fissures.

"Wow!" Angus rocked back on his heels.

The silhouettes of two massive fire dragons had been burned into the wall, imprinted forever like giant scaly fossils. They seemed to undulate around the walls with wings spread wide, talons locked in a furious struggle, flickering flames tangled. Both fire dragons were enormous, far larger than his own, each fiery scale the size of several handprints. He could almost sense the battle that had taken place, as if the storm had also left a lasting impression in the very air around them.

"As you can see, Angus, Bodfish and Stumps were each determined to prove that he had the greater talent and power," Rogwood said. "According to the *Weathervane,* it was an epic battle that lasted all of five minutes before the storm grew too violent and both storm prophets had to be rescued, much to their embarrassment. They were punished for their foolish weather duel and sent straight to bed each night after dinner for a month. It was certainly not their finest hour, and yet each went on to perform quite astonishing acts of bravery when they were older and more in control of their skills. It took every storm prophet some years to use his great abilities wisely and with any measure of control. You, Angus, have been bombarded with new information, images, and ideas about yourself as a storm prophet, and you are feeling an awakening, a

stirring of odd sensations and unfamiliar emotions."

Angus stared at Rogwood, wondering how the lightning catcher could possibly know of the troubling feelings he'd been experiencing.

"You must have some patience, Angus. Try not to expect too much of yourself at this very early stage in your development. And in the meantime, be grateful that you have not yet burned down any part of this Exploratorium."

Angus followed Rogwood back down the stone tunnel a few moments later, still reeling from the shock of the giant fire dragons he'd just seen. When they returned to the stone Octagon, it took several seconds for his brain to register that it was no longer empty. Catcher Sparks and Felix Gudgeon were locked in serious conversation.

". . . been months now, and we still haven't got a clue what the monsoon mongrels are really up to under that vortex," Catcher Sparks said, her arms folded tightly across her chest. "Ah, Aramanthus! Has the weather station resumed taking weather samples?"

"The vortex is still proving to be too dangerous to approach," Rogwood said, joining his fellow lightning catchers. Angus hovered, trying his best to look completely uninterested in the conversation.

"I still say the whole thing's a ruse," Gudgeon said. "Dankhart's using that vortex to hide something bigger."

"Yes, but what, Felix? We've been going around in circles for months now." Catcher Sparks sighed. "If only Valentine had found something before Winnie Wrascal destroyed his office."

Gudgeon grunted. "Fire or no fire, it wouldn't have made any difference. Most of those records were already blacked out, crucial pages missing all over the place. Valentine found nothing useful. We're closer to inventing lightning-proof underpants than we are to finding out what experiments those lightning catchers were performing in 1777." He whispered the last sentence warily, glancing over his shoulder at Angus. "All we know for sure is that it resulted in a huge weather vortex."

"But I cannot believe that is all we know," Catcher Sparks said, frowning. "Surely somewhere there must be records, diaries, letters . . ."

"Whether you believe it or not, Amelia, it might be better to restrict all conversations on the subject to more private areas of the Exploratorium," Rogwood said pointedly. And the conversation came to an abrupt end.

Angus slept soundly that night for the first time since the incident in the Octagon. Smoldering dragons wove their way slowly through his peaceful dreams, his worries soothed by the revelation that the other storm prophets, long ago, had also struggled to control their skills.

The next morning he headed straight up to the library to see if Rogwood had been telling him the truth about Zachary Bodfish's burning it down. Luckily Miss Vulpine was nowhere to be seen. He knelt down to inspect the floorboards carefully behind her desk and felt his heart leap when he discovered several faded-looking scorch marks lurking beneath a wastepaper basket. He raced up to the kitchen, feeling far happier than he had in weeks, and quickly filled Dougal and Indigo in on all the details of the conversation he'd overheard in the Inner Sanctum.

"So you're saying *none* of the lightning catchers actually knows what happened in 1777?" Dougal said, a bowl of porridge lying forgotten in front of him.

"But Gudgeon's been trying to stop us from finding stuff for weeks," Indigo pointed out. "He must have some idea."

"They know there was a weather vortex over Perilous. They definitely think it's got something to do with the one sitting over Castle Dankhart," Angus explained. "But that's all."

"So all this time Gudgeon, Rogwood, and everyone could have been searching for answers, just like us," Indigo said. "That must be the real reason Gudgeon had those documents removed from the research department."

Angus nodded. "That's what they were doing in Valentine Vellum's office when Winnie Wrascal burned it down. But all the documents had been blanked out. Vellum found nothing."

Dougal sat back in his seat, looking flabbergasted. "In that case . . ."

He stopped talking suddenly as Edmund Croxley appeared with the morning's mail, which included a large envelope with Dougal's name handwritten on the front.

"The mailroom asked me to deliver these," Croxley said, dropping several items onto the table, not waiting to see what the large envelope contained.

Dougal ripped it open. "It's a letter from Cradget's. I don't believe it! I've won third prize in the Tri-Hard

Puzzle Competition!" He waved a colouful letter at them excitedly.

"Congratulations!" Angus said stodgily through a mouthful of porridge.

"They've sent the prize as well," Dougal said, delving to the bottom of the envelope. He pulled out a chunky-looking black pen. "There's a spy camera hidden inside it," he said. "You've got to click the top of the pen to take a photo. This is so cool!"

Angus grinned. "You can take secret photos of Clifford Fugg picking the spots on his chin and he'll never know."

"Yeah, or I could get a quick snap of Germ in his yeti-print pajamas and threaten to show it to everyone unless he stops making us test him on scabs and stuff."

Angus turned to get Indigo's opinion on the subject. But she was now grasping a large envelope of her own that had apparently also arrived in the mail.

"Don't tell me you've won something as well?" Dougal said, looking slightly crestfallen. "You never said any-thing about entering Cradget's competition."

"That's because I didn't!" Indigo whispered, and quickly tucked the envelope into her bag.

Before Dougal could grill her any further, Germ appeared at their table with a huge plate of scrambled eggs on toast and sat down next to Indigo.

"All right, little sis? I've been looking for you everywhere." He grinned.

"How are the exams going?" Angus asked. Germ had dark circles under his eyes. His fingernails had been bitten down to the quick.

"Two down, two more to go. I'm moving onto bites, burns, and bruises next," he said cheerfully, pointing to a thick book that was bulging from his bag.

"If you're expecting one of us to test you on lightning burns, you can forget it." Indigo edged her chair away from her brother. "We haven't even finished our breakfast yet."

"That's not why I've been looking for you. I've finally discovered what's wrong with your hand," Germ announced, looking extremely pleased with his own cleverness.

"Nothing's wrong with my hand," Indigo snapped, hiding it automatically under her sleeve. "It's just a stupid rash."

"Not according to my research, and you're, er, definitely not going to like what I've found."

Angus glanced sideways at Dougal as Germ rummaged through his bag for his workbook.

"I looked up all the normal rashes and skin complaints, of course, but nothing seemed to fit," Germ explained, flicking past several pages of handwritten notes. "And then I was doing some reading on freckles, birthmarks, and other kinds of pigmentation, and I found this."

Germ spread his workbook across the table so they could all see the notes he'd scribbled on something called bleckles. "Bleckles are like a cross between a freckle and a blemish. Apparently they run in families. Each family has its own distinctive pattern, and yours"—Germ flicked to the next page, "—comes from the Dankharts."

Dougal almost choked on a mouthful of toast. Indigo stared at her brother horror-struck, biting her lip, a strange, almost guilty expression taking control of her face.

"I copied this drawing from a book by some old dermatology doctor. Bleckles were his specialty. He made a note of all the patterns he'd heard about before he died."

He pointed to a large pencil drawing of a hand bearing the identical marks to the ones Indigo had on her skin.

"As far as I can tell, you're the only one on our side of

the family who's got them," Germ added, showing them his own bleckle-free hands.

"But isn't there anything I can do to get rid of them?" Indigo asked, her voice now trembling.

"'Fraid not, sis. Once they've appeared, you're pretty much stuck with them like big ears or webbed feet," Germ said. "The best thing you can do is keep them covered up. And if anyone asks, I'd blame it on an allergic reaction to Valentine Vellum." He grabbed the book, snapped it shut, and got to his feet again. "Anyway, I've got to memorize a whole chapter on how to treat horrible-hailstone bruises before tomorrow morning. See you three later." And he took his scrambled eggs and joined his friends at a nearby table.

"What am I going to do?" Indigo gulped, keeping her voice low. She was staring at the bleckles on her hand with a disgusted look on her face. "It's like being branded a Dankhart. What if Germ tells someone by accident?"

"He won't," Angus said, feeling confident he was right. "Germ might joke about stuff, but he doesn't want anyone else knowing about your uncle Scabby either."

"But what if the Vellums find out? No one will ever talk to me again. I'll have to leave Perilous!"

"Of course you won't," Dougal said, patting her arm awkwardly. "And you're always telling Angus not to be embarrassed about being a storm prophet."

"So?" Indigo sniffed.

"So it's the same thing with you and your family. Yes, you're a Dankhart."

Indigo blew her nose loudly into a pink handkerchief.

"But you're a Midnight as well." Dougal continued. "You're nothing like your uncle, and that's all anybody needs to know. It's not your fault your skin's got some funny bumps now."

Indigo blinked at Dougal, looking startled by his sudden show of support. But the same guilty expression suddenly swept across her face.

"You-you already knew about the bleckles, didn't you?" Angus said, taking a wild guess.

Indigo paused for a second, looking thoroughly wretched, and nodded. "My mum's got the same bumps on her hand, only smaller. Germ's just never noticed. She keeps them covered up with gloves, long sleeves, and tinted creams, but I saw them years ago. And then, when the exact same bumps started appearing on my hand and they wouldn't go away, I just knew it had something to do with the Dankharts!"

"So that's why you've been staring at Dankhart's picture in the handbook," Dougal said, suddenly putting two and two together.

Indigo nodded again, trying to swallow a small sob. "The first time I saw that picture of Uncle Scabious I knew." She opened her bag, pulled out *The Dankhart Handbook* and flicked to the page devoted to her uncle. On his hand, so small they were barely visible, were the same distinctive bleckles.

"But I don't understand," Angus said. "Why have you been reading all those other books on the Dankharts in the library?"

"I just thought if I could find another picture or discover how to get rid of the bumps . . ."

Angus glanced sideways at Dougal. He had a feeling Indigo still wasn't telling them the whole story. The time had come to confront her about Fawcett Family Tree Hunters.

"Look, Indigo, we—we know about the ad in the *Weathervane*," Angus said, trying to choose his words carefully.

"A-ad?" Indigo gulped, wiping her eyes on the back of her hand.

"You dropped it when you raced out of the kitchens ages ago," Dougal said. "You circled an ad for Fawcett Family Tree Hunters."

Angus took the folded page from his pocket, flattened out the edges, and turned it around so Indigo could read it. "Have you been thinking about getting your own Dankhart family tree?"

"No!" Indigo shook her head looking horrified. "I'd never do that!"

She dived into her bag, grabbed the mysterious envelope that had arrived that morning in the mail, and handed it to Angus. Angus opened it warily and pulled out what appeared to be a weathered-looking family tree. At the top the Midnight family crest showed a deep blue sky dusted with tiny silvery stars. But on the other side of Indigo's family, where there should have been a long list of Dankharts—

Angus took a sharp intake of breath. "According to this, your mum comes from an extended line of chocolate makers from Belgium, and they're all called Anselmus." The Dankharts had been totally wiped from her family history as if they'd never existed.

"That's because I ordered a *fake* family tree from Fawcett's," Indigo explained quietly, pointing to the ad in the *Weathervane* that she'd circled. At the bottom of the promotion was a minuscule paragraph that neither Angus nor Dougal had noticed.

"'Have you ever wanted to distance yourself from your family, to hide embarrassing relations, or controversial connections?'" Angus said, reading the tiny words out loud with some difficulty. "'Have you ever wanted to amaze your friends at dinner parties with your distinguished ancestors? Then send for a new family tree now, complete with authentic detail and family crest.'"

"Wow! This is genius!" Dougal said, sounding seriously impressed. "You could turn your whole family into beekeepers, or famous poets, or medieval knights."

Angus stared at Indigo. "And if anyone ever asks you

about your family or starts getting suspicious about your connections . . ."

"I can show them my family tree," Indigo said, still looking faintly embarrassed. "And there's not a single Dankhart on it. After I found those dreadful bleckles on my hand, I had to do something!"

Shocked at the lengths Indigo had gone to in order to hide her horrible ancestors, Angus studied the fake tree again.

"Maybe next time you should just tell us what you're planning," he said, smiling at her. "We've been seriously worried about you."

"Yeah, we thought you'd lost your marbles," Dougal added, grinning. "Plus we could have got our own family trees done, too. I've always fancied being related to royalty. Prince Dougal of Feaver Street, what do you reckon? It's got a real ring to it."

Indigo continued to brood over the bleckles for the next few days and kept the sleeve of her sweater pulled down over her hand, just in case. But she was now spending most of her free time with Angus and Dougal, helping them think through new ways of discovering what was going on under the weather vortex at Castle Dankhart and what had happened at Perilous during the experiments in 1777.

"There must be somewhere we haven't looked yet," Angus said one Friday afternoon in the experimental division.

Catcher Killigrew had sent Winnie Wrascal on an intensive weather forecasting refresher course, and they had temporarily been placed under the supervision of Catcher Sparks. Their master lightning catcher had set them to work in the very familiar part of the experimental division where they had spent their first day as lightning cubs, removing pockets of revolting earwax from some hailstone helmets. This time she had left them with a huge pile of leather jerkins that had to be washed and waxed, their rips and tears repaired with long needles and thread. Angus had already stabbed himself in the thumb twice, leaving a long trail of dripping blood all the way over to a sink at the back of the workroom.

"We can't give up now," he said, carefully darning a hole in the pocket of a large, scruffy jerkin.

"But Dougal's already searched the library and the research department," Indigo said. She was attempting to

patch up a jerkin that belonged to Catcher Donall, according to the name tag sewn inside it. Pockets, buckles, and chunks of leather had been ripped off the garment by something with extremely large teeth.

"Maybe we should sneak back into the Dankhart archive for another look at that weather sample," Angus suggested.

"We can't." Indigo shook her head. "Catcher Killigrew's threatened to have Winnie Wrascal transferred to a tiny research post in Iceland if she gets into any more trouble, and if we get caught snooping around that archive . . ."

Angus sighed. "There must be somewhere else we can search for answers then. I— Ow!" He jumped to his feet suddenly. "That's the third time I've stabbed my thumb with the same needle!"

"ARGHHHH!" Dougal dropped the leather jerkin he'd been washing a second later and scuttled away from it in a panic. "There's something crawling around inside that pocket!"

It took some time to convince Dougal that all he'd discovered was a prickly pinecone. Angus approached his next leather jerkin with caution, however, turning the pockets out well away from his body just in case. A small collection of smashed snail shells, leaves, and sand tumbled out. It was obvious that the wearer had been helping to clean up the flotsam and jetsam after the third explosion from Castle Dankhart.

The idea hit him like a stray thunderbolt, almost flattening his windpipe.

"The flotsam and jetsam!" he said, still dangling the jerkin at arm's length. "It got collected up in buckets."

Dougal and Indigo exchanged puzzled glances.

"So?" Dougal asked.

"So the buckets got taken into the Inner Sanctum to be searched through for clues."

"I still don't get it," Dougal said, looking mystified. "How's a load of old rubbish going to help us?"

"Forget the buckets. I'm talking about important historical artifacts!" Angus said excitedly. "I mean, I've already seen Veronica Stickleback's leather jerkin and Philip Starling's glasses in there. So what if it's the one place in the whole Exploratorium where we might also find out what really happened in 1777? We've got to search it!"

"Got to search what?" Dougal asked, starting to sound exasperated.

But Indigo's face lit up with sudden understanding. "Oh! The Inner Sanctum!"

14
THE WALKING ENCYCLOPEDIA

"**W**e could let Norman cause a disturbance and then sneak into the Inner Sanctum when no one's looking," Dougal said.

It was two days after their cleaning session in the experimental division. Since then Angus had spent so many hours discussing how to get into the Inner Sanctum with Dougal and Indigo that he'd talked himself hoarse. The most radical idea they'd come up with so far was to trigger the fire alarm, hide until the whole Exploratorium had been evacuated, and then creep through the door in the Octagon. Angus had been quite keen on the idea until Indigo had pointed out that not only would they need a set of keys, but Catcher Sparks would do a head count, realize they were missing, and organize a search party.

Angus sighed. He and Dougal were now standing in the corridor at the boys' end of the living quarters. A late edition of the *Weathervane* had brought everyone out to discuss the exciting news that the last winners' demonstration would be taking place at the weekend in Little Frog's Bottom.

"I wonder why they're holding it there," Angus said. Encouraged by Dougal's Tri-Hard competition success, he was once again attempting to solve the last scare-me-not puzzle, which still showed no signs of self-destruction. Dougal had let Norman out to stretch its wings, and the lightning moth was now zooming up and down the corridor with several of its flying friends like a sparkling silver wave.

"No idea." Dougal ducked swiftly as Norman skimmed the top of his head before speeding up to the ceiling again. "But it's bound to be brilliant. It's happening in the central square. There's a bit in the *Weathervane* about the last of the winners. Here." He handed over the magazine so Angus could read it for himself.

Angus thrust the frustrating puzzle into the pocket of his pants and studied the glossy photos of Lettice and Leonard Galipot. They both looked extremely smug, Angus decided. But their list of achievements was long. They'd already won numerous awards for advanced weather observation. They'd written dozens of research papers over the years and met with Crowned Prince Rufus of the Imbur royal family to collect a prize for cloudspotting. In their spare time, they claimed to be mad fans of iceberg hopping, although, judging by the bulging midriffs they were trying to conceal beneath their lumpy leather jerkins, Angus wasn't convinced they could hop over anything.

"We might just as well go and watch the demonstration," Dougal said, reaching up to catch Norman as it tried to soar past them once again. "There's been no news about the weather vortex for days, and we still haven't got a clue how to get into the Inner Sanctum without being caught and killed by Catcher Sparks."

Angus sighed. Unless they came up with a brilliant plan soon, the other secrets of the Inner Sanctum would stay that way forever.

They were still trying to come up with an idea when they met Gudgeon outside the library early the next evening.

"I've been looking for you three. We've had some news about the weather vortex," he told them, scratching his bearded chin. "It looks like it's finally thinning out."

"What . . . seriously?" Angus said, shocked.

"Some new samples taken by the weather station show a decrease in storm particles, which probably means that whatever's been driving it all this time is running out of steam. And when it does, we'll be able to see exactly what that villain's been doing underneath his cloud."

"But when?" Indigo asked anxiously.

"If all our calculations are correct, it should be no more than a couple of days now," Gudgeon said, checking his weather watch.

"Will you tell us when you know what's going on?" Angus asked hopefully.

Gudgeon nodded. "I promised Jeremius I'd keep you three in the know. Although I doubt even that would stop you from getting into trouble if you put your minds to it."

Indigo flushed a guilty red. "You don't think Gudgeon knows about our idea to break into the Inner Sanctum, do you?" she asked quietly as soon as he'd left.

"How could he?" Angus said. "I mean, we haven't even got a plan yet."

"We might not need one if the weather vortex is finally running out of steam," Dougal said hopefully. "Maybe your uncle Scabby isn't planning anything after all."

But Angus wasn't convinced. Dankhart was an expert schemer. He had once disguised himself as a fake librarian called Mr. Knurling, and spent a whole term shouting at lightning cubs and sniveling about the reference section just to find the infamous lightning vaults. If the Inner Sanctum had any answers about dangerous weather vortices, they had to find a way to search it.

A chance finally came three days later. Catcher Sparks, who was still supervising their duties in the absence of Catcher Wrascal, had sent them to scrape three inches of stinking mud off the soles of two hundred rubber boots. It was hot, sticky, disgusting work, and they were covered in dirt when they left the experimental division at the end of the afternoon.

"I'm so hungry I could eat a whole fog yeti," Dougal said, his stomach rumbling loudly. A delicious smell of roast chicken had been drifting up from the kitchens for hours.

They were already halfway across the Octagon when Angus saw a familiar figure emerge from the Inner Sanctum.

"Hey, that's Catcher Coriolis," he told Dougal and Indigo quietly.

"The lightning catcher who works in the crypt?" Indigo asked.

Angus nodded.

"Creepy." Dougal shivered. "How can anyone sleep in a tomb without having nightmares?"

Catcher Coriolis, clearly suffering from a terrible winter cold, stopped to blow his nose.

"*A-choo!*" He caught the almighty sneeze in a spotted handkerchief, the noise echoing around the Octagon like an explosion. He gave his nose an extra blow, for good measure, and then disappeared down the steps toward the kitchens.

Dougal and Indigo both turned to follow him, but Angus swiftly pulled them back again.

"Hang on a minute."

Catcher Coriolis had dropped something on the floor. Angus darted across the Octagon and scooped up the lumpy object.

"It's his keys to the Inner Sanctum! Catcher Coriolis must have dropped them when he sneezed."

"Urgh!" Dougal wrinkled his nose in disgust. "Germy keys."

"Germy or not, these keys might be our only chance to search the Inner Sanctum," Angus said, quickly making sure the Octagon was deserted.

"You're joking! What if Catcher Coriolis notices his keys have gone?"

"If we're lucky, he won't bother checking for them until he's finished his dinner," Indigo said, "which means we've got at least half an hour." She was already rolling up her sleeves, getting ready to tackle whatever dangers they might face.

Angus swallowed hard. He slotted several keys into the first lock on the door until he found the correct one. The lock clicked open. The chances of their getting caught were extremely high. But the desperate plan had possibilities, and since none of them had come up with any better ideas . . .

He fumbled with the rest of the locks until the door finally swung open.

"Come on!" Angus led the way down the narrow stone tunnel. Indigo followed without hesitation. Dougal flinched as the door closed itself behind them. With a twist and tug they were through the steel safety door in seconds.

Angus headed straight for the door through which the buckets of storm debris had been taken.

"Maybe there's other stuff about the storm vortex in here, too, old stuff that everyone else has forgotten about," he reasoned as he felt along the rough stone wall inside, searching for a switch. He flicked the light fissure on.

"Oh, my!" Indigo gasped.

Books and papers, stacked on ancient-looking shelves and in great tottering piles across the floor, covered every surface. It instantly reminded Angus of Mr. Dewsnap's study, where half-eaten sandwiches and cold cups of tea lay abandoned on top of every heap. These piles, however, stretched all the way up to the ceiling, which was also covered in books, their spines clamped hard against bare rock, their covers flapping open like great colorful bats.

Dangling from the pages within, in long black strings . . . Angus blinked, wondering if he was seeing things. Words were melting off each page. Dozens of stalactitelike sentences wafted daintily in the air.

"I don't believe it!" Dougal said, stunned. "Old Archibald Humble-Pea was right! Remember that secret code I deciphered at the back of our fog guides about what they had hidden in the Inner Sanctum. It said something about melting words!"

Angus gazed at the stringy sentences, shocked that it was actually true.

"But why would anyone want a book with stretchable words?" Indigo asked.

"I don't know." Dougal grabbed the end of the nearest sentence and pulled it out so he could read it properly. "This one says, 'It was only then that Philip Starling decided to ban all future experiments with storm snares as it led to—'"

"As it led to what?" Angus asked.

Dougal shrugged. "Haven't got the foggiest." The words snapped back to their original length as soon as he released them. "That was the end of the sentence."

Angus tried to read some of the words as they passed carefully underneath them, looking for any mention of weather explosions, vortices, or 1777. There was something about storm-force fog, and a thick, elongated sentence that ended with "Fractonimbus."

"Watch out!" Dougal warned, brushing a jumble of vowels and consonants aside. "Some of those words could be deadly!"

"Since when have words been deadly?" Angus asked, peering through the long, drawn-out sentences at him.

"Dad told me about this book he once found in the Little Frog's Bottom library where all the words had been infused with tiny specks of hailstorm. It brought him out in lumps the size of golf balls. So if there're books in here about poisonous fog or venomous lightning bolts, we could be in big trouble!"

Angus quickly flicked a large spidery "sirocco" off his shoulder. He ducked warily under a long, sinewy sentence about fogcicles and froze. Standing directly in front of him, wearing floor-length robes of plain brown, was somebody he'd never seen before. The stranger scowled at Angus with small, beady eyes, his forehead creased.

"Identify yourselves!" he demanded, pointing a crooked finger with a blackened nail at Angus.

"Er, s-sorry, sir. We—we got lost," Angus said, trying to sound convincing as Dougal and Indigo stopped nervously beside him.

"Lost?" The man's face was transformed instantly with a keen, thoughtful expression. "Sir Neville Loxley," he said, pronouncing each word clearly and precisely. "A famous lightning catcher, lost on the Imbur marshes for three days and the first to discover howling, poisonous, and contagious fogs."

"Er." Angus glanced sideways at a puzzled-looking Indigo. "I, um . . ."

He caught the tiny movement from the corner of his eye. The man's robes, billowing around his ankles as if caught in a stiff breeze, had just flickered.

"Hey!" Angus stumbled forward without thinking and prodded the robes with his finger. The figure rippled like a reflection on a smooth pond of clear water. "He's not even real. He's a projectogram, look!"

"Oooh! I know exactly what he is." Dougal rushed over for a closer inspection. "He's a holographic projectogram.

They're just like the holographic histories," he explained when Angus and Indigo stared at him blankly, "only instead of having a storyteller inside a book, these ones are life-size projections. They only ever got to the experimental stage, though," he added. "I think they had a few glitches."

"Like what?" Angus asked, watching as the storyteller scraped at his mossy-looking teeth with his grubby fingernails.

"You couldn't shut them up, for a start. They started following people around like walking encyclopedias, spouting all sorts of useless facts about thunderclouds, Imbur Island, and stuff."

"Imbur Island," the holographic projectogram said as if to prove Dougal right. "An uncharted island lost in a mythical storm, home to the lightning catchers, the ancient Stargazer wood, and the rare crestfallen newt."

"If he's a walking encyclopedia, maybe we should ask him about the weather vortex," Indigo suggested, looking uncertain.

Dougal shrugged. "It's worth a try. According to the tag on his robes, his name's Hartley Windspear."

"Excuse me, Mr. Windspear, sir," Indigo said, her face suddenly glowing with embarrassment, "but can you tell us anything about the weather vortex that's swirling around Castle Dankhart?"

The storyteller stared back at her, his robes still billowing in a holographic breeze, but he remained silent.

"What about weather explosions, then?" Dougal suggested. "Like the one that happened at Perilous in 1777?"

"Perilous," the projectogram said suddenly, making all three of them jump. "A word meaning 'dangerous'; an Exploratorium of Violent Weather and Vicious Storms on the Isle of Imbur; and the only suitable word to describe a famous chicken and chuckleberry pie baked by the Frog's Bottom Bakery."

"Er, I think Hartley Windspear might have been in the Inner Sanctum by himself for a bit too long," Angus said as the storyteller stopped abruptly and began swatting at imaginary flies above his head. "Plus, this is getting us nowhere." He checked his weather watch. It had now been fifteen minutes since he'd stolen Catcher Coriolis's keys. If the keeper of the crypt chose to have a dessert, they might have an extra fifteen minutes. But if he'd already discovered his keys were missing, if he was already on his way back up to the Inner Sanctum with extra lightning catchers . . .

"Come on," he said, leading the way quickly past the projectogram. "We've got to search this place quickly!"

They zigzagged their way past some giant sheets of rippled glass that appeared to contain nothing but a few squashed letters. There were singing weather forecasts, moldy archives full of secret documents that had been written entirely in ancient weather symbols, and a pile of backward-ticking clocks.

Finally, at the far end of the room Angus caught sight of the buckets. He ran the last few steps . . . and felt his spirits plunge. They'd found nothing but the flotsam and jetsam. He'd been desperately hoping there would be *something* else, some crucial information about the storm vortex perhaps.

"We might just as well look through this stuff while we're here," Dougal said, rolling up his sleeves.

"Look for anything odd or out of place or anything that doesn't make sense," Indigo said.

"None of this makes any sense," Dougal said, lifting a

pencil sharpener from the top of a debris pile.

Angus dived straight into the first bucket, pulling out lengths of frayed rope, fragments of seashells, hairnets, and rusty bolts. Indigo took the next bucket, tipped the contents out onto the floor, and sorted through it, grouping everything in piles. There were long splinters of blue glass, a whole heap of silver starlings, and some useless scraps of newspaper.

"This stuff is disgusting," Dougal said, trying to untangle a strip of stinking seaweed from a pair of holey socks.

Angus rummaged through the bizarre collection of storm-battered objects, frantically hoping that a knotted length of elastic or a clump of wiry quills would somehow give them the vital clue they needed, that everything would suddenly fall into place and they would miraculously understand exactly what was going on under the cloud at Castle Dankhart. But as he finally reached the bottom of the bucket, his optimism began to fade once again.

"Have either of you found anything yet?" he asked Dougal and Indigo, already knowing what the answer would be.

"Not unless you think an old toilet seat can solve this mystery," Dougal said, holding up the ancient-looking object. "I don't even want to know how it ended up in a storm vortex."

"Vortex," a voice suddenly whispered behind them. "A swirling eddy or whirlwind with a cavity at the center."

Angus jerked around on his knees. Hartley Windspear had followed them silently to the far end of the room and was now watching them with interest.

"Oi! Clear off!" Dougal said, chucking an old shoe at him. "You're starting to give me the creeps!"

The projectogram glared at Dougal for several seconds, then turned and drifted off with an indignant sniff.

There was a sudden scraping noise from behind them.

"What was that?" Indigo shot to her feet.

"I dunno, but I think we'd better get out of here before Catcher Coriolis comes looking for his keys," Angus said, feeling the whole adventure had been a total waste of time.

They scooped up the rest of the storm debris and chucked it back into the buckets. Then they hurried through the room toward the door. Angus checked his weather watch anxiously and felt his insides squirm. It had now been thirty-five minutes since they'd picked up the keys.

"We've got to get out of here quickly!" he said, breaking into a sprint.

They had almost made it back through the strange melting words when the worst happened. The door up ahead opened, and several familiar figures entered the room. Angus and Dougal scuttled behind the nearest tottering pile of books. Indigo dived behind another, crouching low as voices drifted toward them.

". . . positive I had the keys when I left the crypt," Catcher Coriolis said, shaking his head. "I came in here to return a book I've been reading about crypt fungus, and then I went straight down to the kitchens."

"Catcher Sparks is already conducting a thorough search of the kitchens." Rogwood stepped through the door, joining the conversation.

"Very well." Principal Dark-Angel appeared beside him. "For the time being at least, it seems we have no idea if the keys have been lost or stolen.We must search the entire Inner Sanctum for intruders and double-check that the crypt hasn't been broken into again."

"Might I suggest that we also find Mr. Crevice?"

Rogwood said. "If the keys have been stolen, he would seem to be the most likely suspect."

"That weasel's caused more trouble than he's worth." Gudgeon emerged behind them. "He's had his eye on those dragon scales right from the start. If I ever catch him trying to sell a pricey new bunion cure in that scruffy shop of his . . ."

Dark-Angel sighed. "It appears Valentine has failed to keep the bone merchant out of mischief. I will have to expel Mr. Crevice from Perilous immediately."

Angus turned to stare at Indigo, hoping the lightning catchers were about to leave, and almost passed out cold. The holographic projectogram, attracted by the sound of new voices, had come to see what all the fuss was about. He was now hovering directly behind them with a curious look on his face. Angus nudged Dougal silently in the ribs and jerked his head in Hartley Windspear's direction.

Dougal's face blanched. "That's it! We're dead!" he whispered. "Dark-Angel will have us thrown off the island when she finds us skulking about in here with those keys!"

"Psst!" Angus said as quietly as he could, trying to attract the projectogram's attention. "Please! Mr. Windspear, you're going to get us into serious trouble!"

"Oi! Move it! Clear off! Get lost!" Dougal added, trying to shoo him away without knocking over the stack of books they were hiding behind. But the projectogram stood his ground, folding his arms across his chest.

"Listen, we promise to come back and ask you loads of questions if you just go and stand somewhere else," Angus said, hoping the projectogram couldn't detect a lie when he heard one. He had no intention of ever breaking into the Inner Sanctum again.

The projectogram hesitated for a second, then started to walk away from Angus and Dougal, but it was already too late.

"Ah, perhaps Hartley Windspear can give us some answers." Dark-Angel had spotted the holographic projectogram and was walking over to meet him. "Good evening, Hartley. Tell me, has anyone apart from Catcher Coriolis entered this room this evening?"

The projectogram stared at her benignly, his robes still wafting in the nonexistent breeze.

"Has anyone asked you any questions about the crypt, the storm prophet tombs, or fire dragon scales?"

"Fire dragon scales." The projectogram latched onto the phrase, suddenly coming to life. "Rumored to boost brainpower, cure dim-wittedness, scurvy—"

"Yes, yes, we know all about those particular rumors, thank you," Dark-Angel said, interrupting him. "We are far more interested in any other visitors you may have had this evening."

Angus held his breath, the agonizing seconds ticked by, but the projectogram kept his silence.

"We're wasting our time, Delphinia." The keeper of the crypt appeared at her elbow, wiping his runny nose on a handkerchief. "If Mr. Crevice has stolen my keys, he'd hardly waste his time in this part of the Inner Sanctum. We must inspect the storm prophet tombs immediately for any signs of damage."

"Rufus is right," Rogwood said, already turning toward the door. "We can question Hartley later if necessary. I would also suggest a thorough search of the—"

The door closed suddenly, cutting off their conversation. Angus waited for several seconds to make sure that none of the lightning catchers were coming back; then he scrambled onto his feet.

"Thanks for not giving us away!" he called over his shoulder, giving the projectogram a friendly wave as they sprinted past.

"Fire dragon scales," the projectogram repeated, clearly trying to hold their attention for a few seconds longer, "rumored to boost brainpower, cure dim-wittedness, scurvy, bunions, and pimples."

"Yeah, thanks, we already know about that!" Dougal said.

"Also the subject of a series of top secret experiments conducted in 1777."

Crash!

Angus skidded to a halt, knocking over a small pile of books, as Dougal and Indigo smashed into him from behind.

"What did you just say?" he asked, swiveling around to face the projectogram.

Hartley Windspear pulled himself up to his full height. "Fire dragon scales, the subject of a series of top secret experiments conducted in 1777. Rigorous tests were performed on a number of volunteer lightning catchers to determine if a preparation of powdered fire dragon scales could bestow the skills of a storm prophet on them. Because of some unfortunate side effects, however, including spontaneous drooling, memory loss, and severe bouts of hiccuping, all tests were eventually stopped. No storm prophet skills were noted among the volunteers."

"This is unbelievable!" Dougal said, looking shocked.

"What happened after that?" Angus asked urgently, hoping there was more.

The projectogram paused, and then: "Further experiments were conducted by adding powdered fire dragon scales to lightning storm particles. All experiments were halted, however, following several severe reactions and a large explosion that resulted in the appearance of a spectacular weather vortex. The vortex was declared out of control and raged above the Exploratorium for weeks before it was finally extinguished."

Dougal stared at Hartley Windspear, speechless.

"In conclusion," the projectogram continued importantly, "the lightning catchers noted that fire dragon scales, when combined with lightning storm particles, could produce weather of cataclysmic power. They each signed a declaration, therefore, swearing never to mention the experiments in the kitchens, bathrooms, or communal areas of the Exploratorium."

"That sounds exactly like the declaration we had to sign before entering the storm hollow," Indigo pointed out, stunned.

"They also promised that these lethal experiments would never be repeated, and the fire dragon scales have remained undisturbed in the Perilous crypt ever since."

"Yeah," Angus said, staring at Dougal and Indigo, "until now."

15

THE WEATHER EYE

Angus, Indigo, and Dougal made a mad dash back through the Inner Sanctum before Dark-Angel could return and catch them red-handed. Angus dropped the stolen keys on the floor as soon as they reached the familiar marbled Octagon, hoping that Catcher Coriolis would simply discover them lying there, hoping that Dark-Angel wouldn't have them dusted for fingerprints. They hurried back to the Pigsty, and a night of urgent discussions followed.

"This is so typical," Dougal said, collapsing into one of the armchairs by the fire. "We break into the Inner Sanctum to find out something about the weather vortex and end up discovering loads of secret stuff about fire dragon scales as well."

"I can't believe the early lightning catchers did such dangerous experiments," Indigo said, sitting cross-legged on the floor beside his chair.

"Yeah, what did they *think* was going to happen if they added dragon scales to lightning storm particles?"

"But this doesn't explain anything. We still don't know what's really going on under that weather vortex," Angus said, suddenly realizing it was true. He'd been so convinced that discovering the truth about 1777 would answer all their questions. But if anything, Hartley Windspear's revelations had only confused the issue more. According to the projectogram, the weather vortex had appeared over Perilous only after some highly dangerous experiments involving dragon scales and lightning storm particles. But as no fire dragon scales had yet been stolen from the Perilous crypt—

"It might explain one thing," Dougal said, thinking it through slowly. "What if Dankhart knows about those experiments?"

Indigo pulled her sweater sleeve quickly down over her

bleckles at the mention of her uncle's name.

"What if he found out somehow and now he's getting Crevice and Vellum to steal some dragon scales for him? I mean, if anyone's interested in brewing up his own catastrophic weather, it's Dankhart and his stinking monsoon mongrels."

Angus quickly considered the terrifying possibility that Dougal might be right. If Dankhart carried out his own lethal experiments, if he re-created the calamitous events of 1777 . . .

"Do you think we should we tell someone?" Indigo said, staring at them both anxiously.

"Tell them what?" Dougal asked. "That we stole a bunch of keys from Catcher Coriolis and broke into the Inner Sanctum? Do you want to spend every weekend for the next five years chipping icicles off the snow dome in the Rotundra? Besides, Dark-Angel already knows Crevice is a weasel."

"Yes, but she also thinks Crevice is trying to steal a bunion cure. We could be the only ones who know the truth about 1777. And if Vellum really is helping Crevice, if he's hiding under that coat and breaking into the crypt to steal some dragon scales for my uncle Scabious—"

"But we still haven't got any proof," Angus pointed out. "And we can't just go around accusing Vellum of being in cahoots with Creepy Crevice and Dankhart."

They each stared into the glowing embers of the fire, thinking over the shocking revelations of the evening.

"None of this makes any sense," Dougal said, massaging his temples with his fingers. "Why has Dankhart got a great big cloud of swirling weather hanging over his castle if he hasn't even got his hands on any dragon scales yet? And even if Crevice and Vellum are in it together, how could they get any scales inside Castle Dankhart with that deadly vortex whirling around it?"

Discussion about weather explosions and dragon scales continued long into the night. By the time they went to bed Angus's head ached more than it had on the memorable occasion when he'd been hit by a bombardment of slushy snowballs.

He woke early the following morning feeling even more exhausted. Indigo and Dougal were already sitting at their usual table when he yawned his way up to breakfast a short time later. He grabbed some toast and marmalade, half expecting Dark-Angel to intercept him at any second, demanding to know why he'd stolen keys to the Inner Sanctum and gone riffling through things that didn't concern him. Miraculously, however, none of the lightning catchers eating an early breakfast paid him the slightest attention.

"We've already seen Dark-Angel and Catcher Coriolis," Indigo told him as soon as he sat down. "And neither of them even glanced in our direction."

Angus stared around the room, amazed that nobody else seemed to be aware of their adventures.

"So what do we do now?" Indigo asked. A slice of uneaten toast lay shredded on the plate in front of her. "Do we tell someone about the dragon scale experiments?"

They'd been over and over the same prickly issue dozens of times the night before in the Pigsty without coming up with any realistic answers. They had also discussed Valentine Vellum at length, since they were now convinced he was once again helping Dankhart and the monsoon mongrels with their plans to spread chaos and danger.

"If we could just talk to Gudgeon or Rogwood," Angus

suggested, "maybe we could persuade them to listen to the projectogram."

"Well, we couldn't have picked a worse day to try it," Dougal said.

Angus frowned. "What do you mean?"

"Today is the final winners' demonstration," Dougal said as a stream of lightning cubs entered the kitchens, laughing and joking loudly. "The whole of Perilous is about to descend upon Little Frog's Bottom. We'll be lucky if we can even find Rogwood or Gudgeon. Whatever we're planning to do, it will have to wait until the demonstration is over."

Because it was also a Saturday morning, breakfast took far longer than usual. Jonathon Hake, Violet Quinn, and Georgina Fox joined them at their table, and a lively discussion about the final demonstration followed.

"We've already had shimmer sharks and fearsome fog, so it could be experimental rainstorms next," Jonathon said between large spoonfuls of porridge.

Georgina leaned in across the table, keeping her voice low. "Geronimo Midnight swears he overheard the winners talking about risky lightning cub experiments."

Indigo blushed furiously. Angus turned around in his chair. Germ was laughing and joking with his friends beside the serving tables. He'd been responsible for some of the most outrageous rumors about the winners so far, and Angus hoped there could be no truth in this one either.

After breakfast Angus, Indigo, and Dougal searched the library, the Octagon, and the chilly cloud gardens for any signs of Rogwood or Gudgeon, without success. They peered out across the island, hoping to catch a glimpse of preparations for the last demonstration in Little Frog's Bottom, but a low cloud had descended over the town, and they could see nothing but a few tall chimneys and church spires. They retreated to the warm library instead and spent the rest of the morning trying to avoid Miss Vulpine. Angus made another attempt at cracking his scare-me-not puzzle to pass the time, while Indigo and Dougal flicked aimlessly through the latest copy of the *Weathervane*.

Finally, after a noisy lunch in the kitchens, where excitement levels had once again reached fever pitch, they dressed in coats, woolly hats, and scarves and piled out into the courtyard, onto a packed gravity railway carriage.

"All right, Angus!" Nicholas Grubb waved from the far side of the carriage as it plummeted toward the ground. Angus smiled weakly, clutching his stomach. At the bottom of the tall rock, Catcher Howler shuffled everyone into steam-powered coaches that were already waiting to transport them to Little Frog's Bottom. Half an hour later they arrived in the central square. Angus smiled at Dougal and Indigo. Despite their shocking discoveries in the Inner Sanctum, it was good to be back. The low cloud had now cleared. Cradget's, Brabazon Botanicals, and the Yodeling Yeti café offered tantalizing displays of Imbur buns, colorful flowers, and Grow-Your-Own-Wart kits. The statue of Philip Starling and Edgar Perilous was already casting long shadows across the square as the wintry sun began to dip toward the horizon.

"You will proceed straight to the demonstration tent and stay there until it is time to leave. No wandering off!" Catcher Sparks glared at Clifford Fugg, who was attempting to veer off toward Cradget's. "This is not a shopping expedition. Do I make myself clear, Fugg?"

Angus, Indigo, and Dougal followed a stream of chattering lightning cubs and catchers heading for a large white

tent that had been erected at one end of the square. Inside, seats had been arranged in rows around a raised wooden stage in the middle.

"It's like being inside a circus tent," Dougal said, staring up at the peaked canvas roof above.

Indigo smiled. "Maybe Lettice and Leonard Galipot have formed a flying trapeze act."

"Yeah, or they're planning to juggle with storm globes," Angus said.

The tent was now filling up rapidly. Pixie and Percival Vellum barged past, deliberately elbowing Angus in the ribs. Dougal glared at the twins.

"There's no sign of Valentine Vellum," Indigo said quietly, peering over the heads of the surrounding lightning cubs. "I can't see Rogwood or Gudgeon either."

Angus stared around the rest of the tent. He was just about to give up searching when—

"I don't believe it!" He tugged on Dougal's sleeve excitedly. "Look!" He pointed toward the familiar figure now making his way toward them.

"Uncle Jeremius!" Angus waved. Jeremius greeted him with a bone-crushing hug. He smiled broadly at Dougal and Indigo. "What are you doing here?" Angus asked, feeling immensely relieved that his uncle had returned from whatever mysterious dangers he'd been facing and that he was still in one piece

"I told you I'd return in a few months. It seems I've chosen an interesting day to do it," he said, gazing around the tent. Several lightning catchers waved in their direction.

Jeremius definitely looked thinner, Angus decided, as his uncle turned briefly to speak to Catcher Mint. His chin was covered in a thick growth of straggly beard; his clothes had several new rips and tears.

"But where have you been?" Angus asked as soon as Catcher Mint had moved on. "What have you been doing all this time? Have you heard anything from my mum and dad?"

Jeremius placed a hand on his shoulder. "I'm sorry, Angus. There has been no word in or out of Castle Dankhart for several months now."

Angus nodded. He'd already guessed as much, but it didn't stop his spirits from sinking a notch.

"I'm afraid I can't tell you what I've been doing either," Jeremius continued. "But I hear you three have managed

to stay out of trouble for once. No chasing after monsoon mongrels or iceberg hopping in the Rotundra."

Dougal and Indigo exchanged guilty glances.

"Rogwood tells me your lessons have been going well in the Inner Sanctum, too."

"Er," Angus felt his face redden, wondering if Rogwood had also mentioned the fact that he'd sent some rancid rain chasing after Percival Vellum.

"I do have some news about the weather vortex that you three might be interested to hear," Jeremius said. "According to the latest reports from the weather station, it's continuing to thin out and weaken. The cloud should clear any day now, and we'll know exactly what Dankhart and his monsoon mongrels have been doing."

"We've got something to tell you as well," Angus said, keeping his voice down. "We think it could be important."

At that precise moment, however, Catcher Sparks clapped her hands above her head, calling for attention. Every head turned in her direction.

"The demonstrations will begin in five minutes. If you would all take your seats immediately, please!"

Noise levels increased dramatically as every lightning

catcher and cub began to head toward the seats arranged around the stage.

"Listen, come and find me after the demonstration. We can talk properly then," Jeremius called, already being jostled away from them by the tide. "I'm thinking of asking Principal Dark-Angel if she'll let you three spend the rest of the weekend at Feaver Street with me and Mr. Dewsnap."

"Seriously?" Angus shouted over the moving bodies that now stood between him and his uncle. But Jeremius had already been swallowed up by the crowd.

"This is brilliant," Dougal said, grinning beside him. "I can pick up some spare socks and a few books. With any luck Mrs. Stobbs might bake one of her chicken and ham pies."

"And I've never been to Feaver Street," Indigo said, looking eager to visit.

"Plus we can tell Jeremius what we've just found out from Hartley Windspear," Angus added, suddenly feeling a heavy weight lifting. His mood took a definite upswing.

Jeremius was far more likely than any other lightning catcher to take their worries seriously. And if they could

talk to him properly, away from Perilous . . . It had also been months now since he'd seen any member of his own family. The prospect of a whole weekend at Feaver Street with Jeremius was very appealing.

They found three empty seats behind Violet Quinn, Millicent Nichols, and Georgina Fox. Angus was now looking forward to the demonstration far more than he had been when they'd arrived in the square. A few moments later Principal Dark-Angel appeared onstage to a polite round of applause, and an expectant silence fell.

"Good evening to you all." She began with a weary-looking smile. Angus wondered if she'd been up late into the night dealing with the aftermath of the missing keys. "And so we come to the final demonstration. I have known the Galipots since their early days at Perilous and have admired their work in advanced weather observation for many years. It is my great pleasure, therefore, to introduce the winners of last year's Lightning Catcher of the Year award, Lettice and Leonard Galipot."

There was an enthusiastic round of applause as Principal Dark-Angel left the stage, shaking hands with the two lightning catchers as they passed her on the stairs. A strange contraption was wheeled in from the other side of the stage; it looked like a large unblinking eye sitting on top of a small, square box.

"As the great Edgar Perilous once said, 'Without observation there can be no understanding.'" Leonard Galipot began as soon as the crowd had settled again. "Without observation, we would still be as baffled today by the mysteries of a thundercloud or the power of a tornado as were the early lightning catchers who founded our great Exploratorium here on Imbur."

"He's not going to give us a boring lecture on weather observation, is he?" Dougal whispered.

"Weather observation is still the cornerstone of all work done by every lightning catcher across the globe." Catcher Galipot continued before Angus could answer. "In this modern age, however, we have many instruments and devices to help with such vital work." He pointed to the large eye next to him. "The Galipot portable weather eye is small enough to be taken on virtually any field trip or expedition."

"The weather eye extends all the way up to the cloud base, to storm level," Lettice Galipot said, continuing where her husband left off. "It can rotate through three-hundred and sixty degrees for full panoramic vision. For the purposes of this demonstration, we will project any image seen through the weather eye onto a foldout screen."

The screen was as large as any in a movie theater. Angus shifted in his seat so he could see over the top of Georgina's head more clearly. He was keen to see exactly what the weather eye could do, although he couldn't fight off a slight feeling of disappointment that this demonstration, with its lack of shimmer sharks and fearsome fog, would be nowhere near as dangerous or exciting as the others.

"The weather eye is the perfect instant, mobile weather assessment device for lightning catchers faced with an unexpected storm or emerging weather catastrophe." Lettice Galipot continued. There was murmur of excitement from the audience.

"Now, to demonstrate." She fiddled with a button on the side of the box. A hidden mechanism inside it coughed and spluttered into life. It rumbled and shook for several moments, as if preparing for takeoff.

Whoosh!

The weather eye shot up suddenly through a flap in the tent ceiling, on the end of a tall bendy snakelike pole, and disappeared from sight, leaving several members of the audience gasping with shock.

"As you can see, the Galipot weather eye can be deployed anywhere, night or day. It has already been tested extensively in different weather regions across the globe and through all four seasons here on Imbur Island."

A blurry image suddenly appeared on the screen. Leonard Galipot fiddled with a dial, and the picture sharpened. The weather eye had ascended straight through the top of the cloud sitting directly over Little Frog's Bottom, startling a flock of seagulls. Whiffs and puffs of gray haze floated past as the weather eye waited for its next instruction.

"And now, if I rotate the weather eye to the east . . ."

Leonard Galipot bent down, attached a crank handle to the side of the box, and began to wind it in a clockwise direction. The image on the screen blurred again as the weather eye turned slowly toward the sea. Waves sparkled in the distance. A large bank of fog was approaching the island. Before Angus could tell what kind it was, the weather eye was on the move again, this time facing back toward Perilous, and the familiar building came into focus. It was an impressive sight.

"Each weather eye comes with an optical zoom that allows you to concentrate on any trouble spots."

The lens whizzed in rapidly, revealing a very close-up view of the Exploratorium. Angus squinted at the screen. They were now looking straight through one of the windows in the library, where someone sat hunched over a study table.

"Oh, no! It's Germ!" Indigo blushed beside Angus.

Angus grinned, nudging Dougal. Germ had fallen asleep over his workbooks, his hair sticking up at odd angles, a thin trickle of drool collecting on his chin.

"He's going to be mortified when he finds out everyone's been watching him slobber all over the desk," Dougal said over the sound of sniggering.

Indigo sank down further in her seat, covering her face with her hands. Angus decided that the only thing that would truly upset Germ was the fact that he'd slept through his glorious moment of fame.

Thankfully, the demonstrator turned the lens farther

round and focused in on another window in the lightning catchers' living quarters instead. Catcher Killigrew, who had clearly decided not to attend the event, was busy ironing a voluminous pair of spotted underpants. He then proceeded to trim the long hairs protruding from his nostrils with a small pair of clippers.

"Urgh!" Dougal cringed away from the unsavory sight as the demonstrator hurriedly moved the weather eye sixty degrees to the west.

"Yes, well, I think everyone gets the gist of things. When faced with more challenging terrain," Leonard Galipot said, quickly trying to regain the interest of the audience, most of whom were still snickering at the sight of Catcher Killigrew's underpants, "the weather eye can be extended to even greater heights."

He pushed a button on the side, and the contraption rocked to and fro alarmingly. When the image settled a moment later, a sharp intake of breath swept around the entire audience. The weather eye was now swaying in a high wind, looking down over a range of snowcapped mountains. In the distance, clearly visible for the first time, was the swirling weather vortex over Castle Dankhart.

Angus stared at the disturbing image on the screen, holding his breath. Indigo, horror-struck, was clutching her face with her fingertips.

"Since our arrival at Perilous we have been using the weather eye to help monitor the weather vortex," Lettice Galipot explained.

It was the first time most of the audience had seen a live view of the castle, at storm level or otherwise, even if it was completely obscured by the vortex. Several lightning catchers stood up for a better look. Millicent Nichols fainted in the row in front of them and had to be carried out of the tent for some air. Angus felt his stomach churn. Somewhere beneath the seething weather vortex, his mum and dad were trapped. It was exactly like the weather sample he and Indigo had seen in the Dankhart archive, only a thousand times bigger and far more turbulent than any photograph or description had ever managed to convey. Nor did it seem to be thinning out; if anything, the cloud looked much more violent than the last pictures in the *Weathervane*. Angus glanced at Dark-Angel, Rogwood, Gudgeon, and Jeremius, who were now leaning toward one another in urgent discussions. This was not what they'd been expecting to see.

"If we zoom in, we can observe the cloud in more detail," Lettice Galipot said.

"I can see some of the deadly seven!" Angus stared at great swaths of ice-diamond spores, scarlet sleeping snow, and rancid rain.

"I think I'm going to be sick!" Dougal hissed, shielding his eyes from the lightning bolts, giant hailstones, and countless bits of flying debris.

BOOOOOOOOM!

The ground suddenly trembled beneath their seats.

"What's happening now?" Dougal shot to his feet in a panic.

The whole audience suddenly seemed to be standing; some were clambering out of their seats, and heading for the exit.

"Look!" Angus pointed at the large screen, even brighter and more visible now in the dimming light of the late afternoon. It showed a startling new image from the weather eye.

The weather vortex had doubled in size. The enormous

turbulent cloud, which now whirled with the energy of a thousand violent storms, seemed to be grower bigger by the second.

BOOOOOOOOM!

Another explosion rocked the tent.

"Why does it keep doing that?" Indigo yelled above the screams of panic breaking out all around them.

"I think—I think the weather vortex is finally dispersing!" Dougal explained, his glasses slipping down to the end of his nose in surprise. "It's releasing all the energy and the most dangerous weather that's been tied up at the inner core for months!"

BOOOOOOOOM!

"We've got to get out of this tent now!" Dougal warned as the ground shook forcefully for a third time. "If that cloud gets blown over Little Frog's Bottom, we've had it!"

"No! Wait!"

Angus called Dougal back. Indigo stopped dead in her tracks, and all three of them stared at the confusing images now flitting across the large screen. The cloud had finally been blown clear of the castle by the last explosion. For the first time they could see exactly what was hidden underneath it. There were no signs of any catastrophic weather accidents. The castle stood intact, as tall, dark, and spooky as they'd seen it in the storm hollow.

Gudgeon had been right all along. Dankhart had been using the weather vortex to hide something so monstrous, so huge that it filled the screen in front of them. Angus blinked at the startling image in horror.

"Dankhart's built a lightning tower!"

16

MURDEROUS STINGING FOG

The lightning tower, a giant metal pyramid with an eerie skeletal heart, soared above the dark castle. It glistened and sparkled, drenched in rain and melting snowflakes from the weather vortex. The tower was monstrous, far bigger than the ones Angus had seen with his own eyes through the retrospectacles in London.

"Dankhart's been fooling everyone!" he said, a shiver of understanding shaking him down to the bone. "I should have realized when I saw the towers through the retrospectacles, when I read Edwin Larkspur's name in the *Weathervane*. I bet that's where Dankhart got the idea, from the lightning tower remains!" He stared at Dougal and Indigo, trying to explain. "Edgar Perilous and Philip Starling helped build the towers so they could capture lightning and use it for the good of all humankind. But Dankhart's going to turn it into a weapon!"

"And if you add fire dragon scales to lightning storm particles . . ." Indigo added, understanding instantly.

Dougal turned as pale as a stinging fog. Angus remembered Hartley Windspear's chilling words in the Inner Sanctum: "The lightning catchers noted that fire dragon scales, when combined with lightning storm particles, could produce weather of cataclysmic power."

"It was Dankhart all along. Crevice never wanted those dragon scales for a bunion cure, and with Valentine Vellum's help, Dankhart's going to create his own catastrophic weather!"

"Don't just stand there gawping, you three!" Gudgeon jumped down from the stage and stepped over the emptying rows of chairs until he reached them. "That storm's about to break, and Principal Dark-Angel's ordered an immediate evacuation to Brabazon Botanicals, so shift it!"

"But the crypt!" Angus blurted out, refusing to move.

He had to be sure; he had to know that the storm prophet coffins were still intact, the dragon scales safe. "Has anything happened in the crypt?"

Gudgeon frowned. "I should have guessed you three would already know about that. Someone broke into one of the storm prophet tombs early this morning and stole some fire dragon scales."

Angus glanced sideways at Dougal and Indigo, his worst fears suddenly confirmed.

"Catcher Coriolis raised the alarm, but it was already too late, and this is not the time or the place to be having discussions about the crypt!" Gudgeon added, staring up at the tent ceiling, which was shaking wildly in the wind. "I won't tell you three again. You'd better shift it to Brabazon Botanicals before I carry you there myself!"

He turned away from them abruptly and marched over to shout at some dithering lightning cubs.

They ran, quickly joining a large group of fleeing third, fourth, and fifth years being herded toward the exit closest to Brabazon Botanicals by Catcher Sparks.

"Move along there, quickly now!" she shouted. "And stop pinching Croxley on the arm, Twill!"

Angus tried to turn his head to see who was elbowing him in the shoulder blades and almost choked. Disappearing across the deserted stage, which was now behind them, he was positive he'd just caught a brief glimpse of a lone figure in a long black coat. He ducked under Twill's armpit, trying to get a better look, but the stranger had already vanished.

"The stranger in the coat!" he whispered urgently in Dougal's ear. "I think he's heading for the far side of the tent." He tried to point, accidentally poking a third-year girl in the eye. "Sorry!"

"But what can we do?" Dougal said.

"Find out if we were right about Vellum, Crevice, and those dragon scales, for a start. If they were stolen first thing this morning, I bet Vellum's on his way to deliver them to the bone merchant right now!"

"But nobody will believe us," Indigo said. "Valentine Vellum's a senior lightning catcher. We can't just accuse him of stealing something so valuable."

"They might believe a photo," Dougal said, dragging the spy pen out of his pocket to show them.

Angus stared at his friend. "Dougal, that's genius!"

Indigo nodded. "All we've got to do now is catch Vellum in the act!"

"But what about the weather vortex?" Dougal scowled up at the canvas above their heads. The sky outside was clearly darkening, causing light levels inside the tent to drop dramatically. "We can't just go skipping off into the night with that thing threatening to drop the entire deadly seven on our heads."

Angus glanced with some difficulty at his weather watch, which was now flashing several desperate warnings at him. It would be very close. If they got caught out in the vicious weather, they could be injured, knocked unconscious, or worse.

"We'll have to do it quickly. If we can just prove Vellum's in cahoots with Crevice and Indigo's dear old uncle Scabby . . ."

They twisted around with some difficulty.

"Watch where you're treading, McFangus! That was my foot!" Edmund Croxley complained, glaring down at him.

"Sorry!"

"Ow!"

"Sorry!"

They pushed against the fleeing tide, being knocked and buffeted, pushed and dragged, and for several minutes it was impossible to make any headway.

"McFangus! Midnight! Dewsnap!" An arm shot out from a tight knot of lightning cubs, grabbing Angus by the elbow. "You're heading in the wrong direction," Catcher Sparks said, emerging from the crowd. "You will turn around and go straight to Brabazon Botanicals with the rest of the lightning cubs and do exactly as your uncle Jeremius instructs."

"But, miss—" Angus began.

"No buts, McFangus, and no diversions either. Do I make myself clear?"

She went hurtling off two seconds later to stop three hysterical first years who were attempting to flee through a hole in the tent.

"Nobody's going to listen to us," Indigo said, looking determined. "We've got to see where Vellum's going."

Indigo led the way, breaking through a tiny gap in the crowd, and raced for the exit on the far side of the tent. Outside, the square had grown eerily dark. The weather vortex was advancing across the sky toward Little Frog's

Bottom at a frightening pace. Angus gulped. It had already started to unravel into great long rolls of blackened cloud. It looked a hundred times more deadly than it had on the screen inside the tent.

He swiftly checked his weather watch, which had gone into meltdown and was warning him to take cover, pull on his rubber boots, and flee the island all at the same time.

"We haven't got much time," he said, scanning the square for any signs of life, hoping they hadn't already lost Vellum. He saw a flicker of movement.

"Over there!" A solitary figure was hurrying toward the far side of the square. They ran across the cobbles, keeping out of sight in the deep shadows as they raced past the fishmonger's, Noggins (the hat shop), and the Yodeling Yeti café. All the cheerful displays and colorful awnings that had greeted their arrival had been hastily dragged inside. The shops now looked deserted and unfriendly in the growing gloom, with shutters drawn across the windows. The statue loomed ahead in the darkness, Starling and Perilous watching the horizon as if they, too, were waiting for the deadly storm to break.

CRASH!

Angus flinched as a long streak of lightning struck out, illuminating ghastly bruiselike greens and yellows hidden deep within the clouds. The edge of the weather vortex had finally reached Little Frog's Bottom. It was the most frightening storm he'd ever seen, worse than the one he'd witnessed through the retrospectacles as it destroyed London. Its tar-black edges hovered with menace.

"We're never going to make it!" Dougal yelled above a sudden howl of angry wind. "We've got to get inside now!"

"We could take shelter inside Cradget's!" Indigo pointed to the puzzle shop as it appeared up ahead.

Angus hammered on the door with his fists, no longer bothering to keep his voice down, hoping that someone would hear him and come to the rescue.

"It's no use. The place looks deserted." He stepped back and stared up at the shuttered windows.

"The statue! Head for the statue!" Indigo was already running across the cobbles toward it. But the weather was moving much faster than their legs could carry them. There was an infinitesimal moment of calm; then:

BOOOOMMMM!

Giant hailstones exploded through every inch of air around them. Angus was instantly knocked off his feet, his knees scraping against the cobbles. Fish, snails, splinters of wood, a thick soup of raging weather descended upon the square with a ferocious howl. He scrambled to his feet, shielding his face from great gusts of razor rain that sliced at his clothes and slashed through his shoes as if they were made of paper. Something grabbed his arm. It pulled him forcefully across the cobbles, dodging to the left as a nasty squall of scarlet sleeping snow swept past.

Bang!

He tumbled through a small door and fell to his knees again.

Bang!

The noise of the storm subsided abruptly as the door slammed shut, rattling violently on its hinges. Dougal, soaked to the skin, was bent double beside him. Indigo had guided them both to the safety of the statue.

"Come on!" She led the way up a long spiral staircase to the inside of Philip Starling's head, where windows looked out over every part of the square.

"I can't see anything except foggy hailstones, giant

electrified snowflakes, and that horrible rancid rain!" Dougal said, racing over to Philip Starling's nearest nostril, where another window had been placed.

Angus stared at the deadly weather battering the statue. The rest of the square had disappeared beneath sheets of raging weather. The storm made a dreadful noise, howling, pounding, and snatching at the windows. There was another sound, too, closer, inside the statue. Angus swung around. An open window was banging against its catch.

"Shut that window before the weather gets inside!" He raced across the head to help Indigo, but it was already too late. Long fingers of murderous mist had crept inside. The mist advanced swiftly, grabbing Dougal and bundling him up tightly. Angus swerved to the left, trying to dodge the mist before it could trap him, too, and failed.

"This stuff doesn't feel the same as the mist in the storm hollow!" Angus said, struggling against the tight coils, which had already started to pull in against his rib cage.

"That's because it's combined itself with that stupid stinging fog that Catcher Hornbuckle discovered on the Imbur marshes," Dougal spluttered, barely keeping his head above the foggy curls. "It's murderous stinging fog now!"

"What! How can you tell?"

His question was answered a second later as the murderous stinging fog delivered a sharp stab of pain to the side of his neck.

"Ow!" The fog had a tight grip on him now and was refusing to let go no matter how hard he wiggled his shoulders from side to side. "What's wrong with this stuff? Why won't it give way?"

He could feel it slowly squeezing the air out of his lungs, stinging his arms, face, and legs, paralyzing him with excruciating pain. The fire dragon stirred angrily inside his chest. It was desperate to burst free and help him escape, but something was dreadfully wrong. The stinging fog was pulling in with an iron grip, squeezing the last gasps from his body, the last struggle from his limbs. He twitched and jerked, purple stars now bursting before his eyes as he tried to drag some extra air into his shrinking lungs, but it was impossible to breathe. The room slipped sideways as he fell to the floor. The fog quickly engulfed every part of his body, and a white vapor descended. The battle was almost over.

"Angus?" A shrill voice forced its way through the fog

in his brain. Indigo was leaning over him, a terrified look on her face. "Angus! Are you all right?"

"Of course he isn't! Some mad, murderous, stinging fog has just tried to squeeze him to death. He'll probably never be the same again!"

Angus sat bolt upright, coughing, trying to reinflate his squashed lungs. The inside of Philip Starling's head swam before his eyes. "W-what happened?"

"All the mist suddenly shot across the room and wrapped itself around your body. It was awful!" Indigo told him, looking shaken. "Dougal tore it to shreds with his fingers, and we managed to pull you free."

"Then Indigo soaked up the last of the fog in her sweater and squeezed it out the window before it could start attacking us again," Dougal explained.

"But we thought it was too late!" Indigo added.

"Honestly, we were both convinced you'd had it," Dougal said, sounding shocked by his own bravery.

"Thanks!" Angus took another deep gasp of air, feeling immensely grateful. It was not the first time his friends had saved him from certain injury or worse. "I definitely owe you one for that."

"You owe me more than one." Dougal smiled. "I've never done anything so courageous in my life! I'm definitely sticking to books from now on; *most* of those won't try to squeeze you to death."

They helped Angus back onto his feet as soon as Philip Starling's head stopped spinning around him.

"The weather's getting worse every minute," Indigo said, darting over to one of the windows and gazing at the raging storm outside. Several small toads shot past the window as if to prove the point. "The longer we stay here, the less chance there is of our catching Vellum with Crevice and the dragon scales."

"Isn't the bone merchant's close to this statue?" Angus pressed his nose to the cold glass, wondering if he was even staring in the right direction. "Maybe if we just made a run for it . . ."

There was nothing else for it. They raced back down the stairs and out through the door, where they were instantly hit by another shower of razor rain. Great gusts of tumblewind knocked Angus off his feet and sent him toppling head over heels, carrying him straight toward the bone merchant's. He smashed into a door.

"Ooof!"

Indigo grabbed the handle, and they toppled inside. It took all three of them just to close the door against the fierce winds that were trying to force their way into the shop. Angus collapsed in a heap, no longer caring if they ran straight into Creepy Crevice and a whole gaggle of bone merchants intent on instant mummification.

He brushed some fish scales off his coat and got slowly to his feet. Razor rain scratched at the windows, making horrible screeching noises that set his teeth on edge. He turned away from it to face the labyrinth of shelves and display cabinets covered in thick dust and cobwebs.

"Maybe we're too late," Dougal whispered as Indigo shook sand and seashells out of her wet hair. "Vellum probably scarpered ages ago."

But Angus had to be sure.

"Come on," he said quietly, walking straight past the ugly collection of animal skull table lamps that Dougal had stopped to stare at the last time they'd entered the bone merchant's.

The sound of the weather slowly faded as they moved farther into the shop. They crept past the ornamental

cows'-rib spoons and the gallery of dangling anatomical skeletons. Angus stared straight ahead, determined not to look into the empty eye sockets or accidentally brush the bony knuckles with any part of his body. There was a sudden clatter from behind.

"Shh! Crevice will hear us," Angus hissed, swinging around to find out what Dougal had tripped over this time. Dougal, however, had crashed to the floor, where he now lay snoring gently.

"I don't believe it. He's been hit by some scarlet sleeping snow!" Indigo knelt down to check his breathing. There were several scarlet drops of water on Dougal's coat. "There must have been some stray flakes in the tumblewind."

"He could be asleep for hours. We can't just leave him here," Angus said, staring around the dusty shelves anxiously.

They dragged him carefully into a sheltered nook between two large display cabinets and propped him up against a wall at the back.

"Don't forget his spy camera," Indigo said as Angus riffled quickly through his friend's pockets. "We've got to get some proof that Valentine Vellum has been helping Crevice."

They crept between shelves stacked high with jars full of powdered bone. It wasn't until they reached the end of an eerie alley lined with scrawny-looking rats and weasel bones that they heard the faint sound of voices talking.

Angus pulled Indigo quickly behind a familiar shark's skeleton and peered through a gap in the rib cage. The withered bone merchant was leaning across the shop counter, talking to a figure in a long black coat.

"You took the dragon scales from the tomb of Moray McFangus as I instructed?"

Angus flinched as Creepy Crevice spoke the name of his ancestor, and he felt a sudden flare of anger.

"I took more than enough and at great personal risk." The stranger spoke in nothing more than a whisper, placing a small leather pouch on the counter. "If I had been discovered in the crypt, if Catcher Coriolis had seen my face . . . I trust Dankhart will stick to his end of the bargain?"

"I will pass the scales onto Scabious as soon as possible, and you will hear from him directly."

"But he assured me I would have what I asked for as soon as I—"

"Your bargaining does not concern me," Crevice said, stuffing the pouch into his pocket. "Our business here is complete. You should leave before the cloud clears and you are seen by one of your lightning catcher friends. Imagine being caught coming out of my shop," he said with a sneer in his voice, "after all the trouble I've caused in the Perilous crypt."

The stranger hesitated, clearly wanting to say more. But Crevice had already turned away. He slipped into the office behind his counter and closed the door with a snap.

As the figure turned to leave, Angus grabbed the spy camera from his pocket and gripped it tightly. Now was the moment to prove once and for all that Valentine Vellum was a traitor, that he was in it up to his neck with Dankhart and the monsoon mongrels, that he had betrayed Perilous, the lightning catchers, and every weather oath he'd ever taken, for his own personal gain.

He saw the face beneath the hood for a fraction of a second as the figure hurried toward the door. He recognized it instantly; he'd seen the same steely features hundreds of times before within the stone walls of Perilous, but they did not belong to Valentine Vellum.

Angus sank back onto his heels, accidentally dropping the spy camera in surprise. He fumbled around his feet, frantically trying to scoop it up again, but it was already too late. He turned and stared at Indigo in a state of advanced shock.

The thief from the crypt was Principal Delphinia Dark-Angel.

17

A STORM OF
ANCIENT FLAMES

"**D**ark-Angel?" Angus finally said, waiting until he heard the door shut behind the principal as she hurried out of the shop. "It was Dark-Angel? She's the one who's been stealing fire dragon scales?"

Indigo shook her head in disbelief. "But she's the principal of Perilous, the most important lightning catcher on the planet! How could she do this to us?"

Angus swallowed hard. He'd never seen eye to eye with Dark-Angel. There had been times when he'd had serious doubts about her actions. But he'd never believed her capable of such a devastating betrayal.

"What are we going to do?" Indigo whispered.

"Nobody's going to believe a word of it."

Indigo was right. How would they ever convince anyone else? Angus could hardly believe it himself. In the shock of the moment he'd also failed to take a photo with Dougal's spy camera, to capture Dark-Angel's treachery for all to see.

"We've to get out of here and find Jeremius," Angus said. Jeremius was the only person who was likely to believe them without evidence.

He peered through the shark's rib cage. Crevice showed no signs of emerging from his office.

"Come on!" They crept quietly back through the dusty shelves, past the large jars of powdered bone and dangling skeletons, being careful not to make any noise that would bring Crevice hurrying out to investigate. Again and again the image of Dark-Angel's face flashed before Angus's eyes. He'd been so convinced it was Valentine Vellum hiding beneath the coat that he'd never even considered it could be another lightning catcher, someone who was supposed to be above suspicion, someone who was supposed to be totally trustworthy.

He hurried around the edge of a large display cabinet,

still reeling with shock, and collided with something solid.

Crash!

A tall figure in a long green coat loomed over them. Angus recognized the goatee and shoulder-length hair immediately and felt his spirits plummet. Somehow, they'd just walked straight into Dankhart's chief monsoon mongrel, Adrik Swarfe. But Swarfe was not alone. The man standing beside him was tall and stocky with shaggy brown hair and narrow eyes that gave him the appearance of a ferret. Angus had stared at his picture many times in *The Dankhart Handbook.* His name was Victus Bile.

"Angus, what an unexpected pleasure." Swarfe smiled as if greeting an old friend, but his eyes remained shrewd and calculating. He studied Indigo with interest. "But tell me, what are you and your delightful friend doing in this shop? I assumed you would be attending the fascinating demonstration by the Galipots with the rest of your Exploratorium."

"We—we were sheltering from the weather vortex," Angus said quickly before Indigo could offer a different explanation. "We got separated from the rest of the lightning cubs. The tumblewind . . ."

"Ah, yes, that is a particularly fine weather innovation. I must congratulate you, Victus, on your noble work." Swarfe turned to the other monsoon mongrel and bowed his head. "But I'm afraid we cannot stand around here chatting, Angus. We have an important appointment to keep with Mr. Crevice."

Victus Bile grunted. "We'd better move these two away from those windows before someone spots them." He turned Angus around and shoved him back into the maze of shelves from which they'd almost escaped.

"But what do you want with us?" Angus asked.

"You and your friend, Miss Midnight, will be traveling back to Castle Dankhart with Victus and me," Swarfe said. "I have exciting plans for your future, Angus."

Angus swallowed hard. Swarfe's last plan had involved draining his body of blood to make more lightning hearts. He glanced over his shoulder as Victus Bile hurried them away from the shop windows. Outside, great flashes of lightning filled the square. There was no sign of any search party. Nobody would even realize they were missing until it was too late. He met Indigo's petrified gaze for a second and knew they had both reached the same

horrifying conclusion: Their chances of escaping were virtually nonexistent.

"W-what plans for my future?" Angus asked, desperately searching around the maze, hoping to spot an escape route, a hidden door, an open window.

"As I'm sure you've seen by now, Angus, we have been extremely busy at Castle Dankhart over the last few months constructing a magnificent lightning tower," Swarfe said, leading the way through the dusty shelves. "It has not been easy. We could not allow the lightning catchers to see what we were planning. Under my guidance, therefore, the monsoon mongrels had to engineer a catastrophic weather event so violent and powerful that every lightning catcher on the planet would believe one of our more ambitious weather experiments had gone tragically wrong. I devised a series of perfectly timed weather explosions, masking our true intentions, until the lightning tower was ready to be unveiled. And what better place to reveal our most brilliant accomplishment than in front of a group of so-called weather experts who did not see it coming?" Swarfe said with satisfaction. "What a wonderful surprise for those meddling fools at Perilous."

Angus glanced sideways at Indigo, wondering if Dark-Angel had known about the lightning tower. Had she schemed and plotted just to help Dankhart keep his secret as he built the terrible tower under cover of the weather vortex? He swallowed, feeling sick at the thought of it.

He stared over his shoulder as they continued through the dusty shop, hoping to see his uncle charging to the rescue with Gudgeon, Rogwood, and half of Perilous in tow. But the rest of the bone merchant's stood still and deserted. They would have to plan their own escape. Indigo caught his eye, looking frightened but determined. She was not ready to give up yet.

"I don't understand," Angus said, playing for time. "W-why have you built the lightning tower?"

"It is quite simple, Angus. We intend to finish what the very first lightning catchers started," Swarfe explained, as if teaching a group of first year lightning cubs a harmless lesson on weather theory. "We will use the tower to capture the raw power of lightning in its natural state and then to generate storms of untold force. As I'm sure you already know, pure lightning is far more potent than anything we can produce artificially in a Lightnarium because of intangible elements from the earth and air that it contains."

Angus shivered again, wondering if Valentine Vellum had also played a part in the elaborate plot.

"But this is not just about capturing lightning bolts, Angus. It's about restoring the balance of power. And with such might we intend to overwhelm the lightning catchers at Perilous and every Exploratorium around the globe. The final piece of the puzzle was getting our hands on fire dragon scales from the tombs of the storm prophets."

"Those scales don't belong to you!" Indigo said bravely.

"Nevertheless, Miss Midnight, they were necessary if our plans were to reach completion."

Angus thrust his hand into his pocket, searching for anything that could cause a distraction, just as Swarfe and Dankhart had done with the weather vortex. All they needed was a few seconds of confusion. His shaking fingers found a crumpled handkerchief. There were several useless candy wrappers lurking at the bottom, but nothing more. He quickly tried the other pocket. His hand closed around the scare-me-not puzzle. He'd been carrying it around for days, and it was now shaking. He shot an urgent sideways glance at Indigo.

"Fire dragon scales contain the very essence of the storm prophet they were taken from." Swarfe continued, oblivious. "In 1777, it was discovered by the early lightning catchers that when the scales were added to lightning storm particles, it greatly intensified the ferocity of that storm. We intend to create a weather event ten times more powerful than anything the early lightning catchers could have imagined. And if we then add the dragon scales to the deadly seven . . ." Swarfe said, looking excited at the prospect. "Well, can you imagine an ice-diamond storm that would envelop the whole Isle of Imbur? Or a scarlet sleeping snow attack that could cover the entire southern half of Britain? You have left me with very little choice, Angus McFangus."

"M-me?"

They had finally reached the shop counter. Angus closed his fingers tightly around the scare-me-not, trying to mask the forceful vibrations now coming from his pocket as it got ready to self-destruct.

"Ah, I see that you are puzzled by my words, Angus," Swarfe said.

"Yes." Angus leaped on the fortunate phrase that Swarfe had chosen. "I'm really *puzzled*!" He stared hard at Indigo, desperately hoping she understood the urgent message he was trying to convey.

"Then let me explain." Swarfe continued. "Scabious and I have sought many other methods to control the weather. Scabious attempted to steal the never-ending storm from the lightning vaults, but he was thwarted by you and your meddling friends. You then thoughtlessly destroyed the lightning heart, a precious Swarfe family heirloom of immense value that would have allowed us to create a whole army of storm prophets. We were forced to think again. That is when my thoughts returned to an archaeologist called Edwin Larkspur and his discovery of the lightning tower remains. I had never considered building my own lightning tower, and yet it suddenly seemed like such a simple solution to our problems."

Ping!

Indigo's head shot around in surprise as she heard the faint sound. Swarfe and Victus Bile, however, noticed nothing.

"I could not have designed the lightning tower entirely

by myself." Swarfe continued. "But naturally Scabious and I have made it bigger and infinitely more powerful than the original."

Ping!

Angus gripped the puzzle tightly, getting ready to seize their one chance of escape.

"It is ironic that the strength of the lightning tower, which defeated Philip Starling and Edgar Perilous in 1666, will now crush the lightning catchers once again."

P-ting! P-ting! P-ting!

Angus ripped the scare-me-not from his pocket and threw it straight at Swarfe.

BANG!

The puzzle ruptured in midair, showering the shocked monsoon mongrels in scorched scraps and slivers.

"Run!" Angus yelled.

Indigo was already streaking ahead of him, putting as much distance between herself and the monsoon mongrels as possible. The effects of the scare-me-not would last for seconds only.

They dodged between the skeletons of rats and weasels. Angus skidded and collided with a huge dinosaur's rib cage. It wobbled precariously, threatening to collapse and imprison them both in a cage of bones. But it gave him a sudden idea.

"Quickly, drag one of those jars off the shelf and smash it!" he shouted as they approached the containers full of powdered bone.

They heaved a jar to the edge of the shelf together and pushed hard. The container shattered behind them, sending great clouds of speckled white into the air like a sudden no-way-out fog.

"Angus!" Indigo had tripped and fallen in the confusion. Angus doubled back and hauled her onto her feet. But Victus Bile, covered in white from head to toe like a heavy-footed ghoul, was already emerging through the haze of dust behind them.

"Come on!" Angus pushed Indigo onward, through the rows of dangling skeletons, hands, knees, and ribs clattering around them with the hollow timbre of a xylophone. Victus Bile was gaining on them fast. The monsoon mongrel dived, grabbed Angus by his left ankle, and brought him down with a painful thump!

"Get off me!"Angus kicked out hard with his other foot,

making contact with the monsoon mongrel's nose. He scrambled to his feet again and crashed through the skeletons, toppling them over like a set of sinister dominoes.

"We're almost there!" Indigo yelled as they hurtled past the animal skull lamps and the door came into view at last.

A thick soup of weather still raged in the cobbled square outside, thrashing against the shop windows with the same vigor and might as before. But if they could just make it back to the statue, if they could take shelter until the storm cleared . . .

Angus skidded to a halt suddenly and grabbed Indigo as she went racing past.

"Wait!" His heart was now pounding inside his chest for a different reason. "Dougal! We've left him behind! We've got to go back!"

Indigo gasped. In the alarm and confusion they'd forgotten to rescue their sleeping friend. But it was already too late. There was a disturbance in the air behind them, the sound of more footsteps.

Victus Bile had caught up with them at last. Blood was dripping from his shattered nose. He was still covered in powdered bone, and he was now carrying a gently snoring Dougal in his arms. Swarfe and Crevice appeared behind him two seconds later, and they had now been joined by a fourth figure.

Indigo took a sudden quivering breath. Angus felt his last hopes of escape evaporate. Scabious Dankhart was striding toward them. A large black diamond glimmered from his eye socket, the deep scars on his face made more terrible by the shadows in the gloom around them.

"Enough of this!" Dankhart snarled. "Get the boy. We need to return to the castle before the whole square is swarming with lightning catchers."

Swarfe grabbed Angus by the arm and wheeled him away from the door before he could make a run for it. Angus felt the fire dragon stir inside his chest. The creature was not prepared to give up yet.

"So this is Etheldra's daughter?" Dankhart was now circling Indigo with interest.

Indigo met her uncle's gaze defiantly, chin held high. In the flesh, the family resemblance was even more striking and showed itself in the length of their necks, the hollows of their cheeks. Indigo quickly pulled her sleeve down over the bleckles on her hand. But Dankhart had already seen what she was trying to conceal. He grabbed her wrist tightly and held it out for everyone to see.

"You bear the mark of the Dankharts?" he said, surprised.

"Get off me!" Indigo squirmed, trying to break free of his grasp.

"Leave her alone!" Angus yelled, struggling against Swarfe's tight grip on his arms. Dankhart ignored him.

"Perhaps you are not quite as unpromising as your disappointing mother after all."

"My mum's a Midnight now. She wants nothing to do with you!"

"That may be true, but Dankhart blood flows through your veins, girl. You cannot escape it no matter how hard you struggle and writhe. It is who you are, and you should be proud." Dankhart released her suddenly and lifted his sleeve to reveal an identical mark on his own hand. Indigo shivered away from it, looking utterly revolted. "You have seen with your own eyes what we Dankharts can achieve. You have looked upon the lightning tower, our most magnificent achievement.

Can the Midnights claim such greatness? I wonder."

"The Midnights are a thousand times better than you'll ever be!" Indigo yelled, all the resentment and anger she'd felt at her uncle's existence suddenly bursting out of every pore. "The Midnights would never make razor rain or tumblewind or kidnap Angus's parents!"

Swarfe chuckled darkly. "Your niece shows some spirit, Scabious. I believe she is truly a Dankhart to the core."

Dankhart nodded in agreement. "I will admit she has more potential than I realized."

Indigo glared at them both with absolute loathing.

"The boy McFangus will also prove useful in the months to come." Dankhart turned to face Angus for the first time.

Angus felt shivers of rage and hatred running through him. Once again Dankhart was the cause of all chaos and destruction, the reason behind the weather vortex, the lightning tower, the continued, heartbreaking absence of his parents, and Indigo's extreme distress. The fire dragon burned against the wall in his chest, yearning to be set free.

"Your time as a lightning cub has come to an end,

Angus," Dankhart said. "You will return with me to Castle Dankhart, where you will train with my finest monsoon mongrels. Your talents as a storm prophet will be allowed to flourish. We will waste no more time with history lessons and crypt tours, and soon there will be more storm prophets for you to develop your skills with. Storm prophets have helped us in the past, and now it is your destiny to continue that fine tradition."

"You're lying!" Angus burst out angrily. "The storm prophets would never help you, and neither will I!"

"But I am confident I can persuade you, Angus, just as I have finally persuaded your parents to part with some valuable lightning catcher secrets. They have been most helpful in the building of the lightning tower, their tongues loosened by their long stretch in the dungeons. They will make fine monsoon mongrels once they have completed their training."

"My mum and dad would never help you! They'd rather die!"

"Perhaps that can be arranged. Crevice," Dankhart said, turning suddenly to the bone merchant, who had been listening to the whole conversation with a satisfied smile,

"I believe it may soon be time to revive one of your treasured family traditions. Mummification will work just as well on two interfering lightning catchers as anyone else. Alabone and Evangeline McFangus will make fine specimens for your shop window, unless their son is willing to help us after all."

Crevice sniggered. Dankhart was pulling on his gloves, getting ready to leave the shop. Tumblewind battered the windows outside, rattling the door violently.

"Indigo will return to the castle with us, naturally. I am anxious to discover if her Dankhart nature extends beyond the bleckles on her hand."

"I won't go!" Indigo jerked her arm away before her uncle could grab it.

The door clattered on its hinges again as a vicious squall of scarlet sleeping snow went whizzing past outside.

"What about the Dewsnap boy?" Victus Bile asked. Dougal's head was now lolling against his shoulder.

"He is of no use to us," Swarfe said without emotion, as if they were discussing the fate of a trash can. "Throw him outside and let the ice-diamond spores have him."

"No!" Angus yelled. But his words were drowned out as the shop door suddenly burst open.

Bang!

A gust of giant exploding icicles raced inside. Swarfe loosened his grip for a fraction of a second. Angus tugged himself free, the fire dragon now raging inside his chest.

"Get the boy and bring my niece!" Dankhart ordered, backing warily away from the violent weather he'd helped create. "We must return to Castle Dankhart!"

But Indigo was far too swift for the monsoon mongrel. She ran speedily for cover, skillfully avoiding his grasp. Swarfe turned and made a desperate lunge toward Angus instead. Angus swerved away from him, out of arm's reach, ducking under a heavy bombardment of deadly exploding icicles.

"Enough!" Dankhart roared, launching himself at Angus in a fury.

But this time Angus stood his ground, fists clenched, eyes closed, concentrating hard. He pictured fire dragons soaring over a storm of ancient flames in the Great Fire of London; he saw rancid rain chasing Percival Vellum across the storm hollow; he thought of Moray McFangus, the Bodfish brothers, and their magnificent fire dragon coffins in the crypt. A scorching fire blazed inside his rib cage.

BANG!

The fire dragon erupted into the bone merchant's, filling the cramped shop with its fiery glow.

"Scabious!" Swarfe cowered as the icicle storm intensified. "What's the boy doing?"

But Dankhart had already turned and fled, leaving his monsoon mongrels to fend for themselves.

"ARGHHHH!" Victus Bile dumped Dougal on the floor and ran, leaving a trail of dusty footprints behind him.

Swarfe followed close behind, but the fire dragon was already soaring in blistering pursuit. It dragged the exploding storm of icicles, driving long shards of ice with each flap of its blazing wings at the fleeing monsoon mongrels. Display cabinets shattered and glass jars smashed, their contents mixing with the storm in a white wall of terror and ice. Angus clung to the vision of the creature, feeling each swoop of his fire dragon's body rippling through his own, each drive of its immense burning wings until slowly, slowly the sounds of the terrible storm diminished. He felt the presence of the fire dragon fade, second by second, until he was sure it had disappeared once again.

He sank to his knees in the wreckage of the shop.

18

THE FINAL LESSON

"What's going on?" a groggy voice asked. "Why am I lying in a pile of ice splinters?"

Dougal had finally regained consciousness. He sat up, looking pale and shaken, his glasses askew. But there was no time to explain.

Angus helped his friend onto his feet, Indigo led the way through the smashed wreckage of the door, and they ran across the cobbles in the square without looking back. The worst of the weather had finally blown itself out. Cradget's, the statue, and Brabazon Botanicals were beginning to emerge through the much weaker weather that remained. And through it all a familiar figure was now racing toward them.

"Uncle Jeremius!" Angus called.

"What happened? Where have you three been? We've been searching everywhere."

"It's Dankhart!" Angus said quickly, cutting him off. He had to tell Jeremius exactly what they'd just witnessed before word reached Dark-Angel that they'd been found safe and well.

Angus grabbed Jeremius by the sleeve of his coat and pulled him into the shadows.

"What is it? What's wrong?"

Angus quickly described their terrifying ordeal in the bone merchant's and everything Swarfe had told them about the lightning towers. Jeremius listened silently, his face becoming paler by the second, his knuckles balling into tight fists.

"He's going to use the dragon scales," Angus explained. "They're going to mix them with storm particles that they capture with the lightning tower. We saw—we saw Principal Dark-Angel." He finally managed to spit the words out. "She delivered the scales to the bone merchant. She stole them from the crypt of

Moray McFangus and gave them to Dankhart."

Jeremius stared at him in disbelief. "But you must be mistaken. Delphinia and I rarely see eye to eye, but she would never betray—"

"We saw her. It was definitely her," Angus said, remembering her face in the gloom as she hurried out of the creepy shop. "We saw her talking to Crevice ages ago, too, that day we came into Little Frog's Bottom with you and Mr. Dewsnap; only we didn't know it was her then."

"And you're absolutely sure? You couldn't be mistaken?"

Angus shook his head. "Crevice told her which scales were the best ones to steal. We heard them discussing it. She mentioned something about a special arrangement with Dankhart."

Jeremius ran a hand over his tired face. He turned to stare over his shoulder at the lightning catchers, who were busy organizing a swift retreat back to Perilous now that the worst of the weather had blown itself out. Dark-Angel was having an animated conversation with Catcher Sparks and Gudgeon. She was dressed in her usual leather jerkin. Jeremius stared at her for several seconds and then nodded.

"We can't talk about this now," he said quietly. "Our trip

to Feaver Street will have to wait, I'm afraid. Everyone is being taken back to the Exploratorium. You, Dougal, and Indigo must join the other lightning cubs. Tell no one else about Principal Dark-Angel, understand? Not even Gudgeon. I doubt he'd believe Delphinia is capable of such a dreadful act. If anyone asks you where you've been, don't mention the bone merchant's."

Angus nodded, feeling relieved that Jeremius believed him, that he and his friends would not have to keep such a grave and terrible secret on their own.

"I will talk to Rogwood," Jeremius said, already turned away from him. "We'll come and find you as soon as we return to Perilous."

Their journey back to the Exploratorium in the open-topped coaches was chaotic, with every lightning cub discussing the weather vortex and the dramatic appearance of the lightning tower over Castle Dankhart.

"What if Dankhart's planning to build more lightning towers?" whispered Millicent Nichols, looking panic-stricken.

Jonathon Hake nodded. "What if there's an accident and he sets it on fire?"

"He could sink the whole island if we get a big storm," Nicholas Grubb said loudly over the top of two first years who were arguing about which one of them had spotted the tower first. "He could destroy Little Frog's Bottom, just like the Great Fire of London."

"Don't be ridiculous, Grubb," Catcher Sparks said sternly from the far end of the coach. "Nobody is going to burn anything down."

"I bet that's exactly what they thought in London before it actually happened," Nicholas mumbled under his breath. Edmund Croxley nodded vigorously in agreement.

As soon as they arrived back at Perilous, they were crammed into the gravity railway and then herded swiftly inside the Exploratorium by Catcher Sparks.

"Straight down to the lightning cubs' living quarters now, no dawdling!" she ordered.

Angus and Dougal headed down to the Pigsty, where Indigo joined them only a few minutes later, and they quickly filled Dougal in on everything that he'd slept through in the bone merchant's.

"If I'd known your dear old uncle Scabby was going to make an appearance, I would have stayed in the statue head with the murderous stinging fog!" Dougal said.

Indigo shivered, looking exhausted by the dreadful experience. "Uncle Scabious is ten times worse than I ever imagined! I couldn't believe it when he said he was taking us back to his castle."

Angus still felt sick at the thought of it. They'd had a very narrow escape. If the fire dragon had failed to appear at the last desperate minute, if he'd been unable to control its actions . . .

"I still can't believe Dark-Angel's a traitor," Dougal said, shaking his head sadly. "She must have been planning the whole thing for months, asking Crevice to come in and repair those tombs so he could advise her about which fire dragon scales to steal, sneaking into the Inner Sanctum with her own set of keys."

"And when I caught her in the crypt and Catcher Coriolis marched me up to her office and she asked me all those questions, she was checking to see if she'd got away with it, to see if I'd recognized her," Angus said, suddenly understanding.

"Then she let everyone believe it was Crevice," Indigo added.

They stared into the comforting fire for a few moments without speaking.

"I bet that's why my mum and dad sent the map of the lightning vaults to me," Angus said, thinking aloud. "They must have found out that Dark-Angel couldn't be trusted. They didn't want her getting into the vaults and helping Dankhart steal the never-ending storm."

"She was pretty angry when she found out we'd crept down there by ourselves," Dougal said.

"That's why she sent me home, you mean?"

"But she seemed so relieved when you stopped Swarfe from reviving the lightning heart," Indigo pointed out.

Angus frowned. "Then how do you explain what we've seen tonight?"

"I can't." Indigo shook her head. "It doesn't make any sense."

"Nobody will believe us," Dougal said, thinking it over. "Dark-Angel's the principal. We're just three second-year lightning cubs."

"Jeremius believes us," Indigo said.

"Yeah, but what can he do about it?" Angus said. "If he confronts Dark-Angel and tells her what we've seen, she'll just banish him to an ice shelf in Alaska or somewhere, so he can't cause any trouble."

Indigo frowned. "But we can't just let her get away with it. What if she's planning to help Dankhart with the lightning towers, too?"

"Do you reckon Dark-Angel and Vellum are in it together?" Dougal asked after several seconds of silence. "I mean, none of the other lightning catchers like him, he's always poking his nose into stuff that doesn't concern him, plus he knows everything about Angus's being a storm prophet."

They talked into the small hours of the morning until Dougal finally fell asleep mid-sentence, and they returned to their own rooms. Angus lay staring at the ceiling wide awake, unable to get rid of the image of Dark-Angel's betrayal, of the lightning tower finally revealed, of Dankhart, Swarfe, and Victus Bile plotting to create cataclysmic storms that would defeat every lightning catcher on the planet.

At 4:15 a.m., there was a quiet knock on his door. Angus scrambled out of bed to find Jeremius and Rogwood in the corridor outside.

"Angus, I'm sorry to wake you." There were dark circles under Rogwood's eyes. His voice was barely more than a whisper. "May we come in?"

Jeremius slumped into a chair by the fire. Rogwood remained standing as Angus clambered back under his covers to keep warm.

"Angus, as this might be the only chance your uncle and I have to talk to you in the next few days, we would like you to tell us again exactly what happened this evening," Rogwood said.

Angus hugged his knees to his chest, trying to decide where to start. He told them quickly how they'd followed the figure in the coat across the square, believing it was Valentine Vellum.

"An easy mistake to make," Jeremius said grimly. "I've never met a lightning catcher who looks so much like a criminal."

Angus then described the events in the bone merchant's: how they'd witnessed Dark-Angel handing over the dragon scales to Crevice, the chilling moment when he and Indigo had run straight into Adrik Swarfe and Victus Bile, and the details of Swarfe's plans for the lightning towers and the fire dragon scales.

"Sir, none of the lightning catchers knew about those early experiments in 1777, did they?" he asked Rogwood.

Rogwood shook his head. "I'm afraid I believed the only danger the dragon scales faced was from Mr. Crevice and his desire to obtain a celebrated bunion cure. Had I known what Delphinia was planning . . ." He shook his head again, staring into his beard. "It may well have been Delphinia herself who blacked out all research and reports regarding the events in 1777, covering her tracks so we would not discover her intentions."

It was the sudden appearance of Scabious Dankhart that Angus found the most difficult to describe. He quickly explained about Dankhart's plans to take him and Indigo straight back to the castle and the final spectacular appearance of the fire dragon.

"I think we may need to keep a closer eye on your activities if you, Dougal, and Indigo are ever going to reach your seventh year at this Exploratorium," Jeremius said, looking shocked and pale. "This afternoon's events could have ended very differently, with you and Indigo now trapped inside Castle Dankhart with a band of reckless weather mongrels."

Angus gulped, trying not to think about it.

"I'm afraid Dankhart will now be even more intrigued by your storm prophet skills after seeing you send a storm of exploding icicles chasing after Swarfe, Bile, and Crevice," Rogwood added thoughtfully.

"Sir, Dankhart said something about my parents," Angus said. "He said they were training to become monsoon mongrels."

"I believe Dankhart simply said that to ruffle your feathers, to convince you that he could make anyone bend to his will. I am happy to see he did not succeed."

"It is far more likely that Alabone and Evangeline are doing everything in their power to make his life as difficult as possible, spinning him wild stories, giving him false information," Jeremius reassured him.

When they'd finally exhausted all talk of Dankhart, Swarfe, and their plans for the lightning towers, the conversation returned to Delphinia Dark-Angel.

"I'm afraid we now find ourselves in a very tricky situation." Rogwood paced up and down the room, thinking aloud. "Delphinia is highly respected both here and around the world. Any accusations that she is in league with Scabious Dankhart will be disbelieved at every turn. For the time being at least, the best thing we can do is tell no one and do nothing."

"But, sir—"

Rogwood held up his hand to stop him. "We must not reveal what we know, Angus, before we are ready to act upon it."

"Rogwood and I need time to understand the situation properly, to discover just how far Delphinia's betrayal goes," Jeremius said.

"If she discovers in the meantime that we know of her activities, it will force us into taking action before we are ready and possibly end in disaster. We must be patient."

"But can't you do *anything*?" Angus asked.

"The best thing any of us can do right now is to behave as if Delphinia Dark-Angel were our closest friend and ally, however difficult that may be." Jeremius sighed. "And speaking of Delphinia . . ." He stood up and stretched. His face was more serious than Angus had ever seen it. "She will be wondering where we've got to. I will see you in her office when you have finished, Aramanthus."

Rogwood nodded. Jeremius smiled wearily at Angus and then left the room quietly.

"Angus, I would like us to pay one final visit to the Inner Sanctum," Rogwood said as soon as he'd gone.

"Er, what? Now, sir?" Angus asked.

"Yes. It is an important part of your storm prophet education, Angus, and, given yesterday's events, more vital than ever. And we may not get another chance. I will wait for you at the top of the spiral stairs."

Angus grabbed the same clothes he'd worn the night before, pulled on his shoes, and crept quietly along the corridor, being careful not to wake Dougal. Was Rogwood going to explain more about the dragon scales and the storm particles? Was he going to ask more questions about the appearance of the fire dragon?

He followed Rogwood silently up the marbled steps to the Octagon. Perilous was eerily quiet and deserted.

"For today's lesson, Angus, I must take you to a part of the Inner Sanctum we have not yet visited." Rogwood led him straight into the department and through the door that Angus, Dougal, and Indigo had entered in their search for answers. "This room contains an archive of important information in many different forms," Rogwood explained as he led Angus past the tottering piles of books and under the melting words, which wafted gently around them. He stopped abruptly in front of Hartley Windspear, the holographic projectogram, who was watching them keenly.

Angus swallowed hard, hoping that the projectogram wouldn't reveal the fact that they had already met.

"Good morning, Hartley," Rogwood said politely, as if he were addressing a fellow lightning catcher.

The projectogram stared hard at Angus but said nothing.

"Holographic projectograms were developed may years ago, Angus, as part of the famous holographic history range, but they quickly developed some unfortunate problems," Rogwood explained. Angus tried to look as if he'd never heard this information before.

"They are kept in this particular room to stop them from roaming all over Perilous and making a nuisance of themselves. They are, however, extraordinarily knowledgeable about Perilous and the best source of information for our purposes."

Rogwood turned to the projectogram again. "Hartley, could you please tell us everything you know about

Nathaniel Fitch, Tobias Twinge, and Nicholas Blacktin?"

Angus stared at Rogwood in surprise. This wasn't what he'd been expecting. Fitch, Twinge, and Blacktin were the only storm prophets that Rogwood had told him nothing about so far.

Hartley Windspear drew himself up to his full height, looking set to reveal something big. Angus could feel it quivering in the air, and his heart began to race.

"In the early days of Perilous, after the ravages of the Great Fire, there was much disagreement among the storm prophets over the course their development should take," the projectogram began in a somber voice. "Some of the new storm prophets wished to continue with the dangerous practice of lightning capture. Philip Starling, Edgar Perilous, and the rest of the senior lightning catchers quickly forbade such dangerous experiments, however, and a bitter rift developed. Tensions came to a head when Fitch, Twinge, and Blacktin hatched a terrible plan to unleash the power of the never-ending storm in the lightning vaults, to force Starling and Perilous to acknowledge their power. But the plan went tragically wrong. The storm quickly got out of control and killed Jacob Starling and Fabian Perilous."

Angus stared at the projectogram, the true horror of his words slowing sinking in. "It was the storm prophets? They set the never-ending storm free on purpose?"

Rogwood nodded once but said nothing, allowing the projectogram to continue with his story.

"Fitch, Twinge, and Blacktin quickly fled from Perilous, leaving the remaining storm prophets to contain the deadly storm. But they did not travel far." Hartley Windspear took a deep breath and hung his head sadly before continuing. "They found a refuge for their dreadful talents at Castle Dankhart and were welcomed with open arms. There they were free to follow their most dangerous ambitions and set about their quest to control the weather, to create some of the most deadly and despicable storms known to man. They soon formed themselves into the band of danger-ous weather engineers we know today as the monsoon mongrels."

Angus shook his head in disbelief. "But, sir, it can't be true!"

"I'm afraid there can be no doubt." Rogwood sighed

sadly. "As you have discovered yourself, Angus, the talents of a storm prophet extend well beyond the ability to predict when dangerous weather will strike. Fitch, Twinge, and Blacktin found they could also control and shape the weather, a talent most suited to the ambitions of the Dankharts and the newly formed monsoon mongrels. We have been battling against their weather experiments and terrible innovations ever since. It is one of the reasons the storm prophets are not widely talked about. Everyone knows what can happen when the talent is born into the wrong person. Over the generations, the Dankharts married children of Fitch, Twinge, and Blackfin, so Scabious Dankhart himself is directly descended from those renegade storm prophets and the same talents lie dormant within him."

"Is that why Dankhart could see my fire dragon in the lightning vaults when nobody else could?" Angus asked, suddenly understanding.

Rogwood nodded. "We have known since those early days that any storm prophet could see another's fire dragon. When you asked me at the time, I could not explain it without revealing the full history of the storm prophets. As your talents were still so newly born, it would have been unfair to place such a burden upon your shoulders. But Dankhart has seen your potential from the start and with it the possibility of reviving his own skills. Let me also remind you, Angus, that *most* storm prophets were fine and noble men and women," Rogwood added. "You should be proud to count yourself among them. You have used your own skills in the most desperate of times to save your friends and yourself from certain harm or death. I believe in time your abilities will rival those of the great Moray McFangus himself."

Angus stared down at his shoes, feeling a hot flush of embarrassment burn across his face. "Is that why Principal Dark-Angel wanted to do those tests with Doctor Obsidian, sir, to see if I could control the weather?"

"Delphinia has always been keener than anyone to see how far your talents extend. Sadly it would appear now that her motives have been less than admirable."

"Principal Delphinia Dark-Angel," the holographic pro-jectogram suddenly said, making Angus jump, "senior lightning catcher at the Perilous Exploratorium; head of the global lightning catcher network; chair of the worldwide weather warning committee. Hobbies include gardening and Cradget's crossword puzzles. One known family member, Humphrey Dark-Angel, younger brother."

"Principal Dark-Angel has a brother?" Angus asked, surprised. He'd never heard anyone mention Humphrey Dark-Angel before.

"Sadly Catcher Dark-Angel died some years ago in a tragic accident at Perilous. He was a kind and intelligent man, who is sorely missed to this day by those of us who had the pleasure of working with him. And now I believe we should return to the main Exploratorium before everyone else awakes," Rogwood said, checking his weather watch. "We have some difficult days ahead of us, Angus, and it will not help if we are seen coming out of the Inner Sanctum at such an early hour."

Angus waved at Hartley Windspear as he followed Rogwood back toward the door, wondering what else the projectogram could tell him about the storm prophets.

Over the next few days a flood of new images appeared in the *Weathervane* showing the lightning tower over Castle Dankhart from every possible angle. It was obvious that stormy weather had already started to gather above it.

Catcher Tempest from the London office arrived at Perilous for urgent discussions with Dark-Angel. He was followed by a growing number of experts and senior lightning catchers from around the globe. The gravity railway could be heard, night and day, traveling up and down like a yo-yo. Mrs. Stobbs darted about the Exploratorium with endless trays of tea and biscuits, looking frazzled. Lightning cub duties, however, continued as normal, but Angus, Dougal, and Indigo found it impossible to concentrate on their work in the forecasting department. They spent most of their time instead discussing the shocking revelations delivered by Hartley Windspear.

"I still can't believe the monsoon mongrels were formed by the storm prophets," Indigo said quietly.

Catcher Killigrew had given them a jumbled pile of old weather documents to sort into alphabetical order. Catcher Wrascal still hadn't returned to Perilous.

"All the storm prophets must have died out at Castle Dankhart, too," Angus said, still thinking through everything he'd been told. "That's why Dankhart and Swarfe have been trying to steal never-ending storms, revive lightning hearts, and get their hands on our fire dragon scales."

"Yeah, they must have used up all the dragon scales from their own storm prophet tombs years ago," Dougal said.

Angus was highly tempted to sneak back into the Inner Sanctum to ask Hartley Windspear for more details about Fitch, Twinge, and Blacktin. But another part of him was happier not knowing . . . for now.

To his great surprise, four days after their eventful trip to Little Frog's Bottom, he was summoned up to Dark-Angel's office. He hovered nervously outside the door for several minutes, wondering if she had discovered that he and Indigo had seen her in the bone merchant's. Was he about to walk into the biggest trouble of his life?

He knocked on her door and entered the office with his heart pounding inside his chest. He was extremely relieved to see Rogwood, Gudgeon, and Jeremius had also been called in to see her. Rogwood stood calm and impassive. Jeremius winked from the corner of his eye. Dark-Angel was sitting behind her desk. It was the first time Angus had seen the principal since discovering she was a traitor. She met his stare without the faintest trace of guilt or remorse on her face.

"Angus, I have called you here to tell you what we know about your parents and their situation inside Castle Dankhart," she began, fixing him with a steady gaze.

"Have you heard from them?" Angus asked, instantly forgetting all his other worries. "Are they safe?"

"I'm afraid we've had no word from them directly. But one of our sources inside the castle has sent reliable information that they are safe and sound. Neither Dankhart nor the weather vortex has done anything to harm them."

Angus nodded, feeling immensely relieved. He had feared, after their encounter in the bone merchant's, that Dankhart might take revenge on his parents.

"I realize this has been a difficult few months for you, Angus, with the worry about your parents and your storm prophet lessons in the Inner Sanctum," Dark-Angel said, showing uncharacteristic concern for his well-being. "I hope, however, we can continue with those lessons. Now that you have learned about the storm prophets it is time to consider developing your own skills, under strict supervision, of course."

Angus swallowed hard. Was Dark-Angel simply

following instructions from Dankhart? Was she going to train him up, then hand him over to the monsoon mongrels?

"For the time being, however, you will depart Perilous with everyone else in two days' time at the start of the Christmas holidays."

"C-Christmas?" Angus had almost forgotten. Because of the vortex over Castle Dankhart, there had been no decorations, no carol singing, or any mention of presents.

"Please give my regards to your uncle Max; I'm afraid I've had very little time for writing Christmas cards this year."

"Er," Angus said, wondering how Dark-Angel could be worried about sending cards with such a huge betrayal hanging around her neck.

Despite news that the Christmas holidays were fast approaching, the atmosphere in the kitchens and living quarters remained subdued. Every discussion still centered on the events in Little Frog's Bottom and whether Christmas would be spoiled by the presence of the menacing lightning tower. Germ, however, had finally finished his exams and celebrated his new freedom by organizing a series of thrilling lightning moth races, which came to an end only when Theodore Twill's moth flew straight into Catcher Mint's room and destroyed the contents.

When the morning to leave finally came, Angus, Dougal, and Indigo dragged their bags out into the courtyard and joined a long line of lightning cubs waiting to use the gravity railway. Jeremius joined them as they inched closer to the front.

"I've had a word with your uncle Max, Mr. Dewsnap, and Indigo's parents, and they are all agreed that it would be best for Dougal and Indigo to spend Christmas at the Windmill with you, as far away from the troubles as possible," he told them.

"You're kidding!" Dougal said, suddenly looking excited. "You mean we're going over to the mainland for a whole fortnight?"

"Longer, if necessary," Jeremius said. "Maximilian has agreed to suspend all invention activities over the holidays, so you three should be safe enough," he added, smiling. "You will travel together on the ferry today. Your parents will be waiting at the port to wish you a Merry Christmas before you board," he told Dougal and Indigo. "Dankhart is unlikely to follow anyone to Budleigh Otterstone at the moment with the lightning tower newly unveiled."

"Are you coming with us?" Angus asked hopefully.

"I'm planning to spend a few days at Feaver Street first with Rogwood and Dougal's dad. We need to decide what is to be done about Delphinia," he said, lowering his voice, "and that may take some serious discussion."

"But won't your uncle mind having us to stay, with all that extra cleaning and cooking?" asked Indigo as Jeremius waved good-bye and they were bundled into the gravity railway carriage with their luggage.

Angus shook his head and grinned. "He'll be fine, as long as you don't mind eating curried sprout marmalade and chocolate turkey pudding."

"What, together?" asked Dougal, his smile fading slightly at the thought of it. Even Indigo looked uncertain.

"Er, I wouldn't suggest it if I were you," Angus warned.

As the doors closed and the carriage began to plummet toward the ground, he tried to put all thoughts of his uncle's experimental cooking out of his head.

THE FINAL LESSON

"This is going to be the best Christmas ever!" Dougal declared as they reached the bottom.

Angus was already looking forward to spending the holidays with his two best friends. As for what might happen once the festivities had ended, it was hard to tell. The future of Perilous had never seemed so fraught with danger and uncertainty. Angus knew that no amount of chocolate turkey pudding could ever ease his fears about the lightning tower, Dankhart, and his plans to create the most destructive storms the world had ever seen.